GAMESCAPE

O V E R W O R L D

EMMA TREVAYNE

GAMESCAPE

OVERWORLD

GREENWILLOW BOOKS

An Imprint of HarperCollins*Publishers*

Gamescape: Overworld

Copyright © 2016 by Emma Trevayne

All rights reserved. No part of this book may be used or reproduced in any manner whatsoever without written permission except in the case of brief quotations embodied in critical articles and reviews. Printed in the United States of America. For information address HarperCollins Children's Books, a division of HarperCollins Publishers, 195 Broadway, New York, NY 10007.

www.epicreads.com

The text of this book is set in Versailles. Book design by Sylvie Le Floc'h

Library of Congress Cataloging-in-Publication Data is available.

ISBN 978-0-06-240876-1 (hardback)

16 17 18 19 20 CG/RRDH 10 9 8 7 6 5 4 3 2 1

First Edition

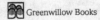 Greenwillow Books

For Heidi, who is a miracle

START SCREEN

This is how the game begins.

Squalling, swaddled, the lights overhead a blur viewed by new eyes. We are conscious—hopefully—but not aware. Arms surround us, and we don't yet know that this is how the game began for them, too.

Fingers tap on a square of light. Date and time of birth. A name, if we have one already. Weight, length, gender.

And just like that, we exist. Officially exist, the details recorded for eternity.

The game is paused then, mostly. Perhaps that's not accurate. Perhaps we are the characters in the castle or the warehouse, cowering in the shadows, waiting for our turn with the wand, the invincibility orb, the gun.

We don't yet know that none of these weapons will help us. We do know that someone is keeping score.

We are wrong about who.

FEED · 1

[Nicholas Lee] Mig, where are you?

[Self: Miguel Anderson] Check my geoloc. Heading in for a few hours.

[Anna Kasperek] C'mon, really? We have that party later.

[Self: Miguel Anderson] God, do I have to?

[Anna Kasperek] Yes. Meet me by the river at 9. Don't you dare lose track of time or I'll come and find you, you know I will.

[Nicholas Lee] He does know that.

[Self: Miguel Anderson] I do know that. *Fine*. I won't be long, I'm so close.

[Nicholas Lee] I'll see you guys at the place. Luck, Mig.

[Self: Miguel Anderson] Later.

LEVEL ONE

You are in a room.

Miguel's laughter echoes off the high gray walls. "Ha. Thanks," he says with exactly as much sarcasm as necessary. The Storyteller says a lot, but she's almost never helpful. His eyes work fine; he can see where he is.

He can't offend her; there's never been any indication that she hears his curses or mocking. Or occasional pleas for help. Conversely, he's certain that every word he utters here is being recorded, uploaded, filed away somewhere. Everything else he does is, but then the flow of information is not just one way. Words, charts, numbers hover in front of his eyes, suspended in the middle distance. Years of practice have taught him to look past them, send them skittering to irrelevance when they're not needed so he can see his surroundings.

He *is* in a room. A new gamescape; he's never been this far before, and the thrill of the unknown makes him want to run, speed ahead. That's a bad idea even if it was possible. He's trapped here, only a meticulous search will reveal the way out.

It's large, well lit, the shadowy edges and corners darker precisely because of the brightness, a tiny fraction of which comes from a high paned window. The door he entered through locked and disappeared the moment it slammed behind him. An echoing silence sucks at his ears, and the air smells musty, stale, unused. Like no one has been here in years. Just one clever trick in an endless stream of them.

He's alone here now; the four figures behind him don't count. Two over each shoulder, the guys a few inches taller than his five-ten, the girls a few inches shorter. If they turned against him, he'd rather take his chances against the guys. He's seen the girls fight.

But they won't turn against him. Loyal to the end. He could reach out and touch them, feel the solidity of their flesh and the guns in their hands, or make them disappear with one quick movement of his wrist. They are no more real than the Storyteller, but he knows for sure they can hear him.

He keeps his arms by his sides, one finger curled around a trigger.

"Split up. Look. It should be about three inches square."

Their boots echo on the stone as they spread out to look, scanning floor and walls swept clean of the last speck of dust. Miguel runs his hands over every imagined crack or lump, crouches down until his knees ache. The room has no purpose but to be a puzzle, and it's difficult to imagine what such a space would be used for outside in the real world. A gymnasium, perhaps; it looks a little like the one at school, painted the same dark gray, the same lights hung from the same visible rafters. The gym has more windows, though.

He looks up. "You two," he says, pointing at the guys only because of their height, then at the window. If they hoist him, he should just be able to reach, reach and not think about what he's doing. They link their fingers, he steps each foot into their pairs of hands, rises up, up to the tiny square pane in the middle of the complicated geometric design of large rectangular ones. Miguel's done something like this before, earlier, and he remembers. Two taps on the middle, and against all laws of nature, it falls inward.

He nearly drops it in surprise when the lungful of fresh air hits him. Another clever trick. Man, dropping it would've sucked. "Ha. Got you. Okay, let me down."

They do, gently, and it's a relief to feel the floor beneath him. That much, at least, is real . . . for a given value of *real*.

A new door has appeared.

A red light blinks about halfway up on the right-hand side. Nearing, Miguel sees the recess in the brushed steel, dimensions exactly the same as the small object he holds. He slots it into place, watches the light wink from red to green, stands back as the door opens.

You are in a corridor. You may go left or right.

"What do we think?" he asks his silent companions, who may or may not be capable of independent thought. On the whole, he thinks, probably not, they haven't been programmed for it, and the burly redheaded male one is dumb as a bag of hammers with a punch like one, too. They're here for strength, in physicality and in numbers, but all the decisions he makes are his alone.

And sometimes, like now, there's no obvious choice. The hallways stretch beyond vision in both directions, spotlights every twenty feet illuminating more dark gray walls.

He passes the weapon from left hand to right and back again. "Status update," he says, refocusing his eyes to one of the input sectors broadcast on his lenses. "Any tips?" There's a keypad on his sleeve, too, but he rarely uses it. Speaking is easier. Officially, cheating isn't allowed, but almost everyone does this for the minor stuff. Usually Miguel wouldn't even bother for this, he doesn't need to, but if he's late for Anna and that godforsaken party, she'll kick his ass. There's no time to run in circles. It takes only a second for someone to check the game's geoloc tag on his message. One word comes back to him.

Wrong.

"Thanks," he says to the helpful stranger. *Wrong*, the

opposite of *right*.

He turns left, his assistants follow.

It's a long corridor, which can mean only one thing. Each step takes them a fraction closer, the dread building a fraction more. He's been close for weeks and now it's here and he wishes there were a few more rooms to search, a few more treasures to unearth. A faint twinge joins every heightened heartbeat. He touches his right index finger to his left wrist, measuring, the results beaming into view just above and a few inches out from his right eyebrow. Yellow, the color as important as the number etched in it. Okay. Could be better, but he's been much worse. It's only the anticipation.

A second red light blinks ahead, and Miguel scans the hall for another glass square before the voice of the Storyteller returns. *There is a keypad in front of you. You must enter the correct code.*

Oh, hell. Miguel steps closer to see the markings on the keys. Numbers, not letters. Fine. He closes his eyes to think. There'd been a puzzle a dozen rooms back, a box locked with a combination that, once solved, had opened to give him the weapon in his hand.

He remembers not knowing whether to laugh or cringe when he'd figured it out. 2-1-0-4. Anna's birthday. As well as he knows these rooms, this building, this world, they know him better. And they want him to know it.

The air smells of stillness, of the point of no return. Too late, as the final number clicks and depresses slightly under his finger, Miguel realizes there is no door. He barely has time to brace his knees before the floor drops out from underneath him. The fall isn't long, exactly the length of time it takes for his stomach to lurch into his throat, for his body to guess—correctly—how much it's going to hurt when he lands. Pain rattles through his muscles and bones, blood pools on his tongue with a copper sting.

After him, his team lands cat easy, already assessing the threat.

It's all around them. The air and Miguel's ears fill with the roar of fire. Heat crackles, rivulets of sweat drip down his forehead and into his eyes, blurring the information broadcast on his visor.

There is a path through the fire.

"I can see that, barely," he mutters, feeling the words form but unable to hear them, though the voice of the Storyteller had been loud and clear. The path leads from the platform they're standing on and is just wide enough for them to slip between the towering flames on either side, if they walk single file.

One step, and the heat intensifies, hitting Miguel like a wall he has to break down, brick by brick. Breath simmers in his lungs. Gasping, half blinded by sweat and haze, he takes them forward, arms tucked in close to his chest. And they haven't even gotten to the boss yet. Maybe he should've gone the other way back in that corridor, found a save point, waited to do this tomorrow. Too late to back out now. Forward, forward. He's never been so hot, so sure his skin is melting off inside his clothes, which are designed to protect him but don't feel like it at the moment.

Come on. Another step. This can't last forever. The metal butt of his gun brushes his chin, and he screams, this sound, too, devoured by the starving fire.

The pain does something. Reminds him. He wheels around, grinning at his helpers. They grin blankly back, mirrors, the firelight reflecting off their teeth. "Come on!" he yells. There's a boss here somewhere. Save points are for wimps. That taste on his tongue isn't a mix of blood and sweat, it's how much he wants this.

Through the red shimmer, Miguel sees the welcome end to the heat, the fire, the sensation that his face has become a featureless pool of flesh. Clever tricks. The next phase is glassy, crystalline, turned glowing orange by the flames. A ledge, a corridor he can't yet see the end of. It can't be as simple as walking into it, of course. This is Chimera. But the gap he has to jump, over a molten, bubbling pool, isn't a big one. He's jumped bigger.

"Back up," he tells the others, getting into a stance for a running start, trying to breathe in enough air for this one effort.

Run. His foot hits the lip at the end of the path. Jump. Land, the front halves of his boots just making the edge on the other side.

Slide.

Not glass. *Ice.* Slick, skidding ice, its surface turned treacherous by the licking heat. His equally treacherous heart rises to his throat as he slips, spins, throws himself flat on his stomach. Made it. He wonders how many people have fallen into the fire, had to go back and try again. They aren't him.

Neither is his team. Two of them don't make it, their programs designed to allow for failure. He blinks, and they're replaced with clones so identical he might not have noticed the switch if he hadn't watched it. Carefully he climbs to his feet, touches his wrist again. Still yellow. A higher number, but that's to be expected. He's fine.

A door appears at the end of the hallway.

"Hang on," he tells the Storyteller. He made it, but somewhere in the slide his weapon didn't. From his cache, he summons everything he's earned that might be useful, everything he can think of. He doesn't know exactly what's waiting for him behind that door, but whatever it is, it won't be easy to bring down. They wouldn't be worth the reward if they were.

Hands and pockets full, he squares his shoulders, glances left and right. Everyone ready? Good.

"Come and get me," he whispers.

Miguel blinks, shifts his back against the solid, slightly bouncy, cool floor of a nearly empty room not much larger than he is. If he stretched his arms and legs, he'd almost touch the walls, but his muscles dismiss the suggestion as too stupid to follow. The burn on his chin is only a memory, and his tongue is fine, injuries that don't translate no matter how real they felt at the time. The whole-body ache is fair, though. He's been running around this room for—he blinks again, and a clock replaces the words in his visor—ten and a half hours straight.

Worth it. So worth it. A smile spreads on his face, turning to a laugh that bounces off the ceiling. He's sore and tired, and if he doesn't get moving, he's going to be late for Anna, but in this one moment, nothing can take away from this feeling. All he'd needed was a solid day with no school or homework to worry about, and wham, he'd done it.

One step closer. Miguel smiles, wider and wider until it hurts more than the rest of the pain dancing around his body. Laughter bubbles and bounces off the walls. That demon had been a real bitch, crawling its way back from the brink of defeat every time Miguel and his team had thrown everything they could at it. Like that mythological creature that kept growing heads when one was cut off, only this creature had just kept growing bitchier.

All the more satisfying when he'd cut its damned entrails out. He'd seen his chance, its arms raised in defense against one of the girls beside him, its eyes suddenly lit with the panicked fire of *mistake*.

One swipe of the knife, summoned from his cache, turned into a second, a third, until its guts spilled onto his feet.

Against everything he knows to be true, he raises his head to look down at the (reasonably) clean toes of his boots. Nothing but street dirt.

Sometimes Chimera feels that real.

Sometimes, like today, the game feels like a nightmare, and he doesn't know what that makes his actual nightmares, the ones from which he wakes blinded and soaked by cold sweat.

Sometimes nightmares feel like victory just because he's alive to have them.

He stands and begins to strip off the sensors, the boots that weren't much help on the ice. Nice try, game, but it wouldn't get him that easily.

Alone, his team ready to rejoin him the next time he comes to play, he tucks his equipment into a hard-shell case. The combination is *not* Anna's birthday, though he has no doubt this one is recorded somewhere with billions of others, each one representing a person who hopes there'll never be a data breach. He checks a glass-doored cabinet set into one wall, but it's empty. Today he's earned something bigger than one of the trinkets that could be left here. In the corner of his visor, a message asks if he would like to receive a new enhancement. Just in case, he checks the list of available options before dismissing it. Not yet. He can't have what he wants yet.

His fingertips brush over the eyepiece as he takes it off and puts it away, remembering the words that had flashed across it.

LEVEL UP.

Billboards glow over the water, reflected fractures of themselves in the rippling waves. His muscles feel like those shards of light; jagged, breaking, re-forming. Every time he blinks, he sees graphics on his eyelids, though he's had the visor off for an hour and hasn't put his normal glasses back on. Once Anna arrives he'll have to go be social, and tomorrow he'll start a new level, but right now he can savor this triumph. On the opposite bank, another Cube shines starkly in the night, this one edged in a vision-insulting lime green that doesn't make its contents any less tempting. Winning only makes him want to win more.

He hears the voice of the Storyteller no matter how loud he turns up the music in his ears, pressing the button with a finger different from all his others.

One of his first rewards, way back when he first started playing. Its advantages are small, in proportion to the size of the thing itself, but necessary. It reacts faster than a normal one would, taking orders from his brain in the smallest fraction of a second, sometimes all the time he has to fire a weapon. Precisely calibrated, it rapidly takes a pulse reading when touched to his opposite wrist. That's more useful to him than it might be to most others.

Chimera. A world of gamers playing for the privilege of turning themselves into hybrids of flesh and machine. He needs it more than most others.

Thanks to the music and her overwhelming perfume, he smells Anna before he hears her. He pulls off the headphones and will never hint that he hates the scent of roses.

"Hey, you." He ignores his screaming limbs to jump to his feet, and she's light in his arms as he twirls her around. Her lips are soft. Kissing her already feels like a memory, but a good one. Some of the best he has.

"Whoa," she says, laughing as he puts her down. "What's gotten into you?"

"Checked my Presence in the last hour?"

"I've been talking to Amanda."

"Ask me how I did."

Her expression changes, augmented eyes sparkling. "You upped?"

"Yep."

Anna holds out her hand, palm facing him. He slaps it with

his own, laughter threatening to overwhelm again.

"Congrats," she says. "How much harder do you think they'll get now?"

"Anna . . ."

"Hey, I'm just asking."

She's not *just asking*. He could die anytime, and not in the way that makes him wake up on a floor, needing to retry the level. The game, killing bosses, makes him feel alive. But they've had this argument before, he's not in the mood for it now. "Oh, can we not? For, like, one night?" He frowns and kisses her again. "I upped. I'm getting closer. Six more. I'll get to the end of Twenty-five before you know it, and boom, there'll be nothing to worry about anymore."

"Fine," she says. "Let's go. I told everyone you'd be on time for once."

"Hey! I was here first!"

"Yeah, yeah." She waves that off, a detail as irrelevant as their relationship is these days, but her mouth twitches back into a smile. "Come on, time to party. Have you eaten?"

"Are you my mother?"

She pokes him in the chest with a sharp fingernail. "Not carrying you if you faint."

"Deal." Miguel turns his back on the river, flicking his ordinary lenses down over his eyes. His feed is full of messages from his friends wondering where he and Anna are—and congratulations on his up—but nobody is surprised they're late. Through the glass, he looks up at one of the billboards and watches it change to advertise a jacket he was checking out online yesterday. Still too expensive, and it's the first day of summer, but he pressed a button to say he liked it, so it's part of his Presence now, stored in the digital library of everything he is.

He takes her hand, which seems softer now that it's inside his, the fingernails tucked away. She has her glasses on, too, and she laughs at something he can't see. Once upon a time the twinge in his chest might have been jealousy, now it's just the mark she left when she poked him.

The streets are clean, and safe, which is a little like prepping for a gunshot wound by taking a vitamin capsule. This isn't a bad place to live, though. Especially at night, when the sun is actually out of sight, out of mind. The sun isn't the only problem, but it's one of them, the biggest, and during the day it illuminates all the others.

Now, the fluorescents spilling out of every window are enough to light their way. There are faster methods, both on the ground and in the air, but Miguel likes the walk, surrounded by real, tangible things, and Anna mostly gave up on hassling him about this weird quirk a year ago. Right around the time she mostly gave up on him.

He doesn't blame her.

Damn, and he told *her* to give it a rest tonight. He should be happy. He *is* happy, more so than he's been in weeks. He refocuses his eyes to scroll through his feed again, blinking to flick the older messages out of the way.

[Nicholas Lee] Mig, man, where are you?

[Nicholas Lee] Hurry up.

Miguel smiles. Nick is a guy who will, with his final breath, ask death what took so long. *Seriously, did you have somewhere better to be? Let's go!*

Okay, okay, they're coming. Anna squeezes his fingers, a gesture of control rather than affection. The neon of another ChimeraCube—violet this time—peeks over the rooftops of the next block. As if he's going to ditch her and run inside. Tempting, but not worth the hassle. With his one strange finger, he touches the thin skin of the inside of her wrist, and the readings appear over his eye. A slight spike, but it calms again once they're past the street leading to the Cube. Wow, she actually was worried.

"I know what you're doing," she says.

"Sorry." He pulls the finger back. "Who else is there?"

"Nick, Taz, Amanda, Seb. Everyone else from our class, but those are the ones you care about."

The *everyone else* is why Anna's having to pull him along. Because *obviously* what he wants more than anything is to spend the night supposedly having fun with the same people he's been trapped in school with for the last ten months. Today was his first day of weekday freedom, the first time since last summer he didn't have homework or have to wait until classes were over to suit up and level up. Or keep trying, at least.

Today that trying paid off.

If he can't be in a Cube, he'd rather be out, walking, feeling the balance between the real and the virtual, wakefulness and dreams. A warm breeze blows south into their faces, scented metallic and damp, tossing Anna's dark hair off her neck. The city feels cracked open, spread and oozing around them, and this surprises Miguel sometimes. Like, there's a whole world out there, across the water and across the land. A whole real world.

It's just not as interesting as Chimera.

It's not nearly as *fun*.

"You won't believe what happens on Nineteen," he says. Behind her glasses, she blinks brown eyes twice in rapid succession, and the blurred reflection of her feed pauses.

"Don't tell me, I'm not there yet. Nowhere near."

"Well, then, you'll be prepared."

"Cheat code alert. Nope."

"Come on, that's not cheating." He nudges her shoulder. "Everyone does it." Half his feeds are people exchanging tricks, clues. The entire damn planet plays Chimera, no way could this stuff stay secret, but that doesn't make it easy. He'd been stuck on Nineteen for months before today, progress coming by inches, and the clock is ticking.

Stop it, he reminds himself. Not tonight.

"I like the satisfaction of a justly earned victory," she says, injecting a tone of distilled righteousness into her voice that she can't maintain, lips cracking into a smile. "Down here."

They turn a corner and see the place just ahead, some coffee bar owned by the parents of a student Miguel's never spoken to. The parents must be in a good mood, to turn it over to a bunch of seventeen-year-olds, but why wouldn't they be? Latest reports, if they can be believed, have coffee beans as extinct in five years, ten at the outside. And like everything else, that just makes people use it up as fast as they can, while they can.

God, a world without coffee. There isn't even going to be a point to living after that.

"Mr. Anderson." Nick flicks his glasses onto his head with a practiced movement as Miguel and Anna step inside, the tinted lenses dark against blond spikes. "You finally grace us with your presence. Too busy celebrating your victory? Good job, man." Something flies from his hand, and Miguel knows what it is before he catches it. A perfectly smooth black stone, heavy for its size. He quickly closes his fingers around it, squeezes for a moment before slipping it into his pocket.

"Thanks."

"What was that?" Anna asks.

"Nothing," he says.

A silence falls as everyone in the place sees him, blood has just enough time to rush to his face before the applause starts. "Thank you, thank you," he says. "Nineteen's a piece of cake."

"Liar," someone calls.

"Okay, cake that takes months to eat." Laughter ripples, and he turns back to Nick, lowering his voice. "I'm here, and wow, it's as dire as I thought. Let's hear it for justified pessimism."

"That's . . . hard to argue," Nick concedes, looking around the retro-trendy altar to all things caffeinated, rough wood tables and brick walls shining off the gleaming steel of the machines behind the counter. People are gathered in the same groups they hung with at school, probably talking about the same things.

Which isn't much. Beyond Chimera, what is there to talk about? Miguel can glance around the room and know basically everything there is to know about each one of them. He follows them all, sees their updates when they fail a test or get dumped or don't want to clean their room, Mom.

That group by the window? The hopeless environmentalists, still trying to save a damned planet. The ones taking up all of a big table in the middle are the bookworms, scrolling through page after page on their lenses and updating one another at the end of every chapter. In the corner is a cluster of Chimera-heads almost as hard core as Miguel, whose eyes narrow. Zack. Guy has no finesse, no style. His constant progress stream speaks of brute force, smashing any obstacle until it moves. Brainless.

There's only one constant. Everywhere, the signs of success. Rewards. Patches of skin that glisten unnaturally under the lights but can't burn in the sun. Eyes with tiny red pinpricks in their pupils, cameras on, recording, uploading. Fingers like Miguel's own, or whole hands, tapping on the tables and holding coffee cups.

"We're back here." Nick leads the way around a wall that partially divides the room. The rest of their friends are relaxing on a couch and a couple of armchairs, displaying varying degrees of enthusiasm about being here. Amanda's happy, smiling into the middle distance or at something on her feed, legs curled up to hide her height. Seb and Taz are talking quietly, and Taz seems grumpy, but that's no indication of anything because she always does. Miguel's pretty sure all the boss beatdowns she dishes out in Chimera are a direct result of her parents' naming her Tabitha.

"Look who's here."

Anna lets go of Miguel's hand as all the others glance at Nick and then the two of them. "Yes, here," Miguel says, "at a party thrown by people who need to use their handy, instant access to a dictionary. Go ahead," he says a little louder, "look up *party."*

"Shhh." Anna slaps him gently.

"It's not that bad," says Amanda. "It's nice to hang, since I'm guessing tomorrow we'll all be busy playing . . . and for the rest of the summer. I'll have to get used to seeing only your avatars again."

"Like every other vacation since we were twelve," says Nick. "And evening. And weekend. But okay. Let's be mostly flesh-and-blood humans for a while."

"Wait." Taz holds her hand up. "Something's happening."

Miguel sees it, too, a flashing red alert in his feed. Nick drops his glasses back down. The whole coffee bar falls silent, voices fading one by one at first and then in a rush.

Attention, Chimera gamers of the world! We are your Gamerunners, and in just one hour, we will have a special announcement for you. It's something we've been working on forever, and finally we're ready to unveil it. In just one hour you'll never look at Chimera the same way again.

Stay tuned.

CUTSCENE:
BLAKE

The two men meet on a hill overlooking a city. It doesn't matter which city. They could be in Manhattan, Berlin, Tokyo, Jerusalem, London. It's the same everywhere, and so the where is unimportant. What matters are the enormous mirrored Cubes, edged in lines of neon red, blue, green, yellow, scattered like dice across a board throughout the landscape below.

These men know better than anyone else what goes on inside those Cubes; they designed the game.

Both tall, both pale, they have often been mistaken for brothers, and it's true that in many ways they are the same. In others they could not be more different, and so maybe it's a surprise they managed to work together long enough to make it out of alpha testing. It's even more of a surprise that they've been partners much longer than that. They both had the things necessary for exactly such a collaboration: a few common goals and, for each, a deeply held and private belief that he was smarter than the other. That each had the advantage.

"You got new eyes," one comments. He's dressed all in black, fading into the night. His own eyes are hidden behind dark glasses, which don't obscure his vision even a little.

The other shrugs. "Enhancements are always moving forward."

"Even for us."

"Yes."

"You called, Lucius," says the one in black. "Why?" He thinks he knows, in fact he's sure he does, but it never hurts to let the other side think you're stupid, especially when it knows you aren't. Keeps them guessing.

"You've seen the way it's going," says the other. "It's time."

"The systems are ready. Coded and loaded."

"I know. I checked." New bright blue eyes stare without blinking. "And added a few new features of my own."

"Oh, really? Fluffy bunny rabbits and sparking rainbows, knowing you."

"That's genuinely unfair, Blake." The expression of hurt is fake, an affectation.

Neither one of them can feel pain. Examined by any of the many doctors on their payroll, both would be labeled sociopaths.

Blake, the one in black, surveys the city and smiles. Chimera is a huge success, has been for years, and is about to be an even bigger one. The world's governments are happy with the myriad benefits the game provides, and the resultant tax breaks are *incredible*. Success is a beautiful thing.

But the game isn't over yet, and there are only two ways to keep people interested, keep them playing: make them wait for a new adventure until they're about to snap, or give them what they want before they even know they want it. Blake was all for waiting for them to snap, but this way had intriguing possibilities, too.

"How much of the original story did we steal, in the end?"

"Just enough to pay tribute to it," Lucius answers. "More the idea than anything. If the source occurs to people, we don't want them thinking they know what's coming next."

Blake nods. "I'll send out the announcements," he says, removing a tiny keypad from his pocket and tapping swiftly. An hour's warning will be enough; word will spread online, across the world, in seconds. Technology is a wonderful thing as well, and none of what they're doing would be possible without it.

"Can I trust you?" asks Lucius.

"You have until now."

"Not in the slightest."

"Well, then." Blake grins. "Look where that's gotten you. Nothing to worry about."

They shake hands and head in opposite directions. Alone,

Blake steps onto a hoverboard, calm as it takes off into the air. Flying without wings, possibly his secret favorite item in the wealth of toys at his disposal. He skims the treetops at speed, fear a thing for lesser mortals, heading for Chimera's nearest office. This one is in a cluster of identical buildings, with no hint anywhere outside of the business that goes on within. The last thing he's ever wanted is a bunch of people knocking on the door looking for tips on how to pass whatever level has them stuck.

Inside, it's empty of human life, and that has nothing to do with the time of day. Only on paper does Chimera have thousands of employees spread across hundreds of cities. There are some, but they are mostly medical personnel and cleaning staff. He and Lucius take care of the coding themselves.

Blake tends to think of this building as headquarters, if only because it's the address given on official documents filed with various governments, and that because it was the first one.

They'd been having lunch, he and Lucius, at some place on the waterfront that Lucius especially liked for some reason that wasn't entirely clear. Blake had sent his food back twice, though the second time had just been to see Lucius's eye start to twitch. Both were looking for a new project to occupy the hours, and it wasn't the first time they'd worked together. After a wave of brilliant ideas, about half of which were Blake's and all of which he takes credit for, Chimera was born.

Since then, it's been a bigger hit than either imagined.

The building hums, thousands of computers whirring away, tracking Chimera-related statuses, running the game in all the Cubes, recording every player movement, win, loss. He sits down at one—despite Lucius's misgivings, yes, Blake can be trusted to do this—and waits, watching the minutes count down the promised hour.

Three, two. His fingers hover over the screen. One.

Hello again, Chimera gamers of the world. Are you ready?

The official Chimera feed fills instantly with replies in the millions. Excellent. He doesn't read a single one of them.

Until now your Chimera experience has been a singular adventure, a solitary endeavor. You, against the monsters and the clock, your own quest to defeat each level, aided only by your virtual team. You have earned your rewards, gained the experience necessary for the next challenge.

Well, Chimera gamers, the next challenge is here.

Technology progresses. We, your Gamerunners, have been working on the next phase of Chimera, and now we need your help. Before it can be revealed to the whole world, we must make sure it works. We are in need of beta testers, and we thought we'd make the process as exciting as possible.

Starting tomorrow, the selection process will begin for our first Chimera competition. Two hundred gamers worldwide will be chosen, and each will be given a team of real fellow Chimera players to assist them on their path. Those selected will be given a ChimeraCube for their teams' personal use for as long as it takes, but we anticipate two months. First to the finish line wins, and the world will be watching, following each team's status online, cheering . . . or not.

The risks will be higher. The challenges greater. The gamescapes unfamiliar. And the rewards will make your current enhancements look like toys. Oh, yes, there will be rewards. As our thanks for your assistance, not only will we grant rewards at random times throughout the game, but the members of the winning team will be allowed to choose any enhancement of which we are capable, whether they have reached Level Twenty-five in the regular game or not.

Blake pauses. Another five million or so replies stream in.

We will announce details of the selection process in—he checks his watch—*twelve hours. Until then . . .*

Game on.

Blake sits back, reading a message from Lucius as it pops up. Let the fun begin.

LEVEL TWO

The coffee bar is silent as the final message scrolls across thirty pairs of lenses and for a few seconds after that. Then: the swell of noise, of too many voices speaking at once.

"A competition," whispers Miguel. No one hears him, but it doesn't matter. They're all saying the same thing.

"That'll be different," says Nick, Guardian of the Obvious. Miguel can't think about giving him shit for it. *Rewards that will make your current enhancements look like toys. Whether they have reached Level Twenty-five or not.*

"Think it'll look like the normal game?" An endless stream of puzzles, quests, monsters to defeat. A fantasy world, born from the Gamerunners' imaginations. A Chimera. They'd named it well for more than one reason.

Maybe not endless, if the point of the competition is to have a winner.

Anna catches his eye and shakes her head. No. She never

answered him earlier, when he asked if she was his mother. He has one of those, and he already knows he's probably in for a discussion when he gets home. Maybe he should practice his arguments on Anna first, but he still looks away, around the room, for something that'll delay what he knows is coming. It's probably the only time since he was eleven that he's been happy to see Zack walking toward him.

"You entering, Mig?" Zack asks, curling a biomechatronic hand, the older brother of Mig's finger, the plastic composite flexing and bunching almost like real skin. "Hope you're ready to be disappointed."

"We don't even know how they're choosing people yet," Nick says, "but Mig kicks your ass at Chimera, and you know it. I've seen your updates. It took you how long to pass Thirteen?"

"You know why I have this?" Zack holds up his fist. "It's so that when I punch you, it doesn't hurt me."

"Yeah, I'm entering," Miguel says, realizing his mistake as soon as the words are out. Anna's sharp-again nails dig into his upper arm, her earlier promise to give it a rest tonight definitely abandoned now, the weight of her perplexed anger in her fingertips.

Better get it over with.

"Need permission from the girlfriend, huh?" Zack laughs, watching Miguel stand and move away with her. Miguel ignores him, but Nick gets in a last dig as he pushes past Zack to follow them.

A light rain has started to fall, blurring neon edges. The false atmospheric layer above, thinning by the day, diffuses sunlight but isn't a solid bubble. The three of them gather in the doorway of the darkened store beside the coffee bar to shelter from the drops. They *say* the chemicals in the water are still at safe levels for skin, but they say a lot of things.

"Tell him he's crazy," Anna says, glaring at Nick. "God knows he won't listen to me."

"You're crazy," Nick says dutifully. Miguel's jaw tightens. They met because of him, when all three were kids, and now they're joining forces? He opens his mouth, Nick cuts him off. "You're crazy, but not for the reason she thinks. Anna, if it were me, I'd be doing the same thing."

"Then you're *both* crazy. His heart could crap out at any minute, but he spends all his time running around Chimera, shot up on adrenaline and endorphins and who knows what else buzzing around what passes for his brain, and now he's planning to do it more?"

"I'm still right here," says Miguel through gritted teeth. "But I'm leaving. Please feel free to continue this without me because my presence is obviously not required."

"Mig." Her voice gentles. "Don't you know how much we worry about you?"

This is the thing she's never understood: that it's not nearly as much as he worries about himself, so it's not that he doesn't appreciate it, but it's all noise swirling around the piercing signal in his own mind. "Don't you know how much you wouldn't have to, if I can get a new heart through the game?"

"We should wait and find out more of the details," says Nick. "The rewards might not help him anyway. There might not be any point."

Rewards. That's what it's all for. All the best doctors are on Chimera's payroll, replacing skin and eyes and limbs and lungs with enhanced counterparts. Since video games began, and Miguel's studied their history more than most of the other things his teachers think he needs to learn, they've been based on a system of gathering items, enhancing the character to aid progression. Chimera has taken that, like everything else, and turned up the volume.

So he plays. Because even if he had the money, he can't find one who isn't working for the game that he'd trust to cut him open again. They're all back-street hacks with bandages and prayers. He's looked. His parents have looked. A couple of years ago they even petitioned the Gamerunners to be allowed to use the rewards they've earned on him, though he's not supposed to know that. They didn't tell him in case the answer was no. Which it was.

"You should be glad about this," he says. Anna raises her eyebrows in questioning challenge. "What would you rather, that I spend a couple months doing this or a couple years getting to the end of Twenty-five?"

"They said this would be more dangerous," she protests.

"If I die trying, well, I was going to sometime anyway. We're *all* playing for our lives, turning ourselves into cyborgs bit by bit because robots stand a better chance on the planet than humans do. I'm just on a slightly accelerated time scale."

Anna winces and turns away, gazing across the street at the last few drops of rain splashing into a puddle. He touches her shoulder. She's smart, it's one of the things he loves about her, but emotions aren't always. It'd taken him longer than it should've to realize she's human, a part of her had hoped she could fix his broken heart by loving him enough.

He's human, too. He'd hoped she could.

"Want me to take you home?" he asks.

She shakes her head. "I'll stay for a while."

"Okay."

Nick claps him on the back, and Miguel steps out onto the sidewalk, heading for the nearest hoverboard hub. The tiredness takes him like this, sudden and violent, but it wasn't the time to tell Anna that, or to admit he doesn't have the energy to walk home. A few blocks away, a line of the silver disks, locked on their edges in a steel rack, curves like the lashes of a blinking eye.

Always watching. Nothing anyone does is hidden,

invisible.

He types a code on the keypad at the end, and the screen lights up. ANDERSON, MIGUEL. PAYMENT ACCEPTED. The latch on the nearest board clicks open, and it rises, flips, waits a few inches above rain-slick concrete.

"Higher," he tells it. It drifts to waist height, its surface molded to allow for sitting or standing. Not that seeing little old ladies surfing the air currents isn't its own kind of funny, but not everyone wants to do it.

Great, he's become his own grandmother. Excellent. But he sits anyway. "Registered home address," he says, and it takes off.

A competition. Winners. Prizes. It would be cool to win, and here, coasting on a breeze freshened by toxic rain, he spares a second of time to think about it. The whole world knowing how good he is at Chimera. That would be pretty awesome, but if he has to choose, he doesn't care as much about winning as he does about living. That's why he spends so much time in the Cubes to begin with. The biomech enhancements help in the game, sure, but they aren't shed with the protective clothing, sensors, visor at the end of a session. Outside, under a burning sun in thinned, poisoned air, those same enhancements are every human's best shot.

Level Twenty-five. He can see it looming ahead, almost feel what it'll be like to call up the overworld and see its icon waiting for him to open it and step inside. One boss later, he can choose whatever he wants from the entire list of what the doctors are capable of, his reward for making it a quarter of the way through the game. There's never been a question of what he'll choose.

But now . . .

As he'd said to Anna, he could spend two months in the competition, get his heart, and get his life back. A life he'd spend in the game because it's better than the real world, but a real *life*. Running around, earning all the enhancements he wants instead of unnecessary surgeries being too dangerous to risk. He could even try to be the first person to beat the game completely.

The soles of his shoes brush the tops of the trees, the leaves rustling realistically enough to pretend they're growing, living things. He's never seen any of the few remaining forests; in this city, as in all of them so far as he knows, trees are merely glorified pixels.

Nice, though. Something to look at. He's not sure whether caring that things *look* pretty is the best use of the government's time, but then he checks himself in a mirror before he leaves the house, so maybe he can't judge.

The hoverboard loses height by inches, a familiar rooftop sliding into view like the next cutscreen. By the time it stops outside his house he just has to point his toes to touch solid ground. Cargo delivered, the hoverboard whizzes off to plant itself back at its hub for recharging as the lock on the front door responds to the touch of Miguel's artificial finger. The finger is useful, but he got it because his parents insisted. He would've gone for something else, an eye camera possibly, but they'd said that if he was going to play, he needed to keep track of his heart rate and not just guess. Every time he measures, it's transmitted to them, too.

"Mom? Dad?"

No answer. Either asleep, out together, or in a Cube. Neither takes it as seriously anymore as Miguel does now, but there's still a tiny wasp- sting of envy that they're both further on in the game than he is. That they've been playing longer, the game having been introduced to their generation, is kind of a weak excuse. He's looked back in their Presences, they both were great players when they were younger. But now . . .

His dad sometimes goes for a walk in his slippers and often comments on news articles online, for god's sake. Anyone who does that should be beatable at a video game.

More out of laziness than electricity conservation, he feels his way to his room in the dark. There a faint glow from his computers illuminates a mess. Clothes, most of them earned in the game, cover the floor more thoroughly than the unseen carpet underneath. Sprawling on an unmade bed, he blinks to activate his feed again and reads a random selection of messages, everyone talking, guessing, debating what the Gamerunners have planned and how they'll choose the teams. Everyone certain he or she will be picked.

"Good luck," he whispers into the darkness, unsure if he's saying it to them or himself. It's a little more than ten hours until the Gamerunners deliver their next updates, and while he'd like to stay up to count down the minutes, the day has taken its toll. He sends out an update to his friends, as if any of them care that he's falling asleep, and folds the glasses away.

Seen from overhead, Anna, Nick, and Miguel form a triangle on the not quite natural green of the grass, Nick's hair an especially incongruous splash. The roof over the park lets in the kindness of sunlight with none of its cruelty, glinting off composite leaves, plants, flowers that change and die with the seasons outside. There's some cool software behind that, but again it feels pointless, the focus wrong.

All around the three of them, people are gathered in similar groups, talking and reading their feeds at once, a festival of multitasking. Miguel can't hear them, but he can guess. The subject is the same everywhere.

"It's like one of those personality tests," says Anna. "I took one online once."

"Did it say you're a pain in the ass?" asks Nick. "Ow."

Anna rubs her elbow. "You have bony ribs. Eat a

cheeseburger."

"That's not very ecoconscious of you."

"You two." Miguel shakes his head. He could say more, but a new status distracts him. Zack, digging at him again. It's been constant since the Gamerunners last updated.

"Personality test. Yeah, kind of, I guess," he says finally. Next week almost anyone who wants to will be able to choose an entirely new level, designed to assess them all as competitors. It's open to any Chimera gamer who has passed Level Ten, probably as more of an age than a skill cutoff . Most people hit that around sixteen. He hit it a month after his fourteenth birthday.

"So a week to play this weird level. Another for the medical exams, then the selection."

"Mig—"

"I know," he says to Anna. "Let me play the level first. Who knows, they might not like my style there, or however they're judging that, and the medical won't even matter. Look at it like this: I'm going to spend next week in a Cube anyway, so doing it playing a level a toddler could pass is healthier than the normal game, no?"

Winning an argument with her, even a small one, is rarer than his heart condition. He grins at her glare.

"That's the part that doesn't make sense to me." Nick twirls a blade of fake grass between his fingers. "They've never made us pass a health test before, and the normal game is hard, physically. Why now?"

"Because everyone's going to be watching, duh," Anna answers, taking the words from Miguel's mouth, adding more of her own. "Even more than they are now. Yeah, sure, your friends follow your progress, maybe other gamers in Paris or Shanghai or wherever if you're on the same level, but this is different, the Gamerunners said so themselves. They're putting on a show. Someone dies from exertion in an anonymous booth in a Cube somewhere, big deal. Who's going to notice or complain? Their families? We're not forced to play. But someone kicks it during this competition and Chimera's in trouble."

"Yeah." Miguel blinks away another stupid jab from Zack. "Too many people complain to the government that Chimera's dangerous, and they can kiss good-bye to the tax breaks I'm sure they get for keeping us all amused and out of trouble. And healthier than we'd probably be otherwise. Chimera makes us exercise, see doctors regularly for upgrades . . ."

"Point. Okay, want to go play?"

A few quick blinks. "Cube Cobalt has room." If that's the nearest, everyone must be wanting to practice. That, and school's out, but it's usually not this bad. Walking's out, if they want to get there before people steal their spots, so they hoverboard it halfway across the city to a building edged in blue. Miguel stands this time. If he so much as yawns, Anna will get on his back about resting. The lopsided weight of their gear cases threatens to tip the disks off-balance, though it's been years since the last report of that actually happening.

Everything moves forward. Technology especially. And nowhere more so than in the Cube in front of them and its brethren across the world. Miguel doesn't know how the Gamerunners have coded half the stuff in here, and at home, alone in front of his computer on the nights he can't sleep, he's tried to figure it out.

"Right, Thirteen, time to die," Anna says, swinging open the door.

"I can't believe you're ahead of me."

"And I'm ahead of both of you," Miguel says. "Catch up."

"Luck. Meet back here at six?"

The clock hovering in front of his left eye says a bit after noon. Decent session, they can have a break for dinner, and Miguel, at least, can get another few hours in before heading home. On a glowing blueprint on the wall, they locate three empty rooms on different floors and part ways, Miguel heading for one on the opposite side at the top of the Cube.

This room looks exactly like the one he was in yesterday, like every one he's been in over the past five years. There'd been worldwide agreement on that—you have to be twelve to play, and Miguel hadn't slept at all the night before that birthday. His inaugural Chimera experience had been marred with stupid mistakes born of exhaustion, but he got better.

A lot better. Fast.

Surrounded by gray-painted concrete, under a single blue spotlight, he taps in the combination and opens his case. Strips of sensors wrap around limbs and chest, ready to communicate with their counterparts on the walls. He waves his arm, and they awaken, a thousand pinpoints of light, too organized to be a constellation, but they look like stars.

For the first time in months, he doesn't have to spend this moment going over everything the level has thrown at him so far, everything he'll have to repeat. He can, and has, done this in his sleep, waking up sweat soaked and gasping.

His stomach flutters. Now he gets to imagine the unknown. Twenty will build on Nineteen, patterns repeating in the enormous, complicated, colorful mosaic of Chimera challenges. And one of the patterns is that there'll be things he's never encountered before. Shit will get real . . . or virtually real.

He exchanges his glasses for the visor, putting them safely in the case, the case in the cabinet on the wall so he doesn't trip over it. Back in the middle of the small room, he slides the visor slowly down over his eyes.

"Select: start," he says. The scent of the air is the first thing to change, from a cramped, adrenaline-stained room to something fresher than outside, clean and safe. Next comes the sound, as computers somewhere close and far away do their work, and it is no sound at all, emptiness ready to be filled by roaring flames, screams, the voice of the Storyteller. His team appears behind his shoulders, determination on their rendered faces.

"Cache," he says. The room around him becomes an armory, a collection of every single treasure, weapon, helpful item Miguel has ever collected. From a rackful of them, he selects guns and hands them out to his helpers before holstering one of his own. That would be the strangest thing if he got into the competition, if he was chosen to lead a team. Would he give the same orders? Sacrifice them as easily as he has dozens of virtual ones over the years?

One step at a time.

Speaking of steps . . .

"Overworld," he commands, and his stomach flutters. The room changes instantly, years of rewards replaced by years of progress. A map, blue because it always matches the outside of whatever Cube he's in, draws itself in light around him.

And at the end of the line there it is. A twentieth large hexagon, the start points of every level he's achieved, joined by strings of smaller save points to which he can return.

Sometimes he spends minutes here, reminding himself how far he's come. Not today. He steps to the end of the map and touches the last hexagon with a finger. It ripples as if it were the surface of a pond, and the room changes. Disappears. The level forms in every dimension. He's expecting the change, the new gamescape, still vertigo tips his belly as gravel on the mountaintop crunches under his boots. Clouds tickle the exposed skin of his face with freezing fingers.

He's never been on a mountain, but it looks . . . like it must actually look, somewhere out there in the real world. Chimera's cleverest of all its tricks. Forests, cities, that perfect blue lake he sees in the distance, all are indistinguishable replicas of the things they imitate. When it's a building, it's impressive. When it's a monster that one of the Gamerunners dreamed up, it's terrifying. If they really existed, they'd look just like that.

A path curves down the mountain. It leads to a hidden doorway.

"Got it," he tells the Storyteller. "Come on, guys."

Grinning, his team in step behind him, Miguel aims for the door with pointed focus. It might take him weeks or months to reach it, but somewhere on the other side of that door is a demon to slay.

LEVEL THREE

He is breathless. Exhausted and sore. Blood pounds through natural veins that themselves seem to hurt; he hasn't had any of his replaced. Yet. They'll have to be, if and when he gets his upgrade.

If, if, if. It could hardly be anything *but* an upgrade. A downgrade would be . . . death. And he feels close to it now, collapsed and alone on the floor of his room in the vast ChimeraCube. Somewhere, unheard and unseen, Anna and Nick are waging their own battles. His visor hits the wall with an echoing crack.

He knows what this is. After every victory, like yesterday's, the end of Twenty-five is close enough to touch. After every stumble, he'll never reach it. Starting a new level's always tough, almost a punishment for any hubris brought on by the previous success, but this had been evil. He got through the door on the mountaintop okay, since then he's been trying to get out of the room it opened into. Enclosed spaces are not his thing.

He checks the time. Five-thirty. There's no point in going back in to try again. He knows himself, he'll lose hours in a few short minutes. So he's waiting outside when Nick and Anna blink their way into the harsh reality of the late-afternoon sun.

"Stop moping," Nick says, pointing at Miguel.

"I didn't say anything!"

"Your face did."

"Well, your face. . ." Yeah, he's got nothing. Nick grins, and Miguel turns his attention to Anna instead, leaning down to kiss her cheek. "How'd you do?"

"Meh. Progress, but I got trapped in that cathedral like six times."

"The one in the woods?"

"Yeah."

That one was tricky. He could tell her how to get through it, but it's more fun not to. Plus she'd probably whack him, albeit gently, which means it's doubly more fun not to.

"Food," says Nick.

A crowd heads inside the Cube, passing them as they leave. It's prime Chimera hours now, when everyone finishes work or school or whatever it is people do all day. Gaming is free, but they need to earn money somehow for other stuff, like food and all the products companies pay to advertise in-game. A week earlier Miguel would've been streaming in with them, the day's calculus and physics already forgotten. He'd play until nine or ten, go home, eat, homework, crash out. Weekends were better, he could usually get in a solid ten or twelve hours, both days, with quick breaks to eat, and he'd finish just in time to be late to meet Anna. Summer vacations are the best. All day, every day.

It doesn't look like he's going to get long sessions like that anytime soon. After last night's announcement people have more reason to play than ever. The Cubes will all be rammed full.

There's no guessing what the new level will be like. Even in the normal game, Miguel's never managed to predict much of what lies ahead, though that doesn't mean he's always unprepared. He's gathered warnings, tips, tricks from people who've gone before him. That can't happen this time. The Gamerunners have made it clear that anyone who shares information about the testing level will automatically be ruled out of consideration for the competition. As will anyone who reads the cheats, even accidentally.

It's not fair, but it doesn't have to be. There are probably a metric ton of agreements between the Gamerunners and every government in the world, and Miguel would bet one of his more minor—read, easily replaceable—bodily organs that none of them require the game to be fair. Fiscally beneficial, yes. Fair, no.

Speaking of unfair . . .

"Ugh," says Anna, lifting her lenses. "Zack's bragging again."

"So?" Nick shrugs. "Fiction is meant to be entertaining."

Miguel laughs. The fantasy of Zack's getting his ass handed to him on a platter of silver pixels makes his food taste even better than an afternoon of running does. He cleans his plate in three minutes.

"We going back?" Nick asks, swallowing his own last forkful.

Anna blinks, frowns, her eyes go wide. "Um, nope."

"Oh." Nick's shoulders fall slightly, eyes darting between Anna and Miguel. "Hot date, you two? Should I get out of here?"

Miguel kicks him under the table. Nick knows how things are between him and Anna.

"It's not that," Anna says, eyes studiously focused on her lenses, body shifting an inch farther away from Miguel. "There is literally not a single free space in the city, let alone three. *Everyone* is practicing, holy shit."

"Wait, seriously?" Miguel does some rapid blinking of his own. He'd guessed it would be busy, but not this bad. She's not exaggerating, and *holy shit* just about covers it. Never in the five years since he started playing has he been unable to find a place. Sure, sometimes it's in one of the more inconvenient Cubes, too far to walk to, but that's what hoverboards are for.

"Expand search," he whispers, and his own eyes widen. He's damned if he's boarding two hundred miles to the nearest available room. At least not tonight. If he can't find space in the morning, he might have to reconsider his options.

"So, what now? You guys want to come over?"

Anna shakes her head, Nick shrugs a "sure," and Miguel smothers the sense of relief. White lies never hurt anyone, but it can be exhausting to pretend. He and Anna haven't had a hot date in months. Having her around is still nice, obviously, that's never changed, but things get so . . . weird . . . so easily, so abruptly. And the *when* is, like Chimera, unpredictable. In his darker moments Miguel knows exactly why that is.

Planning for the future isn't a preferred pastime for someone who might not have much of one, and his efforts to extend his life are what has driven them apart.

He and Nick part ways with Anna under thankfully clear skies.

"Let's walk," suggests Miguel.

"I will never understand you. You have the best excuse in the world to be lazy and you don't take it. Come on, let's board, like we used to."

"We don't fit anymore."

"Sure we do. Where's your sense of adventure?" Nick leads

the way to the nearest overboard station. They are definitely too big these days to share a single-person board the way they did all the time when they were kids, but they make it work. Miguel's legs dangle over the edge, Nick standing behind him with a death grip on his shoulders as they skim the trees and tip the board almost vertically into the wind, laughing.

Once again, the house is empty. "If my mom gets a spot in this competition and I don't, I'm gonna be pissed," Miguel says, though he wouldn't be, really. Not much. Not superpissed anyway.

"Dude, for real. My dad took the day off work to play." Nick blinks. "And has apparently been trying to beat the same demon since eight A.M."

"Level?"

"Fifty-one."

Progress slows, partly game mechanic, partly consequence of real life. Rewards get better, more valuable with each successive, lengthening level. Jobs and kids give people less time to try.

There is no one on earth who has completed the game. For years, status updates have bragged of their posters getting close, but it's all wishful thinking. No one is anywhere near.

Nick wanders through the house, practically his second home, peering into rooms to double-check they're alone. "So," he says when he's looked everywhere, "how's it coming?"

"Bedroom."

It doesn't have a name. At even a third glance from someone with decent skills, *it* doesn't exist, hidden away on a secret partition of Miguel's computer, blocked by enough firewalls to burn anyone who tries to knock them down.

It could probably get him into trouble, though he's never been too sure, or thought too hard, about what kind. Legal, since there might be copyright issues at play, but even if they let that go, it's a safe bet the Gamerunners wouldn't be too happy about *it*. Miguel wouldn't be too happy about having other players beating down his door to give *it* a try either. That would be a special kind of hell.

Years ago a music teacher had told his class that Mozart could hear a piece of music once and instantly, perfectly repeat it. Miguel's never been particularly musical, but he has talents.

Like Chimera. And computers.

The simulation boots up, pixels on a screen. The graphics are a little crude, but they're recognizable, they work. Every level he's played is here. Inside a ChimeraCube, going back to retrace his steps is a waste of time, going forward is more important. Here, though, in the darkness and hum of his room, every spare moment he has, he can go back and retrace his steps, learn from his mistakes, find faster ways out and through.

"Can I take a look at Thirteen?"

"Sure." Miguel types rapidly and retreats to his bed as Nick takes the chair. He'll help if Nick asks, which he sometimes does, but for the moment he relaxes, watches his friend. Nick's wrong; he can be lazy when he wants to.

It's cheating, for sure, and wrong, but like the coded status updates, it's not blatant. It's actually way more of a secret than those. Nick is the only other person who knows of the sim's existence, and it's going to stay that way. Publicizing it might make Miguel rich—for about five minutes. Then it would make him dead, quickly or slowly. Neither is an attractive option.

Miguel slides on his visor. He checks the clock in the corner of his lenses: 4 hours, 240 minutes, 14,000, 400 seconds in which to defeat the testing level.

Some hours are more valuable than others. Minutes, seconds, years, same thing. Time is humanity's greatest and costliest asset because there is no choice but to spend it, and no guarantee of ever getting more.

These hours pass in the span of a heartbeat, and he is back in a tiny slice of real world, a gaming room like any other. There is nothing else he can do, no more skills he can display to the Gamerunners. He finished the level with ten minutes to spare and spends it lying on the floor as he usually does, trying to catch his breath.

He kicked ass. He knows it. Whether the Gamerunners agree is up to them. If they don't, well, that's their problem, and he's no further behind than he would be if they hadn't come up with this competition thing.

All he can do now is wait. He leaves the Cube and walks home, pushing his way through the people waiting for their turns. It'll be another few days before all the prospective entrants have played the testing level. The night before it opened up, everyone who had registered interest had been given a time slot in the nearest Cube, four hours in which to try to pass it.

It's Wednesday, the level closes on Saturday. He can't even play more to kill the time; all the Cubes are being used.

The real world is bright and crystalline, solid but oh so fragile, just like the people who pass him on the sidewalk. Visible biomech gleams in the sunlight or creates its own illumination, winking dots of red or green to show the machinery is functioning.

The only choice now is to adapt because it's better than outright surrender. Submit to the razor-edged knife of future, wake up with parts of metal or plastic where there was once flesh.

The front door opens, a pair of camera lenses focus on him, aperture irises expanding in the lesser light. The mouth below them smiles, the throat behind them leading to a pair of biomech lungs.

"Hi, honey."

"Hi, Mom."

He waits while she carefully sets down her bags, heavy with fragile equipment. She uses handheld cameras most of the time, but her eyes give her the ability to capture whatever she sees, the moment she sees it.

Taking photographs for the end of the world. Miguel's never much seen the point in it, but they're all beautiful, in the way only dying things can be.

Her pictures of him are good, too.

"How did it go?" she asks. As always, there is a subtle thread running through the otherwise evenly woven fabric of her voice when she asks about the game. It's the same thread Anna has, but it's a lot more forgivable from his mom. He knows she worries, she and his dad both do. They just can't argue with his reasons for playing.

"Okay, I think? I don't know. We're not allowed to talk about it."

"I know," she says, motioning for him to follow her into the kitchen. She likes routine. Home, put bags down, make synthmint tea, no matter how hot it is outside. The paperlike substance, infused with chemical peppermint, dissolves the instant she pours boiling water into her mug. "It seems like they're being pretty strict about that."

"Or it's that no one's taking the risk." Enforcing a rule works pretty well if no one dares break it.

"Whichever. I haven't seen anything in my feed about what the level's like."

"And I'm not going to tell you, either." Miguel grins.

His mother's shoulders deflate a little. "Damn. I bring you into the world, and this is the thanks I get. Worth a shot, right? I'm only curious, since I'm not playing it."

"I thought that's where you were, practicing."

"Nah, just having some fun. So?"

"It's a level." Miguel closes his eyes and sees . . . things. Teeth and screaming mouths. Endless corridors and landscapes so vast they create their own kind of suffocating claustrophobia.

There hadn't been a boss at the end, just a puzzle. A damned hard puzzle. He'd had to kneel down on the sand of the beach he'd ended up on and trace all the possible answers into it with his finger for a good half hour before being halfway sure he had the right one. "It wasn't that hard."

She probably knows he's lying, but lets him get away with it. "I guess if they make it too difficult, they won't get all the people they need," she says. "When's your medical?"

"Day after tomorrow."

"Okay, honey. You home for dinner?"

"Yup." He nods, and his mother starts pulling farmed, created, manufactured ingredients from cupboards. Nothing is wild, nothing is fresh. Once he'd spent hours on an early level stuck in a wheat field and not knowing what it was until he searched online when he got home. Nothing is grown like that anymore, out in the open, under the sky.

Which is probably a good thing. No one likes to be poisoned. It makes for a bad day and maybe a last day.

The computers in his room hum gently, making it a little warmer than the rest of the house, which is kept cold by law. His parents have an exemption because of his heart, but even that allows them only two degrees more than everyone else. He hums along with them for a second, a one-note symphony.

His keyboard is a projection of light on his desk—or whatever flat surface he chooses. Sometimes it's the wall, when he's too restless to sit, or the floor if he's bothered to clean it recently. But for now it's on the desk, and he closes his eyes again, letting his fingers type while he loses himself in memory. He'd had to dig his way from an underground cave, with a violent, shrieking creature waiting for him on the surface. He'd killed that, and then . . . yes . . . crossed the river, that's right.

That's when things had gone bad, but they could've gone worse. He'd needed to know if being splashed by the water would be dangerous. *Yes* was the answer.

The way the water had melted his team member into pixels would stay with him for a while, but he felt no emotion over it. She hadn't been a real person, and sometimes sacrifices have to be made.

His fingertips go numb from their tapping as he codes,

designs. Again, it won't be polished like Chimera is, smooth and seamless, indistinguishable from reality, but it'll be enough for him to go over, figure out what the Gamerunners were trying to test. What skills they were looking for when they designed the special level.

The puzzle, that's a definite one. The whole game is full of puzzles, but they aren't often quite that hard. The Gamerunners want the competitors to use their brains. Not surprising.

The creatures . . . well, a lot of Chimera is about fighting. Choosing the right weapon, the right stance, the right split, flickering second to strike.

The river.

Risk and sacrifice.

How badly do you want this? Will you kill for it?

For a moment he is even more aware than usual of his heartbeat.

The front door opens, closes, and a few minutes later Mom calls him for dinner. Miguel can't actually remember the last time the three of them sat down to eat together; at least one of them is always in a Cube or at school or work. Mom has a thing for shooting in the evening light, something about the way the chemicals and gases burn on the horizon, setting the world on fire.

Too late he realizes they've planned this.

"So," says his father. "We wanted to talk to you about this

competition."

"What about it?" Miguel asks around a mouthful of powdery mashed potato, as if he can't guess. If Anna is predictable, his parents are a certainty.

His mother's eyes cut to his dad's. "We weren't going to stop you from entering," she says. "There was no harm in playing the testing level, or at least no more than usual."

"But you don't think I should take the medical."

"We don't think you should go through with it if you pass and you're selected. Seeing one of Chimera's doctors might not be a bad idea. Maybe they'll have an idea of something we haven't tried yet." Miguel's father doesn't look hopeful as he says this. With good reason. Miguel's mother frowns. They've always done their best to tell Miguel the truth about his condition, keep him informed as much as they are, the detail of their honesty increasing with his age and comprehension.

"What if this is my only chance, huh? They don't hand out new hearts like they do eyes or fingers, even in Chimera."

"You can still play the regular game," says his mother.

"Rosa—"

A loudly silent look passes between his parents. Miguel's mouth drops open. "Are you thinking of stopping me from doing that, too?"

"We understand why you play so much," says his father, "but it's only going to get more dangerous for you. This competition—"

"You wish they'd waited five years?" Miguel guesses. Optimistically. His father winces. Target achieved. His aim has gotten better, thanks to Chimera.

"Sometimes I wish that damned game had never been invented," his mother mutters. "Then all the good doctors would still be working in normal hospitals."

"And we wouldn't be able to afford them anyway." Miguel stands, no longer hungry despite the day's exertion. Fear blackens his mother's already dark eyes.

"Calm down, please."

"I'm calm."

"You're not."

"We're going to argue about how I feel now? I'm going to take my medical, I'm going to pass it, and they're going to let me play," says Miguel, trying not to let his face betray the pain in his chest. It's harder when he's angry. "But first, I'm going to lie down."

They don't stop him. They never have, and it's probably cruel that he's used this to his advantage for as long as he's known it would work. They like it when he rests. And this time he actually does, instead of using it as an excuse to escape back to his homemade sim. The pillows crush under his head, and he stares at the ceiling, watching the orange glow of sunset fade and darken across the paint.

LEVEL FOUR

He doesn't know what time he falls asleep, only that he's done it in his glasses and when he wakes, statuses are scrolling past, full of mundane crap no one cares about. Why anyone needs to know what even his closest friend eats for breakfast, or that he's happy it's not raining, is beyond him. But speaking of closest friends, he blinks quickly, checking for Nick and Anna, who are both tackling the level today. He wishes he could give them hints, but that would destroy his chances, if he has any. They're smart and good at Chimera. They'll get it.

He checks that the house is empty before leaving his room by the simple expedient of the geoloc tags on his parents' last updates. Dad's at work, Mom's out shooting halfway across the city. Her last picture is beautiful, a study in angles and contrasts of the skyscrapers downtown. In the far background, blurred by depth of field but identifiable, is a Cube, glowing violet.

It's been less than twenty-four hours, but his feet itch to be back in one of those rooms. Another few days and they'll open up again, the testing complete. Of course some of them will be put into use for the competition, but mostly things will return to normal, the Gamerunners say. Maybe this is all part of the plan: put them all through Chimera withdrawal for a week so they're desperate to get back to it.

If the Gamerunners *have* a plan. When his history classes cover the origins of Chimera, the *whys* are glossed over. That the Gamerunners thought it was a good idea seems to be as much as anyone knows, and they didn't predict how popular it would get. How it would take over the world. You'd think there would be better places to use the money, the sheer genius that go into it, like, oh, Miguel's not sure . . .saving the planet? Maybe the Gamerunners knew it was too late for that, so they might as well give people something fun to do on the way down.

It's been a while since he last went a whole day without playing, that because of an unplanned hospital trip. It's been five years since he could go wherever he wanted and couldn't choose to spend the time in a Cube. The sim beckons, but it'll just make him more annoyed that he can't do the real thing.

He dresses, leaves the house to walk, his glasses back home on his desk, as disconnected as he feels. This street has been home his entire life, a string of small artificial boxes in the shade of tall artificial trees. His house had always seemed to be in a slightly darker shadow than the rest, a cloud hanging over it.

But he's been happy here, especially with nothing else to compare it with. He has friends, family, the school he's about to walk past on the other side of the road. Funny, he doesn't think about that very often. There are no more roses to smell, haven't been for generations, he only knows the saying as a curiosity, but he wouldn't have stopped anyway. Since his twelfth birthday he's thought of little but Chimera and getting through every day. And Anna, the past few years, but her not as much as he should have. He just crossed the corner on which he kissed her the first time. Time had felt infinite in those few seconds.

Realistic as the game is, in its mythical monster way, it's a great place to hide from reality.

"Mig!"

He stops, startled, turns in the direction of the voice, also the direction of the sun, which burns his eyes. A tall figure is running toward him, but only when she's inches away does he see who it is. "Oh. Hey, Amanda."

"Hey yourself. Haven't seen you since the party. What's up?"

"Nothing. Been busy." It's not as if they've ever hung out that much outside school, but she's one of the more bearable, funnier people in his class. "What are you doing here?" She lives farther from the school than he does, has clearly just come from inside it. "Did you forget it's summer vacation?"

"Ha. No. Taz and I have an extra credit project. Not sure what we'll do if one of us is picked, though. You entered, right?"

"Yeah. Did my test yesterday. Medical tomorrow."

"Mine, too. You'll pass, though, strong dude like you."

He is temporarily more aware of his heartbeat. "Sure."

"You want to come in, chill with us? Taz and Seb are fighting again, so I wouldn't mind some happier company."

He's flattered she thinks he would be. Although he is happy, curiously so given that he's not inside a Cube. Sometimes the outside world has something to recommend it. "Sorry, I told Nick and Anna I'd meet them after their tests."

If she recognizes the lie, she doesn't let on. "Oh. Okay. Well, I should get back in there. Wish me luck."

"Luck," he says, watching her turn and jog back inside the low red building in which he's wasted far more than half his available life. He might as well go meet Nick and Anna, see how they did even if they can't really talk about it. The Cube they're in is a couple of miles away. The walk will do him good.

There aren't as many Chimera hospitals as there are Cubes, here or anywhere, but there are still several in the city, their edges also etched in different colors, and everything inside is as state of the art as the game. Androids, incapable of making errors, perform minor procedures on their own and major ones under supervision. Miguel knows from experience that the human body is as unpredictable and badly behaved as a Chimera boss, bleeding inconveniently when science and logic dictate that it shouldn't. He's pretty glad that when it's happened to him, the figure standing over him was capable of creative, human thought. Nanobots scuttle over every surface, invisible to the naked eye, chewing up atoms of dirt. The only place they don't touch is a towering apple tree in the glass expanse of the atrium, a rare, growing thing. A projected plaque in blue light blathers something about its being a symbol of life and rejuvenation.

"Miguel Anderson, here for my medical," he says into a speaker at a desk. A series of arrows flicker to life on the floor, guiding his way through the maze of hallways. Man, he wishes the game had that.

The arrows guide him deep into the building and onto a square of floor, indistinguishable but for the lack of ceiling above it, that rises when it senses his body weight. Four floors up, it slides left to join another hallway and let him off. More arrows take him to a small waiting area arranged with empty seats.

He has yet to see a single person. That makes sense, it always has. Limiting human contact here minimizes the chance of infection, though the risk is already small. The doctors here are the best, and their proprietary drugs kill anything that might damage their ingenious work.

"You may enter," says a mechanical voice before he's given time to sit. Yet another arrow, likely the last, appears over a door.

"Good morning," says the doctor when he's half inside the examination room. Shit. He hadn't expected her to be young and female, though there's no reason why. He certainly hadn't expected her to be so pretty. He didn't think about it at all, but now he's thinking a lot about how to make his body behave. He reminds himself that she's a doctor, good enough to work for Chimera. Let her do her job. Putting up with teenage boys can't be fun for her, and her week is probably full of them.

"I'm Dr. Spencer. I have your file."

He hears the tone of . . . something . . . in her voice. Surprise that he's entered the competition at all? Curiosity over why he hasn't been "fixed" yet? Longing to perform the surgery that will cure him? He's not sure, but he'll bet she doesn't usually sound like that.

"It's a big file," he says. Dr. Spencer nods.

"Well, let's get started," she says. "Shirt off, please."

"Uh. Okay." He'd expected her to say something. Fine, shirt off. It's been a long time since he's been half naked in front of a woman, and then it was only Anna. Luckily the color of his skin slightly hides the blush. Not completely, but a little.

Nothing hides the scars.

He is no stranger to doctors, hospitals, the tests they put you through that seem to make no sense. He tracks a point of light with his eyes, touches his fingertips with his thumb, bends over to reach his toes. She points to a section of floor in the corner, different from the rest. More like the floor in a Chimera room, slightly springy, but this one is moving on its own, scrolling at a smooth, brisk walking pace. The sensor she sticks to him itches; she motions for him to step on, eyes already on the screen to see the dismal readings.

He doesn't know anyone else who's had their medical yet, and so he doesn't know whether the two hours it takes is normal. He touches machines and climbs into them, is scanned, prodded, stuck with needles that fill with precious blood. After the initial introduction, he doesn't speak to Dr. Spencer except to answer questions or agree to her instructions. There's no point, and he doesn't want *argumentative* added to his history, though it's likely already there. Tantrums had been forgiven in the early days. Who would expect a child to understand? But when he'd gotten old enough, and did understand, well, then it'd just been unfair.

"All done," she says finally, her full lips twisting. Her mouth opens and closes, and he waits. "You know," she says. It's not a question.

"Yeah."

"And that's why you play."

"Yeah."

"I don't blame you," she whispers, nearly inaudibly. She clears her throat. "But you need to stop."

"What?"

She looks away, choosing one blank spot on the wall that is apparently more interesting than all the others. "How much time were you given?"

He doesn't need to pretend to remember. "The last doc I saw said I'd probably make it to twenty-one. Age, I mean, not level."

"He might've been right about the level," says Dr. Spencer. "You're very good. But I think the other thing was . . . optimistic."

The filters suck all the air from the room. "Excuse me?"

"I'm sorry," she says, dragging her eyes back to his. "If you stop placing so much strain on yourself, and by that I mean you go home and start eating your meals in bed, you might have another year. I can't recommend you for the competition. I can't recommend you play at all."

"You're wrong," he says, pulse thundering in his ears. He won't measure it here in front of her. "I'm already at Level Twenty. I can make it."

"If I told you I could take you downstairs and give you a new heart this minute, would you trust me to cut you open?"

He wants to say no. Maybe she's a terrible doctor. But she works for the game. "Yes," he says.

"Then you need to trust me now."

No. No, he doesn't. He stares at his feet, teeth clenched.

"I'm sorry," she repeats. "I wish it were different. I always do, in these situations. We could have helped you."

"See, that's what I don't get. You all know how to do this stuff, but instead of being out there"—he points out the window—"fixing sick people, you sit in here and wait for them to earn it. They don't even have to be sick, they just have to want dumb shit, like—"

"A biomech finger?" she asks, pointing at his. "If you think Chimera is the reason the best doctors are available to only a few, I suggest the first thing you do when you stop gaming is read a history book."

"You could still be a doctor out there."

"I could, but do you think I'd have the time to heal everyone, or the equipment? They're good at many things, but biomech happens in Chimera hospitals."

"And that's the only thing that's going to help me."

She doesn't answer, doesn't need to. "I can't recommend you for the competition," she says again, as if saying it twice will make him realize she's right. She *does* almost sound sorry. "You must be aware of the danger of it."

"I am." He wants to curse her, takes a deep breath. *He*

understands the danger, what does she care if he dies playing? But Anna's right, the world is going to be watching this, and that would be bad publicity the Gamerunners don't want.

He's known the truth for a long time. He knows how hard his parents tried to find some alternative, the endless medications and surgeries that gave him only the hairline scars that cross his chest.

"You are going to die, Mr. Anderson," she says. "If you don't stop playing *now*, it could be very soon. If you insist on continuing, you should at least find the time to say good-bye to your loved ones. Because of confidentiality, I can't tell them anything, but I suggest you do."

Spots dance on his eyes. He blinks them away to stare at her. "You're serious," he whispers hoarsely.

"Yes." A heavy silence vibrates between them.

"I won't make it."

"No."

He's gotten bad news before, but it was always distant. Not tomorrow or next week, so he could ignore it.

"Okay," he says, standing. It's not okay. Nothing's okay. "Thank you."

He's not grateful.

The arrows reappear to lead him out; he's never been sure whether it's to prevent him from getting lost or to stop him from looking around. But he's not curious now, not today.

Outside, he drops his lenses down and scrolls through more updates. Both his parents are still out, and an empty house is unappealing.

Everything is.

Hoverboards zoom overhead, tiny electric cars cram the streets, their horn volumes set on high. No one cares about noise pollution anymore, it doesn't matter as much as the other kinds.

He stands on the corner, frozen in the warmth.

Well.

Game over.

He, Anna, and Nick are back in the park. It's almost as if time has been rewound to when they were wondering what the test would entail, when excitement over the competition was swelling but hadn't yet reached its pitch. That's what makes the now *now*, the heightened buzz of the chatter around them. Contestants will be announced at midnight, and a bizarre calm has stolen over Miguel in the week since he had his medical. He knows he won't be chosen.

More details have emerged: The Gamerunners will choose leaders, the contestants who'll all be aiming to guide their groups to victory. From the pool of everyone else who passed the testing level, the leaders will be given teams, replacing the artificial companions that aid the normal game. That'll definitely be weird, playing with real people who can argue back and won't blindly follow orders. Then again, more brains will only help.

"I think I've got a good chance," says Nick. Miguel smiles. That's probably true, his friend could do really well. "There's one thing I don't get, though. Why are they letting such a wide age range in? Won't anyone younger get their asses kicked by people who've been playing for decades?"

"I've been thinking about that," says Anna. "You'd think so, but maybe not. First, anyone younger has less biomech, but probably more energy. Plus anyone who's been playing for forever is going to be so used to playing alone. They'll be slowed down by having to figure out how to play with anyone else. It's never exactly been a team sport."

Anna pretty obviously cares less, entered more because everyone else did, but even she has a light in her eyes as she guesses what the competition could be like.

"And everyone will be watching, you know? You won't want to make a mistake, the 'verse will be full of people laughing at you."

"No pressure," says Miguel, voice mild.

"Sometimes pressure makes people do great things," she counters. "Coal into diamonds, or something."

"Like you've ever seen a diamond."

"Manufactured ones, sure."

"Not the same thing," he says. Life must've been so different back then, before the earth was pillaged, robbed of every last scrap of value. True, some things can't be destroyed, but they can be hidden away in case of . . . what? Nothing is going to get better. One day, no matter what the clever Chimera doctors can do now, they'll stop being able to produce lungs that can cope with the air, skin that will last a lifetime under the sun.

And what then? Nothing but androids, maybe. Human brains in jars, or digitized and uploaded to a collective consciousness. That was sort of starting already. Experiments were progressing, largely with the help and expertise of Chimera's doctors. But the androids would eventually break down, there'd be no one to maintain the computer systems, and then . . . nothing.

The end of the world. At least if *world* can be defined by the people on it.

These thoughts have been weirdly comforting since his medical, which he told Nick and Anna went fine. He'd only be delaying the inevitable, so it doesn't matter, right?

"Yoohoo," says Anna, waving her hand in front of his face. "Going to come back from space?"

"If I could go to space, no, I wouldn't come back." Earth had given up trying to find a planet people could move to long ago. Resources for rockets and the fuel to power them were needed here now. The space race was another history lesson.

"Ha-ha. What were you thinking?"

"Stuff. Nothing important."

"You know, you're pretty Zen about all this. You were all fired up for this competition, and now it's like you just don't care."

"I care." Way, way too much. "I just can't do anything to improve my chances."

"You okay, man?"

"Totally fine."

Nick squints at him but doesn't argue.

By some unspoken agreement, they all lie on their backs and watch the sky darken through the glass ceiling. They used to spend whole nights like this when they were little, talking, playing stupid games. Dinnertime passes, Miguel half expecting to hear his mom call the three of them to come eat, but she doesn't, she's at home, and none of them mention food. Especially from Nick, that's unusual. The park doesn't empty like it ordinarily does at dusk. Conversely, it's getting busier, people gathering in groups for the announcement.

When the clock in the corner of his left lens hits ten, Miguel sits up.

"I've gotta go."

"What?" Anna blinks, curses. "Close window," she orders her lenses. "I thought we were going to wait together."

Miguel shrugs. "I'd rather be alone when they don't call

my name, okay? Or see how happy you are when they don't."

The teasing is meaner than he intended, and the hurt in her eyes stings him. "I'm sorry," he says, taking her hand for a second. Nick looks away and back again, pretending he didn't move in the first place. "I'd really just rather be on my own. I love you. Both of you."

He means it. Her concern for him *is* concern, it's never been pity. She makes him laugh. She makes him smarter.

"You too," she says, rising to give him an awkward hug. "See you tomorrow?"

"Sure."

He's almost out the door when Nick catches up to him. Fuck. "Mig, you really okay?"

"I really am."

They'll understand with time.

"You know, it's okay with me."

"What is?" Nick has the good grace to look puzzled.

"You and her."

"I don't—"

"You hide it from me, but I see the way you look at her. And the way you look when I touch her. More important, I see the way she looks at you, even though she feels guilty about it. I know her, Nick. And what you want wouldn't matter shit if she didn't want it, too, but she does. What you guys do is up to you, I'm not, like, giving *permission* or anything. You've got to get that from her. But I wouldn't be pissed, okay?"

"Mig—"

"I'll see you tomorrow." The lie is a little easier the second time.

"Okay, I guess."

The streets are almost empty now. The Cubes are open to everyone again, but for the first time he can remember, people are choosing not to play. Even those who didn't enter the competition, who have no vested interest in the outcome, are waiting to find out who they're going to be cheering for or booing at over the next two months.

He gets a hoverboard from the nearest station; he can't walk where he's going. Like he told Nick and Anna, he wants to be alone when they broadcast the results.

Hoverboards are programmed to ascend only to a certain height, but it's enough to get him onto the roof of a building near the river. The water's dark, rippling surface looks eerily like a river in the testing level, the one to which he'd sacrificed a teammate. Maybe he shouldn't have done that so easily, readily. Like that's what would have stopped the Gamerunners from choosing him.

He measures his pulse for a minute, two, with his tiny piece of biomech. If Mom and Dad are monitoring, their next breaths will come easier. Doing it has always been soothing anyway, when it should have been terrifying; never knowing if the next one would come, reassured when it did.

He's never been calmer. This is the right place to be. Going home would have made everything more difficult, so it's better this way. A message will be delivered to his parents at a scheduled time. It doesn't say much more than what he said to Anna and Nick, but that's really all he needs to say.

The minutes tick down. The fragments of light reflecting off the water look like seconds, winking in and out of existence. Like heartbeats. Like people.

Everything is beautiful: the glow, the living city, the strange shapes of the clouds. Religion isn't a common thing anymore, mostly people stopped pleading with the sky when it began spitting acid at them, but maybe this is what it was for, this feeling. This sense of something larger, its purpose to show Miguel how small he is. Small is good. Unimportant is good.

Small means no guilt when he leaves.

Forty-three minutes. It's almost silly to wait, but it feels... symmetrical, somehow. Neat, even, as defined as the edges of the nearest Cube a few blocks away behind him. Chimera is the most fun he's ever known, full of adventures he'd never have experienced otherwise. His parents wouldn't have let him climb mountains, swim lakes, run through labyrinthine buildings as fast as he could. But in the game it was okay, it was just Chimera, and who knew? Maybe it would help him earn the heart he needed.

But not now. He can't sit by and watch the competition, or ignore it while he tries to make progress that will suddenly feel slow. Ignoring it would be impossible anyway, it's going to be everywhere.

And if Nick gets in, Miguel will be that much closer to it.

Enough. In a few minutes none of this will matter anymore. His useless heart can finally give up, like it has threatened to do for years. He can rest. Everyone likes it when he rests.

He's ten steps from the edge of the roof, give or take, and he needs all the remaining minutes to drag himself that short distance. Life doesn't give up willingly, he learns. There is no reset button, he won't wake up on the floor of a small room with a message asking him if he wants to try again.

But he's there. He steps up, and his toes curl over the ledge.

CUTSCENE:
BLAKE

Blake is still deciding. He has one remaining hour in which to pick his candidates, half the chosen ones for the competition. Lucius is elsewhere in the building, surely making those same choices.

Actually Lucius has probably had his chosen since the final medical report came in. That's the kind of man he is. The type to do his homework early so that he can go over it again to make sure he's done it right.

Blake prefers instinct, but his is giving him some trouble right now. Really, he's picked most of his, but he has one spot left to fill and two potentials with which to fill it. One did all the right things on the testing level, the other . . .The other is an interesting case.

He still has time.

At Chimera headquarters he steps onto the private tile in his office that will raise him up to where Lucius chooses to work. He doesn't warn of his arrival, he never does. What would be the fun in that?

Lucius is used to it. He's difficult to surprise.

"Are you ready?" Lucius asks.

"I will be. You?"

"Of course. I was just reading a book."

Blake simply shakes his head. Of course he was. Something heartwarming, probably. He'll never understand his friend's taste.

Friend is the wrong word, but it's close enough.

"I think this will be exciting," says Lucius. "I'll win, of course."

"Dream on. No, really, do dream. You've always been so good at it."

Lucius smiles. "Making them come true has always been more my specialty."

"Yes, yes, you're a regular saint. I've seen how much you donate to charities from the company accounts. I need to go out for a while. I'll be back in time for the announcement."

"Make sure you are, or I'll fill the list with everyone I like."

"You wouldn't." But Blake isn't *completely* convinced of that. It would go against Lucius's nature, but Lucius hasn't hung around him all this time without picking up a few tricks.

Blake has no plans to speak to either of the people he's going to visit, but much can be learned from observation. The first is almost boring, easily found from geoloc tags, sitting in a park, holding hands with a girl. He watches them from overhead, staring down through the glass roof. The second is more of a challenge, but tracked down soon enough with Blake's collection of fancy toys. He hasn't updated in hours, which makes it only slightly more difficult. There isn't much Blake can't do when he wants to.

And he's glad he wanted to. Well, well. This is much more interesting. He watches the boy from another rooftop, augmented eyes seeing clearly across the distance. It's evident what the boy intends to do, and it's clear why. His medical exam gave Blake a lot to think about.

Desperation can be a beautiful thing.

True to his word, rare in itself, he is back at headquarters with time to spare, though not much of it. Lucius meets him in the lobby, in front of a wide expanse of touch panels. Together, as the clock ticks midnight, they begin to type. Blake hopes the boy pauses just long enough. He needs only a few seconds.

"Congratulations, Miguel Anderson," he whispers as his fingers move. "Let's see how far you'll go."

LEVEL FIVE

Miguel's foot slips as his name flashes across his lenses. His stomach turns over. Scrambling for balance, he falls back, hitting the roof with a painful crash. Pain is good, pain is life. It spreads around his limbs, background noise as he watches the feed, waiting for the punch line. He'd only kept them on for the time.

What if he hadn't kept them on at all? Cold sweat beads on his skin. What had he been about to do?

His name is still there. He's in. Oh . . . my . . . god. But Dr. Spencer had told him he wouldn't be; he doesn't understand.

The answers aren't going to come on this roof. Shakily he stands, distrusting the legs that nearly slipped out from under him on the ledge. This view of the city was nearly the last thing he ever saw. Across it, closer and yet in the unreachable middle distance, his feed fills, messages from Nick, Anna, his parents scattered among names he doesn't recognize. His parents.

Shit. He cancels the scheduled message to them.

Names are still being announced, two hundred of them. All the team leaders. He doesn't pay any attention, there'll be time for that later. Time. He still has some. For now he needs to get off this roof, and the hoverboard has long since gone back to the station it came from. Sometimes he imagines the voice of the Storyteller narrating his actual life.

You are on a roof. There is a door leading to a stairwell.

Thankfully it's unlocked. Jumping had been a good way out, but it wouldn't be a good way down. His lockpicking skills aren't bad, but his tools for it are inside his Chimera cache and can't be summoned into the real world. His mind races in time with his feet, boots ringing on the steps. Dizzy from all the turns, he arrives in an atrium, running, running both toward the unknown and away from it. Toward the adventure of Chimera, away from the horror of what he'd nearly done.

The light turns red. A siren wails, tripped by motion sensors that expected intruders to come in the front door, which is only polite. He swears under his breath, eyes casting around for an exit. He has to get out of here, find out what's going on, get as far as he can from the roof. The sealed doors are glass. His boots, earned in the game but now almost permanently fused to his feet, are capped with steel.

Well, he's sorry.

Glass rains like snowflakes. The alarm cries louder for a

few seconds, then stops so abruptly it takes him a second to realize a man is standing at the keypad on the outside, another waiting by a small electric car on the curb.

"Miguel Anderson?"

"Yes?" He's about to be arrested, surely.

But that's not a police car. A stylized *C* adorns the driver's door. And both of their uniforms.

"Please come with us."

"But—" He turns back, the glass crunching under him.

"We'll take care of it." The man by the car smiles. "Seriously, don't worry. Congratulations, you're one of the leaders."

Yeah, but he doesn't know why.

"We're just going to get you home safe," says the other, finished with his business at the keypad. "I'll stay here, watch this until someone comes to fix it," he tells his partner. "Get in the car, Mr. Anderson."

"I—okay." It might not be a good idea, but it's a better one than staying.

"How did you know where I was? I haven't posted anything. No geoloc tags," he says as the car moves silently through near-empty streets. The driver shrugs.

"Just following orders."

Huh. His glasses do have a tracker on them, but it's illegal for anyone to follow without permission from the government or the users themselves, granted by the act of posting an update. Miguel hasn't posted anything public in hours. So the Gamerunners have permission, or they're not playing by the rules.

Neither would surprise him.

"And you're taking me home? Why? I figured I'd be going to, I don't know, a Cube or something." As much as he'd thought about it at all. So many things are careening around his brain it's hard to grasp any one of them.

"Just following orders," the man repeats. So he doesn't know, or won't say.

Again, neither would surprise Miguel. He falls silent, letting reality sink in through the windows.

He's in the competition. He must have done well on his test, impressed them. They think he's good enough to win.

His smile fades a little at the sight of his parents when he steps inside the house. Nick runs from behind them to high-five Miguel, hard enough to sting. Anna stands by the window, her face an unreadable mask.

"I know what you're going to say," says Miguel, shaking out his hand to get the feeling back. "Mom, Dad, please let me do it. I made it in! This is a great thing!"

"No." His mother shakes her head. "It's too dangerous. I want to talk to the doctor who gave you your medical and ask what the hell they were thinking."

Yeah. So does Miguel, but he tries not to let that show on

his face.

"Maybe you're getting better," says Nick. "Maybe they've been wrong all this time." His hopeful expression is ironically heartbreaking.

No, that's not it. Dr. Spencer told Miguel to say good-bye to his loved ones. Probably imagining a scene much like this, everyone gathered in a living room. He could tell them right now.

Sure.

"Mom, Dad. Please."

His parents exchange a glance.

"If it gets too dangerous, I'll stop. You know I know my limits. I'm still here, aren't I?"

Tears well in his mother's camera eyes. Oops. His father puts his hand on her shoulder and leans in to whisper something in her ear. Miguel holds his breath and looks at Anna, who looks away. What is her problem? Was she only okay with his entering when she thought he wouldn't get picked?

He turns to Nick instead. It's not Anna's choice.

"Okay." His mother wipes her eyes, moves to hug him. "We're not going to stop you. You're almost an adult. You've always kind of been one, even when you were little, so serious about everything. So serious about Chimera. And we do understand why. You have to *promise* to stop if it starts being too much."

"I promise," Miguel whispers, hardly believing what he's hearing.

"We're worried, son, but . . ." His father trails off, rubbing his face with his hands. "Your life is yours to do what you want with."

Miguel's stomach turns over again, foot dangling over the ledge. He'd nearly thrown it away.

"This is *awesome*," says Nick. "Don't worry, you two. He'll be okay. He'll be amazing."

"So that's it?" Miguel asks, smile growing back to face-stretching proportions. "Time to celebrate?"

Anna turns from the window. "Not quite. Can I talk to you for a second? Alone?"

He nods, leads her to his room, Nick's eyes on his back. To her credit, she waits until he's closed the door before she turns on him, keeping her voice low, simmering with anger. "You coward."

What? She doesn't know what he'd planned to do on that roof. Does she? Can she read him that well?

"Did it occur to you to maybe break up with me yourself?"

Oh. *Oh.*

He breathes deeply. "So many times. I just . . . I couldn't."

"So you thought you'd get Nick to do it for you?"

"No." He moves around her, paces as much as the messy floor will allow. "No. I thought I should . . . get out of the way."

Truer than she'll ever know. He'll never tell her.

"Without asking how I felt about it."

"I know how you feel about it. I know you, Anna. I know how you feel about him. You think I haven't seen it, and felt like shit every day for being the reason you weren't together?" He faces her again. "You're one of the best people I know, one of the strongest. If I were *any other guy*, you'd have dumped my ass ages ago, and you'd have gone after who you wanted like you go after everything else. Good grades, medical school, chocolate."

She cracks the tiniest of smiles, but her eyes are wet.

"But I'm not any other guy, and you're too nice. You've never wanted to hurt me."

"I still don't," she whispers.

"You won't be. Hey," he says, reaching for her hand. "Don't think you're easy to give up."

"Oh, trust me, I don't."

He laughs quietly. "Good. Like I told him, what you guys do now, or not, is up to you. But I love you both."

"Me, too." She squeezes his fingers and drops them, the motion more significant than it should be. "So, the competition. You are going to be careful, right? I may not be your girlfriend anymore, but I'm still your friend, and I will kick your ass if you hurt yourself doing this."

She doesn't make empty threats. "I'll be careful, promise.

Let's go back out there before my parents wonder what we're doing in here."

"God, yeah. Your mom loves to make me blush."

Miguel groans, smile back once more. His mother catches everything with her camera eyes as he and Anna reenter the living room, knowing glance replaced by confusion as she watches Anna move to Nick's side and lace her fingers with his. Miguel shakes his head a fraction. Leave it. There'll be questions about that sometime soon, but not tonight. Both his parents have apparently decided to fake a celebration they clearly don't feel, and the charade is fine with Miguel. He *is* thrilled, excited, happy. And exhausted. The simulated alcohol handed out in tiny glasses spins his head as it tries to grasp the swing of the evening, from death to a second chance at life.

His ears are ringing. He is in a room filled with people and screens, uniting the Chimera contestants around the world. Three from his city, the highest concentration, the rest scattered across the globe. Another lurch rolls his stomach, the moment he was about to step off the roof, one foot in the air.

Who would they have chosen if he hadn't seen his name just in time?

"Congrats," says a girl. She has long red hair and a sharp face. Her clothes are Chimera chic: combat pants and a black vest that shows off toned arms. Pretty, but older than him by several years, and he has to remember she's his rival. Sarah, that's her name.

"You, too," he says. "Good luck," he adds because he thinks he should.

"Yeah," she answers. Apparently she doesn't think the same.

The screens and people all are talking. "Welcome," says a disembodied voice, and as one they all shut up. Like someone's someone has hit a mute button, it's that immediate.

"You are our successful contestants, our leaders," says the voice. "You will be playing our brand-new Chimera. Over the next three days we will assign your teams, and you will be given another three days to practice together before the competition starts. We are aware that playing with a group of living people will change the dynamic. Remember, however, that *you* are the leaders. You have been chosen to make the decisions, and they will be important ones. Take charge of your groups."

The murmuring starts again, but to Miguel it just sounds like more ringing. The voice is like a male version of the Storyteller, cutting through everything, the only thing that makes sense. Everything else is background. He's ready. He wants to play.

You are in a large gray room. Your parents are waiting outside, quietly freaking out. Your best friend and his girlfriend, who until yesterday was your girlfriend, are with them awed.

Miguel grins. He hasn't stopped smiling, even through the

memory of what he almost did, the late night, the tiredness.

"You will be given equipment on the morning of the official start." The voice cuts in again. "You will have to learn to use it as you progress. We may be fair, but we are not going to make it simple. This competition has been designed to test you, to challenge you more than Chimera ever has. It is up to you to decide how much you want to reap the rewards we will offer and the lengths to which you will go to earn them."

Standing in this room, Miguel thinks there is no limit. He doesn't know why they've let him into the competition, but he knows Chimera.

He still wonders why they let him in at all, but now that's just a distraction. He's not going to let his curiosity get in the way of winning.

A uniformed woman, the same stylized Chimera *C* on her pocket, takes his arm, the third time since last night someone has guided him to where he needs to be. In the game he'll be able to make his own choices. She places him in front of a lens, the other two local competitors put into position on either side of him. On 197 screens, close-up shots of other rivals appear, ranging in age from a little younger than Miguel to a few who are about his parents' age. They'll have experience on their side, but maybe not the energy of youth.

"Meet your competitors," says the voice. "Congratulations, everyone."

There's no way to tell how good any of them are without checking two hundred Presences, but they can't beat him. They don't want it as much as he does.

Win, and he gets anything he wants. The Gamerunners' promise.

Win, and he gets to live. What could any of them need that compares?

Maybe one of them needs a new heart, too, or something. Maybe they all do.

Screw it. He can't think about that. He stared into the eyes of death last night, deep and black as if they belonged to a real person, a walking, talking death that was reaching out his hand to claim Miguel for its own.

Their fingers came so close to touching.

Another twist, deep in his belly. Nobody knows what he almost did on that roof, and nobody ever will, but he can use it. He's never wanted to live so much, never wanted so badly to beat anything and anyone that might stand in the way of it.

And he thought he was obsessed with Chimera *before*, but it's not only the game he wants to beat now, it's Dr. Spencer's prediction. His whole life, doctors have been telling him he's going to die, she had just been the last, and the harshest. This competition was how he would prove them all wrong.

"We suggest you all return to your homes, rest, spend time with your loved ones. You won't be seeing them much for a while after we begin. We will summon you individually to meet your teams when they have been assigned. Wait for our message."

Nick joins him as soon as he gets outside. "Zack? Seriously? That asshole?" he says as Miguel spies his parents and Anna and sees Zack talking to Sarah in a cluster of reporters behind them.

"I'm trying not to think about it." Miguel grimaces. The reporters catch up, and Miguel can picture his face appearing everywhere online, captured by their eyes.

"Mr. Anderson, how do you feel about taking part in the Chimera competition? Are you ready for the challenges the Gamerunners have promised?"

"More than ready. I didn't see anyone in there who makes me worry," says Miguel, loudly for Zack's benefit, grinning for the camera's. He's sure every one of the two hundred others have said exactly that, or close enough, in twenty-five languages.

"And you're ready for the world to be watching you? Following your status updates and cheering you on?"

"I guess I'd better give them something to watch, huh? Don't worry."

"Well, congratulations, we look forward to seeing you play." The cameras move away.

"Handled that well," says Nick. "Anyone'd think you'd

been famous your whole life. I put a tag trace on your name this morning. A *million* mentions between breakfast and now."

"Fuck." He's glad he didn't know that before speaking to the cameras. "Seriously?"

"Look for yourself."

He blinks. Jesus. Okay. He can do this.

"You can give your place to me if you're too nervous, you know. Keep playing like normal."

"Please. You got the girl, you want my spot as well?"

Nick blushes.

"That's what I thought," says Miguel. "Come on. I'm supposed to spend time with people, right? Let's do this." *Say good-bye to your loved ones,* says Dr. Spencer's voice in his head, and he shakes it free. She was wrong, she must've been or they wouldn't have picked him. Some other doctor looked at his test results and overruled her. He has nothing to worry about. Now he just gets to play. To win. He pushes through the crowd to Anna and his parents, his mind already on his team. He hopes they don't all suck, that's the last thing he needs: a bunch of idiot deadweights who can't Chimera their way out of a box. And the equipment they've promised . . . what will that be? He's used to his clothes changing the moment the visor goes on, the heft of a weapon in his hand. It's mildly concerning that he won't have time to game with the new gear, but part of the fun for the spectators will be watching the competitors do dumb shit while they're learning, and it probably makes things more fair if none of them have warning or time to practice.

Still, it would be nice to know. Then he could code the stuff into his sim, get a head start.

He can't have everything, and he *has* just been given the thing he wanted most, or the chance to get it.

[Zachary Chan] **Miguel Anderson** Ha-ha I am going to kick your ass.

[Self: Miguel Anderson] You can try. I'd kick yours, but I'd need to earn myself a bigger foot first.

[Zachary Chan] You suck.

Miguel blinks away the messages. It is now officially the longest he's ever gone without playing Chimera since he was twelve. He wonders, again, if this is part of the plan. Get them all itching, twitching, so the start is as explosive as possible. When he'd had his first free day, he'd gone for a walk, enjoyed the real world for a while, but the real world is now something that happens to other people. Reporters have been camped outside his little house for two days, kept at bay by another Chimera uniform, who clears a path for his parents when they need to leave the house.

He blinks, opens a window on his lenses, speaks for the benefit of the mic, sends a fourth message today to Nick, who still isn't answering. Anna's quiet, too, and he's fine with it, really, but couldn't they wait just a couple of days? Spend time with your loved ones, sure. His have ditched him to spend time with each other.

"You hungry?" His mother knocks on his open door.

"Nah. Thanks, though."

"You need to keep your strength up."

He turns his head on his pillow to look at her. She seems older than she did a few days ago. "Okay, sure," he agrees.

His mouth is full when the knock comes, the uniform steps inside. "Mr. Anderson. Time to go meet your team."

Miguel pushes his chair back so quickly it falls over. "Will I be coming back here?"

"Yes, it should only take a few hours."

No need for good-byes then. He gives his mother a brief hug and follows the uniform, a lackey who either knows nothing or is a very good liar, his face blank to all of Miguel's questions. But he's strong, pushing his way through the cameras to create space for Miguel to get in the car. They shout questions through the glass, but Miguel can't answer them because he doesn't know what's coming. He has nothing else to say.

The Cube he's taken to is edged in green. The one just across the river. He's played in it before, but when he steps inside, he sees instantly that they've changed it. Usually a Cube's front doors open onto a small lobby containing only a map on the wall of where to find an empty gaming space in the maze of floors. The map is still there, but it's different.

Hundreds of tiny rooms have been replaced by a single huge one taking up most of the ground floor. One flight up, five large rectangles fill the square footage, divided by hallways. The floor above that is marked only with a *C* superimposed over a single red cross. He knows what that means.

There's no time to inspect the rest too closely. The uniform nudges him toward the inner doors that lead to the large room, they slide open a few inches from his toes.

A gaming room, the biggest he's ever seen. Spots on the walls ready to flare to life and read the sensors that will cover his body. One step inside, the floor springs gently under his feet.

It isn't empty. Miguel's eyes adjust to the light, and a grin splits his face. "You're kidding," he says.

"Thank fuck it's you," Nick answers. "I was afraid I was gonna get Zack."

▪LEVEL SIX

"I mean, the Gamerunners would probably frown on killing your leader, right?" Nick continues.

"I would," says Miguel. "So don't get any ideas."

"Never. Come on, meet everyone else."

Right. Time to look. He closes his eyes briefly and prays that the Gamerunners haven't given him a couple of morons.

Two girls. Good. Sure, it's different with a virtual team, but he knows how tough they are. Excitement grows to match his intrigue at the idea of having teammates who can think for themselves. They aren't just here for muscle, though they'll be that, too. Miguel can't remember the last time he bested Anna in any problem that called for logic. And a guy, shorter than he is but stockier, hair cut short and dyed blue, a choice that doesn't look exactly right on him. But Miguel doesn't care what he looks like.

"Uh. Hi. I'm Miguel," he says. He really needs to remember

to sound more like he's in charge, especially the first time he gives them an order.

"Grace." Tiny and blond. Telltale pupils betray camera eyes.

"Leah." Almost his height, hair as black as his own but her skin a much deeper olive.

"Josh." He of the blue hair.

Their physical characteristics are all he has to go on right now, the only things he really knows about them. That in itself is weird. So much of his life has been lived in words on a screen, personalities rising over the physical, real people just objects moving around him. Most of the rest of it has been spent alone, in a Cube like this one, though this one is different now. His parents, Anna, and Nick are almost the only sustained, meaningful human contact he's ever had. He's had other friends, and teachers, but they don't feel like they count.

And doctors, but there haven't been many of those since the last one gave up on Miguel, and Miguel on him.

"Welcome," says a voice, not the same one that presided over the gathering of all the leaders. Everyone knows there are two Gamerunners, maybe they're taking turns. "Please turn to face the cameras. Step forward when your name is called."

On one gray wall a bank of tiles slides up to reveal a row of blinking lights, red eyes staring at them beneath a line of screens.

"Citizens of the world, Chimera players, our audience. Please meet Team Eighteen, who will be assigned to their city's Chartreuse Cube. We request that you use the Team Eighteen tag in all communications to and about them during the competition. Send them messages of luck or criticism, let them know how much they are entertaining you . . . or not. Our leader, whom you have already met, is Miguel Anderson."

Gulp. But he isn't stepping off the same kind of ledge. The floor is flat, slightly bouncy underneath him.

"Nicholas Lee."

Heat radiates off Nick beside him.

"Grace Morgan." She only comes up to Miguel's shoulder.

"Leah Khan."

"Joshua Cunningham."

"We are very excited about our Team Eighteen and look forward to tracking their progress. Thank you."

The red eyes blink out. The voice goes silent.

This is it.

His last night at home.

The dinner table is silent. Both his parents have tried to make conversation, but to Miguel it feels more like the night before one of his surgeries than just going off to play Chimera. And yeah, he knows it's different, he isn't taking off to the nearest Cube for a couple of hours, but there's no reason for the kitchen to feel like a funeral parlor.

"I'll be fine," he tells them. "Don't worry so much. It's only Chimera."

His mother inhales. "It's not," she says. "But you're right, we said you could do it, we're not going back on our word. We're just worried about the exertion."

"Don't. I push myself in the normal game anyway, and I've been fine so far." They don't need to know what Dr. Spencer said. She was wrong.

He is tired, his chest does ache, but he blames that on three days of gaming with his new team. It's been . . . interesting, which is always a good word when nothing else quite fits. Not good or bad—yet—but interesting.

"Well, at least we'll be able to see what's happening," says his father.

It's hard to imagine that. It's one thing to know someone is reading his updates, seeing where he is in the game based on his geoloc tags and their own knowledge of Chimera, another to know he's about to be a rendered image, broadcast on his own dedicated feed to anyone in the world who wants to watch him. Productivity is going to go way down, he bets. People sneaking off at work to check on how their favorite team is going, comparing with the others.

Will he be anyone's favorite? *Someone* has to like him. His parents and Anna will be watching him for sure, though in

Anna's case she'll be paying more attention to Nick.

"What are your teammates like?"

He shrugs. "You know Nick. The others I don't know that well. I checked out their Presences, their feeds, but knowing what kind of cereal someone likes or seeing the messages they post on whatever board isn't the same as actually knowing them."

"You have everything you need?" Typical mother.

"You should see it," Miguel says. The living quarters in the ChimeraCube are the swishest place he's ever been. A bed big enough for a dozen people, smooth glass and soft carpets everywhere. Someone's been working hard to make the players comfortable—and ensure they don't have to leave the Cube for anything during the competition. A button, pressed, will summon food. A spoken word will fill an enormous bath, like water conservation doesn't matter inside the Cube. A closet is full of all the clothes he's ever lusted after in the game or online, brand new and his size.

"You'll have to take breaks. Come and see us."

"I will. And it won't be that long. Summer always passes too fast." The Gamerunners estimated two months. They've underestimated him. He's beaten every level he's ever played before the projected time, that's not going to stop now.

It's going to suck for the Gamerunners if they've made it too easy. Built up this whole worldwide comp only to have it end in a week. But he's pretty sure they haven't made it too easy, the testing level alone had been kind of a bitch. Then again, they can't have made it impossible, either. Chatter online theorizes that the only way the Gamerunners got permission for this, the extra bandwidth for heightened traffic, to occupy so much of the media, was to assure the worldwide governments that anyone under eighteen would make it back in time for school. Because that matters.

Education for the end of the world. It's weird what people will cling to.

Like hope. Hope that it all can somehow be reversed. That somewhere in some classroom is an undiscovered genius who will know what to do.

"Gonna go pack," he tells his parents. His room at the Cube has everything he needs, but not everything he wants, hard as they tried. Some Chimera minion somewhere had trawled through his Presence and put his favorite soap in the bathroom, loaded a tablet by the bed with his favorite books, stocked some distant kitchen in the underbelly of the building with his favorite foods. They know a *lot* about him. But they can't duplicate the leather wrist gauntlet he'd earned way back in his first week of playing, broken in to fit like another skin and thick enough to offer some protection from a boss's blade. It had been the first thing he'd ever seen in the game outlined in green light, embossed with the Chimera logo. And they can't find another strange blue rock like the one Nick found the day Miguel had defeated his first level and had designated as a trophy. Miguel knows every smooth side and sharp edge of it in his palm.

On the street outside his bedroom window, sunset turns camera eyes to red mirrors. The pack of reporters looks like a group of Chimera demons in the twilight. He's lost count of the number of interviews he's given over the past few days, every time he goes anywhere, all saying the same thing. All *not* saying the same thing.

Nick he knows. No worries there. And playing with him has felt like having a double, an extension of his own mind.

Leah is wicked smart.

Josh goes to his school, though it took Miguel a day or so to remember that. He's seen him around, another person, another thing that's not as interesting as his feed or the inside of a gaming room.

Grace he could throw pretty far, petite as she is. Farther— by a long way—than he trusts her.

He can't say why. She turns away, typing on her sleeve or talking as if posting a status, only for nothing to appear in her feed. Private messages, maybe, but why be so secretive about them? While they've been practicing, she's right there, concentrating as if eager to help solve the puzzle in front of them, then the answers never come from her.

She never meets his eyes.

He's briefly entertained the thought that she could be some kind of Chimera plant. It feels unlikely, not right somehow, but it gives him pause. None of them really know what the Gamerunners have planned, what their aim is for all of this, if they have one. A beta test, sure, they said that, but they didn't say why. The normal game works fine. It's like they're counting on the players—and the spectators—being too excited to ask many questions. Grace could be watching them from inside the game, reporting back on what they think.

Miguel *is* excited.

He'll just have to keep an eye on her.

His parents insist on going to ChimeraCube Chartreuse with him, like it's his first day of school or something. Ridiculous, but when he arrives, the others have brought their families, too, everyone milling around on the street in front of the green doors. The gaming room will unlock at exactly nine. Wherever the Gamerunners are, whatever time zone they're operating on, at least this is bearable. Miguel feels a little sorry for anyone on the other side of the world who has to start at two in the morning or whatever, but they've presumably had enough time to adjust their biorhythms to be fresh and ready. And if not, well, sucks to be them.

So he's not *that* sympathetic.

The chorus of good lucks merges into one voice as Miguel

and his team gather together. Good-byes have been said. Silly, really. He can leave and go home whenever he wants, he just doesn't think he's going to want to.

He is the first in the gaming room, itself almost a living thing, waiting to see what they'll do with it.

The floor bounces gently, ready for running, jumping feet.

"Hey."

He turns. "Hey," he says, and Leah smiles, a real, excited smile, bright in the dimness. Like him, she has spent a few minutes in her suite, changing into clothes that will translate well when rendered by the sensors: sturdy boots, pants with lots of pockets, close-fitting shirts that won't catch or snag while they wick sweat from skin. "I think we shop at the same place."

"Ha. Yeah. You're not going to get us killed, right? In the game, I mean?"

"I hope not."

"Comforting, from our leader."

His shoulders stiffen. "And could you do a better job?"

"Sorry," she says, taking a step toward him. "I didn't mean it like that. Sometimes I forget I don't know people well enough to tease them. You're good, from what I've seen."

"But we don't know what's coming."

"Right."

"Cool, though, isn't it?"

"God, yeah. I can't wait. The hell are the rest of us?"

"Right here," Nick answers, stepping inside, Josh and Grace close behind. "There was a note in my room about not bringing my gear down with me. Are we getting new stuff?"

There'd been one waiting for Miguel, too, broadcast on the blank wall over his new bed. "In there, I'm guessing," he says, pointing to the cabinets that have appeared on the opposite wall. As one they move forward to solve the first puzzle the game has to offer. After swapping places with Josh and then Leah, Miguel finds the one that opens with his fingerprint, re-created perfectly at the tip of his biomech.

A new, uncracked visor sits on a shelf at eye level, between new gloves and strips of sensors, laid out in rows. He swaps his glasses for the visor; it fits as if he'd been measured for it, the molding snug against his brows, not too tight around the back of his head. A speaker tucks into one ear. A microphone on the nosepiece is ready for any command he sees fit to give.

Inside it, for now, is only blackness, a deep, empty blackness that can hold a whole imaginary world. He doesn't want to take the visor off, but he does, none of them are ready yet. Also, it's a good idea to move away from the glass. He knows how to jog in place, move in the game without moving his actual body more than necessary, but still. He's broken cabinet doors in a couple of gaming rooms before, kicking out too hard against a boss.

"Good stuff," says Nick, inspecting the outside of his own visor, tapping it with his knuckles. "Strap up?" he asks.

"Yes." Miguel takes the sensor strips one by one from the cabinet, buckles them around calves, thighs, forearms, biceps, waist. He reaches behind his back to snap the final one into place across his chest, it slips from sweaty palms to the floor.

"Here," says Leah, her own sensors already taken care of. "Turn around."

He thought he was the one supposed to be giving orders. But he does as she says and barely feeling her fingers she deftly clicks the two ends together. A shiver runs down his spine anyway, and he feels a puff of air on the back of his neck, a silent laugh at his reaction. Hey, he wants to say, it's been a long time since anyone but Anna touched him. It's been a pretty long time since even she had, and it was never going to happen again.

But she doesn't know who Anna is, and it doesn't matter.

It's time to play. Finally.

Finally.

"How does this even work?" Josh asks as Miguel leads the way to the open space in the middle of the room and directs everyone to stand in a circle, each several feet apart. "Do we know? Did you get any instructions?"

"Nope," says Miguel, hating the edge of defensiveness that creeps into his voice. As if the Gamerunners had offered to tell him what to do and he'd refused, preferring to figure it out for himself. Did Josh think he was an idiot? Maybe. "I'm just going to do it like normal, see what happens. Gloves and visors on."

Blindfolded by the visor, he waits until he can hear that everyone's stopped moving. "Select: start," he says.

The air changes. His wrist burns, and his leather bracelet vanishes. Okay, noted. He can't bring anything in from outside, even things earned in the regular game.

Normally he'd go straight to his cache. Normally he knows where he's going, has a pretty good idea of what he'll need there.

"Chimera: overworld," he whispers. The sudden burst of green light makes him blink inside the visor, and when his eyes refocus, a globe is spinning gently in the center of the circle they've made. Through its transparent glow, he sees Nick's eyes widen, the visor, gloves, and sensor strips made of materials that don't render in the game. He just looks like Nick, albeit the surprised version.

"Well, that's new," says Grace.

A few weeks ago Miguel's overworld was a string of hexagons that looked like the DNA strand of a mythical creature, now it's a globe like the ones he's studied in geography. That feels so far away.

Welcome, says the Storyteller. That's new, too. They aren't in a level yet.

You will find that this is only the first of many ways in which the Chimera that awaits you is different from the one you have experienced in your playing careers. You are accustomed to a game in which your own goals, and your own enjoyment, are the only things that matter.

Miguel glances around the group. Everyone is silent, listening, curious.

Rest assured you will still have the opportunity to earn the rewards you seek, better ones than ever before, and you may find similarities between the competition levels and what you already know. Challenges, mental and physical, are designed to test you. Puzzles and bosses brace themselves for your attempts to defeat them.

Okay. He's used to that.

But the similarities end there. Gone is a game seemingly without end, where you are battling only for personal gain.

No one has ever completed the normal game. It's rumored to be theoretically possible, but the amount of time it would take is more than anyone has. More than Miguel has, for sure, so he hasn't spent much time guessing what would happen if he did. Probably nothing. He'd be more biomech than human, though, after a hundred levels, a hundred upgrades.

The earth outside is damaged beyond repair, you know

this. Whatever your age, you have grown up with this as truth. Chimera is not the real world, and anything can happen here. The virtual world before you is damaged, too, but you have the chance to save it. It has been invaded by a demon, a demon that has laid traps for you. A demon that lies in wait, biding its time. If you do not defeat it, it will rise up and take over, and nothing will ever be safe again.

Scattered across the world, hidden in often disparate and unnatural landscapes, are the tools you need to break into the demon's lair and destroy the threat for good. Some will be guarded by monsters familiar and not, some difficult to find or obtain. You must get them all. You must save the world. Every choice you make will matter. Some paths will lead to personal reward, but away from your ultimate goal. Others lead to nowhere, and you will have to retrace your steps. Yet others will end in disaster.

You have the chance to stretch your rendered limbs beyond the reach of humanity and become like the mythical gods of old, ruling and reshaping the earth. Every decision will inform the next, will dictate how quickly you reach the finish line, now that there is a finish line. You have twelve levels to defeat before you get there. Some may take you hours, some may take you days. Some will have to wait while one of you receives an enhancement. On all but the last level, there is an item you must collect, in addition to any rewards or enhancements you might win, or bosses you must kill before you can progress. Reach the final level, defeat it, before your rival teams, and you will be admired, worshiped, revered by everybody watching. And everybody is watching. Good luck.

Miguel's mouth hangs open for several seconds after the Storyteller finishes the longest message he's ever heard from her. On the bright side, the best time to look like an astonished idiot is when everyone else around you does, too.

And the more he thinks about it, the more it does make sense. It's kind of genius, really.

"We have to save the world?" Grace asks.

"Just this one," Miguel says, pointing at the green globe. "It's called a story mode. They've totally stolen this from older video games. I've always wanted to play one. What?" he asks, catching Grace's dubious expression. "I read."

"Okay. Where do we start?"

Leah, on the other side of the globe, glances at Nick. "There," she says, fingertip an inch away from a spot glowing slightly brighter than the rest.

"Excellent. Fine. What was it the Storyteller said?" Nick asks. "Let's go be gods. Easy."

Miguel grins. Yeah.

Easy.

LEVEL SEVEN

The overworld is different, but the cache looks mostly the same. Emptier, though, and the weapons and gear that fill the racks aren't as sophisticated as stuff he's used recently; all that has to be reearned.

As in the gaming room currently housing their bodies, there are five cabinets along one wall. Private compartments, one for each of them. Some of the things they find will be theirs alone. Good to know.

"Twelve levels," Leah muses.

"Does that matter?" he asks her.

"I don't know. Probably not."

"What do we need?" Grace asks, moving from one shelf to the next, inspecting. Miguel studies her perfectly rendered profile, accurate as one of his mother's photographs. Pixels don't alter how much he trusts her; he'll have to keep an eye on her. But it's Nick who picks up a gun, fires it at a blank expanse of gray wall. The bullet ricochets, glass shatters.

Miguel ducks, instinct overruling his brain as the volume of his heartbeat cranks up. The readings on his visor are for his real heart, not his rendered one. One breath, two, he calms it before raising his head to stare at the hole in the door of what must be Josh's private cache, if they line up the same way as they do outside.

"Oh . . . my . . . god," says Leah.

Nick gazes at the weapon in his hand as if he's never seen it before. "Sorry, Josh."

Josh glares at Nick, finally shrugs.

"The bullets are real?" Leah asks.

"Maybe not real exactly," Miguel answers, stepping closer to the destruction. "But that's new, the game shouldn't react like that." Normally when you shoot something inanimate in Chimera, it repairs within a few seconds, a clear message that you made a wrong move. "I think it's telling us that whatever we damage stays damaged." He thinks for a second. "That would make sense. We're supposed to save the world, not break it more."

"Including us?"

He looks at Grace. "Inside the game, I'm guessing so. Outside, who knows?"

"Well, we're not going to be shooting each other," offers Josh, "so it doesn't matter, right?"

Right. Sort of. They won't be, and they won't see the other teams—he thinks—who might have reason to kill them, but the bosses are a different story. They've killed him too many times to count. If the harm they cause is real, and permanent, this really is a very different Chimera.

The greatest risks. The greatest rewards.

"Like a dream."

"What?" he asks Leah.

"Even if it is only inside the game . . . what is it they say? When you die in a dream, you die in real life?" A shadow crosses her face.

She's right. There's always been something very dreamlike about Chimera. Jump off a building, feel yourself falling, wake up on your back in a room, pulse racing, unable to remember the exact moment of impact but certain it happened. Step back into the dream and do it again.

Game over here could really mean . . . game over.

"Okay. We take the guns and we be really fucking careful, got it? I know you all know how to use these things, I've seen you when we were practicing. They're the same models we're used to."

"Got it, Captain," says Nick, holstering the one he fired and slinging a rifle over his shoulder.

"Armor up, too." Miguel checks out a vest. It's the good stuff, spun from harvested, genetically modified spider silk.

For now they leave the tents, sleeping bags, boxes of matches, but their presence in the cache is interesting, another thing that points to enhanced real-world effects. They can *sleep* in the game if they want to. Whether it would be restful is a different question, and heading for their suites and huge beds after hitting a save point will probably be way more appealing, but it's worth noting.

There is water, though no food. So the Gamerunners don't actually want them to play 24-7, unless the first 'scape is a tavern stocked with bison and mead, served by Vikings. Hell, it might be.

"Come on," he orders, aiming it more at Grace than the others, irritated with her and himself for his uneasiness. It would be easier if he had something more than a gut feeling, something she'd actually done during practice that he could point to when asking the Gamerunners to replace her. But there's nothing, and he has no idea what would've happened if he'd made the request. They might have laughed or ignored him altogether. Come to that, he doesn't know whether it's the Gamerunners themselves who are monitoring the special inbox he's been given in case of issues.

He refuses to be the first leader to cry like a baby the first time the game doesn't go his way. They let him in. They believe that he can do this, or at least that he'll be entertaining while he tries.

They could be generous, benevolent dudes who want him to earn his new heart and know what he hasn't told anyone: that he won't pass through the regular game fast enough to do it.

They could be *anyone*.

And whoever they are, they've invented a hell of a fun time.

"Ready?"

A chorus of agreement sounds. His digital assistants never spoke. "Chimera: overworld," he says again, expecting the room change, the violet globe, but still awed by it. He finds the place Leah spotted first, slightly brighter than the rest. In the real world it would be several hundred miles away. Here it sits just under his hovering biomech. He waits for the others to gather behind him pretty sure they're not going to step right into the jaws of a demon. If they were, he'd send Grace first.

He closes his eyes and touches the globe.

The room changes.

It's a city street. Not his city, which is definitely by design. Don't want anywhere too familiar, anywhere he might know the way. Somewhere in Melbourne or Florence, a team might be outside the park he hangs out in with Nick and Anna. He'll check later, that would be funny.

Skyscrapers tower overhead, their roofs from this angle looking as though they touch the heavy rain clouds.

"Status update," he whispers. The mic in his visor picks up the command, a red light blinks in his field of vision. "We are in a city. Let the game begin."

A bleep in his ear lets him know it posted successfully. If anyone out there is paying attention, watching, replying, he'll read it later.

"Which way?" Leah asks. "We have no idea what we're looking for, or what we're supposed to do. The Storyteller said we're supposed to find something, but what?"

True . . . and not. "Right. And what usually happens in Chimera when you don't know what to do next?"

"You find a map."

"Exactly." Miguel scans the landscape, turning his head left and right, up and down a street filled with moving but driverless cars. His team is behind him, protecting, Grace angled slightly away as they look. There's always a sign, always a way forward for the sharp eyed and smart.

A faint aura of light outlines a building a few blocks ahead. Not the tallest, but eye-catching. An ivory tower of white marble and mirror glass.

"There. See?"

"Yesssssss," says Josh.

They head toward it. Into difficulty or danger, because Miguel's damn sure it isn't filled with sunshine and girls in bikinis, but whatever's in there isn't going to be the worst thing they see. It's only the first level.

There are no people on the streets. If there were, it would be hard to tell that they were in the game, but there's nothing and no one to block their way. Miguel could be out for a walk in the real world, though if he were the silence would be eerie. He sets the pace, they reach the tower in minutes.

Locked doors.

"Well, shit," says Leah. "We haven't found any codes or keys yet."

"Which means we don't need them," says Miguel. "It's something else."

"Or we ran straight past whatever it is," says Grace, frowning.

"I doubt it. Let me think."

"Do we have that kind of time?"

Miguel elbows Nick in the ribs. Not hard, but hard enough. "Oof."

There are no keypads, no slots, and nothing to put in them. No fingerprint sensors or retina scanners. He taps the tiles around the doors, fine red threads running through the white marble like trickles of blood along flesh. They don't give way.

"Hold up," Leah says. He doesn't turn, but he listens. "Who says we have to go in the front door?"

Wordlessly they run around the outside. The tower backs onto a filthy alley, blocked with chain fences that give way easily to Josh's brutish shoulder. Miguel nods thanks and jogs along, looking.

Another door, steel instead of glass, a handle that turns at the slightest touch.

"Good job."

Leah grins. Okay, they're in, but that doesn't solve the

whole puzzle.

You are on the ground floor of a building. It is filled with offices. Somewhere there is a map.

"I was wondering when you'd show up in here," Miguel says to the Storyteller. She doesn't answer.

"Screw this," Grace says. "It could be anywhere."

Miguel ignores her. He'll listen when she brings something useful to the game, and she's wrong.

"It would take us—any of the teams—weeks to go through every office. It's somewhere important. We're in an office building. Where are the important decisions made?"

"Boardroom," says Leah.

"Exactly. Let's find the tile."

In the lobby a square of marble floor is slightly darker than the others, just large enough for the five of them to cluster together away from the edges. The ledges. He leans ever so slightly into Nick and concentrates on each shallow breath until the tile reaches the top floor, slides sideways, and docks into place.

It's nice for a guess to be right. The boardroom is easy to find, windows dimmed by dark glass but lit by the map on the huge screen on the wall. It's of a building, but not this one.

"We're going to need it later," says Josh. "Can we make a copy?"

Miguel turns to Grace. He'd known the first time he saw

her eyes.

"Fine. Everyone get behind me so you don't block my shot." She blinks. Click.

"Send it to me," he says.

"I will."

"Now."

She doesn't look happy, not that he knows what that'd look like, he hasn't seen it yet. But a tiny corn appears in one corner of his visor.

"Thank you," he says, pressing a blue button under the monitor. A save point.

"Yeah."

"Status updates and let's go. Don't say anything about the map, just that we're making progress."

The first challenge down. God only knows how many to go.

His first Chimera level was like this, some others have been since. Less battle, more treasure hunt—the nickname they're often given in status updates. All about finding things that will help later. After locating the map, they spend the rest of the day exploring the city. Leah discovers a pair of antigravity boots in her size that will allow her to scale walls. In an unlocked store Miguel finds a couple of weapons more like the ones he's used to.

"How are you feeling?" Nick asks, the others ahead, turning over wooden crates, scattered to look like trash.

"This? This is easy. I was expecting it to be a lot harder."

"Me, too, but that's not what I meant."

"I'm fine."

"You're still not going to tell them?"

Miguel cuts his eyes at his friend. "I still don't see why I should."

"It's the right thing to do? Especially now that we know the goal. Oh, hey, by the way, if I run too fast I might faint or die or something, just so you know."

That there's some truth to what Nick says only makes Miguel scowl. "It's none of their business. There could be something fatally wrong with any of them—hell, with all of them—and they're not telling me."

"That's not right, either."

"You're way too concerned with what's right."

"You're way too concerned with winning."

"Yup."

He gets Nick's point, but he can count on one hand the number of people who know, other than doctors required to keep his secret, and he's not about to use the other one on a couple of people he just met. Especially not Grace. He stares across the street at her for a little too long.

"You don't like her."

"I don't trust her."

"Yeah, me neither."

They always agree on the important things.

Night falls, streetlights illuminate their way and turn the level into a game of shadows and glow, shadows in which anything could be hiding. Treasure hunt levels are meant to help; they're also meant to lure the player into a false sense of security. He resists the urge to check his feed too closely, read the tags and see how the other teams are doing. Either they're behind, which means they don't matter, or they're ahead, which he doesn't want to know.

But this is too quiet. Too easy. Even though some levels have always been this way, about preparation, gathering, he can't shake the feeling in his belly. They're all on a ledge, and something's coming. After years of the game, he knows better than to rush forward to find it. That's a good way to get dead. If *dead* is only an inconvenience, he doesn't want to start over, and their last save point was at the map. Their cache is full of things they've found, having to find them a second time would be a waste. He remembers the bullet. It might not be only an inconvenience.

Either way he doesn't have the energy or life to spare.

He slows down. Turns over everything he can lift to inspect the ground for items underneath. Makes note of any numbers that might later end up being essential codes. Watches the shapes of clouds for the faces of monsters lying in wait for them.

When the ground begins to shake, he's almost not surprised. The road begins to crack. At first a hairline fracture, it soon splits before him to an unhealable wound, the vibrations rising through the soles of his feet and up to rattle his teeth.

"Everyone on this side!" he shouts. Nick is with him. Leah and Grace hear him, process his words in time to leap the swelling gap. Josh drops the light car he's overturned, fear darkening his eyes from storm cloud gray to hurricane black. A hungry wind swallows his curse.

"Cache!" Leah shouts. "Boots!"

Miguel can see every feature of her face, but he knows that in the real world she is wearing a visor that displays their armory, her feed, a clock, anything else she's set it to show. The boots appear in her hand, summoned in a rendering of pixels from their database of items. The line between digital and real blurs to irrelevance. She throws them across the gap. "Put them on!"

"They're too small!"

"Would you rather die in comfortable ones? Come on!"

It's cruelly funny, watching him run in them, wincing with every step, but Miguel doesn't laugh. The gap is far too wide to jump now, but it's small enough—just—for Josh to hit the wall nearest them about thirty feet down. Nick anchors Miguel as he peers over the edge, watches the suction come to life and Josh limp, grimacing with the effort of holding his body level, up the sheer surface and away from the fathomless black below.

He and Nick help Josh the last few feet, as soon as they

can reach his outstretched hands. The moment he steps over the lip, the ground shakes harder. Windows fall from above, hitting the ground around them and throwing up hailstones of jagged glass. One slices Miguel's cheek, hot blood sliding fast over sweat-slicked skin.

It tastes real.

The air grows warmer. You look down.

"Where the hell have you been?" Miguel screams at the Storyteller. But he obeys, so do all the others. The hollow chasm isn't hollow anymore. Flames lick up both sides of the fissure, and in the middle, running all the way down the long street, all the way through the city, is a path.

"You've got to be kidding me!" yells Grace.

"It's not! You haven't reached Nineteen yet!" Miguel answers. But it's not exactly the same. "How the fuck are we supposed to get down there?"

He can't think. It's too loud. The roar of flame and the breaking glass and the wind. Metal in the throes of torture, screaming.

A damaged world. One he's supposed to save.

"Did we find any parachutes?" Nick screams.

"No!"

The map. Miguel blinks, opens the image across his visor, blocking out the reality in front of him. He inspects every line, turns his back on the flaming road. "In here!" he shouts, running to the building behind him, its rows of empty window frames grinning toothlessly into the night.

This time the door opens at a touch. Four pairs of thudding feet follow him. Down. They need to go down as far as they can, but he's sure as hell not getting on a tile while the world is threatening to split in two.

The cracks around the stairwell door glow faintly. The stairs behind it descend much, much deeper than any ordinary building would need them to. They passed the *basement* two minutes ago, but there's no way out, not yet, unless they go back the way they came. Which is so not a choice it's not even worth thinking about.

Miguel's chest screams like the twisted steel. He pays it about as much attention. Noted. Move on. Keep going.

Finally a door. The heat hits him first, a blast furnace of hellfire.

"Anyone have any heatproof gloves?" Nick asks over the noise.

"I found some! Cache! Gloves!" says Josh, eager for redemption. They appear in his hands, are on them an instant later, and he reaches for the searing handle.

"Stay away from the flames if you can," Miguel orders. "Remember, if we get burned in here, I think we have to heal naturally."

They have to go single file., and even then they have to be careful. Blinding fire stretches on each side of the path as far as he can see, which isn't actually that far, his vision stained orange and red. And he has to go first.

Amid the flames he grins. His team. His glory. And he's done this before.

As in Nineteen, the path is tolerable if he isn't stupid about it. Not cool, but the heat washes past him on each side and dissipates. His face and hands are fine as long as he doesn't get too close. His clothing is still in one piece. It's a devil, but one he knows.

No one talks as they walk the path, too focused on staying in line, away from the fire. Miguel watches the clock in his visor because of the many things he's learned in Chimera, one is that it is always, always smart to know how long something takes. He makes a bet with himself, is gratified when he wins, the obvious save point beckoning as the end of the chasm comes into view. He steps out of the flames onto a shelf of rock, panting, relieved, and waits for the others to join him.

"We can stop now and pick up tomorrow, or we can keep going," he says. High overhead, a pinprick in the sky, the moon shines from behind a distorted, scowling cloud. "There'll be a boss waiting for us in the morning."

"Keep going," says Nick. The others nod.

Miguel punches the save point. If something happens now, at least they'll never have to cross through the fire again. Not *this* fire anyway.

Beside the save point, a grate, just large enough for a

person to fit through, is set into the wall.

"Looks like it leads into an old sewer system? I've read about these," says Leah. "Our feet might get wet."

Wet feet are a lot more miserable than they sound, Miguel knows that from experience, but he'll deal. "What else were these used for?"

"Moving water and waste around."

"Gross."

"Yeah, well."

"Have you ever noticed that?" Grace asks, stepping aside to let Josh and Miguel pull the grate free. It groans with halfhearted protest but doesn't take much strength. "A lot of Chimera is . . . old stuff. The way the world used to be. Weird for the crazy technology the game uses, isn't it?"

They're the most words he's heard Grace string together, and it's an interesting thought, one that's occurred to him before.

"We've seen the past, but not the future?" he suggests. "We know what history looks like, but stuff like this is new because we haven't actually seen it before?"

"I'm not sure that's it," says Leah, stepping through the grate ahead of the others. Her next words echo. "It's that we do know the future. The world's going to end. What's the fun in playing a game about it?"

"Maybe," says Miguel. "Yeah, fair point. Except . . . we are."

CUTSCENE:
LUCIUS

Chimera headquarters is quiet. It's always quiet. He and Blake have had some disagreements about that in the past. Blake likes chaos, noise, but Lucius always wins those spats. Blake can find chaos outside Chimera's walls if he wishes. He's perfectly adept at creating it if he can't find any conveniently located uproar in which to delight.

The competition is going well thus far. No one has been egregiously injured, and no one will be. Lucius hopes. One of the competitors concerns him, but then, one of his competitors concerns Blake. Fair is fair.

Lucius likes fair.

Sometimes he wonders whether Chimera itself was a mistake, but he must remember that he and Blake are only tools. True, they'd come up with the idea in that delightful little café, but if it hadn't been Chimera, it would have been something else. Their superiors demand results.

Right now their superiors are *thrilled*. Or at least Lucius's are. Blake says the same, and Lucius believes him. He absolutely doesn't put lying past Blake, but Lucius knows him well enough by now to tell the difference.

He hopes.

It was simpler in the early days. There were fewer players, for one thing, and the timeline stretched so far ahead of them both that it wasn't worth thinking about. Time is elastic, and only at the very end does it snap. Truth be told—and he tells the truth whenever he can—he'd spent large swaths of time doing pretty much nothing because there wasn't much to do. All around him people got on with their lives while he watched.

Things are more complicated these days, which is to be expected, and is both exciting and slightly terrifying. This competition is the fruition of everything he and Blake have worked toward for so long. After this the game will change beyond recognition.

Status updates scroll past on the screen in front of him. Each team already has its own set of supporters and detractors, but the messages all say largely the same thing, with varying degrees of sarcasm. *Good luck.* It's too early for anything else. Thus far all the competitors seem to be obeying the rules about cheating and sharing information. He'd told Blake that would happen, though he doesn't discount the possibility that as the game progresses, everyone will become more lax.

That's always the way; people desire to do the right thing until it becomes too difficult. Most of them don't *want* to cross the carefully drawn lines, and to Lucius's way of thinking, intent counts for a lot.

He and Blake have had many arguments about that, too, over the years. The way Blake sees it, how they get to the wrong place doesn't matter. Journey versus destination.

Well. They'll see who is right in the end.

Lucius turns his attention from the updates to much more mundane tasks. They've had to hire several hundred additional actual employees for the competition—neither he nor Blake can be everywhere at once, even if they wanted to be. The players need to be taken care of in their Cubes, fed, guarded, their sleeping quarters kept clean.

"What are you doing?" Blake asks from the doorway. It's been a long time since he caught Lucius by surprise.

"Paying our assistants. You weren't going to."

Blake smiles. "I was going to *tell* them I had. Can't trust computers, you know. Things always get lost in the system."

"Hence why I'm doing it."

"You take away all my fun."

"Not all of it."

"I suppose."

"How are your teams doing?" Blake asks. Lucius smiles.

"Well, but I'm sure you know that. Yours?"

"Same."

"And are you certain the leader of Eighteen was a good choice?"

"He was the *perfect* choice, old friend. He is exactly what the competition needs, and his team is perfectly balanced, I saw to that. One of each type, and he fits ideally into the middle. I know you think I simply want the ones who will stop at nothing, the brutal ones, but he is much more interesting than that. Already he's making some very intriguing choices. Are you worried about his health or his skill?"

"Both," Lucius admits honestly.

"His skill is well matched by your favorite."

Yes. Lucius is proud of him. He, too, is young, but he's seen examples of his dogged protectiveness and his blistering intelligence.

"Don't worry. The teams will be fine. I notice you edited my piece of code that allowed for actual death."

"I left the injuries," says Lucius, "and the penalties if one of a team makes a grievous error, but actual death *did* seem unfair. They *can* still shuffle off this mortal coil, but only if their minds convince them they've died. It won't be our fault."

"Softy."

"Perhaps. You know there's nothing I can do if the leader of Eighteen overexerts himself, if he damages himself too badly."

"You mean there's nothing you *will* do. Good. I'll be

downstairs if you need me."

Were there any casual observers, it might seem strange to them that Blake had come upstairs simply to chat, but who else did they have to speak to? Lucius understands why humans have devoted so much energy to forms of communication, just so they could reach out for someone who understands..

Lucius presses a few keys that will ensure that all appropriate hospitals are well stocked. Small medical centers, set up in each Cube in the days before the competition began, can cope with minor ailments brought on by stress or obstacles, and he checks that these, too, are fully equipped.

The computers around him hum, joining the chorus that runs through the whole building, server upon server huffing with the effort of running Chimera's complicated interface. If any other gaming companies had still existed, like they used to, their owners would have given several essential organs each to get a glimpse of the proprietary software upon which Chimera is built. Lucius and Blake oppose each other on a great many things—almost everything, when it comes right down to it—but each admires the other for the brilliance that created Chimera.

And between them, inside the huge near-silent building they have made their home away from their respective homes, behind walls that shut out the rest of the dying world, a very, very different game is being played.

LEVEL EIGHT

"**A**re you all right?"

Miguel jumps. He didn't expect her, or anyone, but Leah stands in the doorway of his room, shoulder leaning slightly against the frame.

"Why wouldn't I be?"

She points to his face. Oh, that.

"It's nothing."

"There's a doctor here, you should get it checked out."

He's been through that before, the laser running over a split in his skin, his flesh, drawing the two sides together. The scars are faint, but he sees them every time he takes his shirt off.

"Nah. I'm good."

She drops it. But she doesn't leave. "So, Miguel Anderson," she says, stepping a few uninvited paces into the room, "who are you?"

"Excuse me?" She's close enough to smell, and she's showered with something scented. He thinks of oranges and the tea his mother drinks, paper dissolving into steam. They'd hit a literal brick wall in the level and decided to sleep, try again in the morning. He's not the only one who didn't go straight to bed.

"I think you still think of us like a normal Chimera team. We exist, you know. We're actual people. Obviously you and Nick are friends, but maybe you should get to know the rest of us?"

"I've seen you play. Today and while we were practicing."

"And that's all that matters?"

Kind of, yeah. He doesn't say it aloud, but her . . . disgusted? hurt? . . . expression tells him she gets it anyway.

"Tough," she says, standing taller. "If you expect us to follow and help you, you should know us. And we should know you."

His suite has a small seating area; he goes to it without asking her to join him, knowing she will regardless. His bones ache along with his chest. They'd given up an hour into exploring the sewers, an hour they'll have to repeat in the morning.

He shrugs. "I'm an only child. My mom's a photographer. My dad's a chemist, works for a lab that synthesizes flavors."

"I have four sisters," she offers. "You can blame the

population problem on my parents."

He gives her the laugh she's looking for. They both know it goes back a lot farther than that.

"Had you really reached Twenty before this all started?"

"Yep."

"Nice. Then why just the finger? Or do you have other things I can't see?"

His stomach flips. Answer carefully. Keep your face blank. "Haven't earned anything else I've needed so far."

"Ohhh," she says, eyebrows raised. "So you're *that* good at Chimera? You don't need the help the rest of us do?"

"Something like that, sure."

She shows off her own enhancements, he admires her patches of impervious skin, the scars behind her ears that hide sophisticated cochlear implants. She can sense vibrations for miles. Useful for detecting bosses in the game. Useful for quakes in the real world, admonitions from an angry planet. It's been a while since the last one. They say a big one is coming soon.

"Should I whisper?" he asks. She laughs.

"No, you're good. Do you think we can win?'

He *knows* they can. "We have as much chance as any other team," he says, shrugging.

"Yeah."

She looks good, curled on the couch. Toned and tough.

He hasn't been alone with a girl since Anna, who is probably talking to Nick online right now. Thinking about that is a dumb idea.

"You should get some sleep. So should I."

"Okay," she says, rising. Watching her stretch is a dumb idea, too. "We're not done here."

"I didn't think so, but we have all summer."

She smiles. "Fair enough. We're going to meet a boss tomorrow, right?"

"I think so. You know how it goes. Chimera ebbs and flows, gives and takes. We had to find the map. But then just got to wander around looking for stuff. Then the earthquake and the fire path, now we're just mooching around the sewers. Something's coming. So eat breakfast."

"Ha. Will do. Good night, Miguel."

"Night."

His bed is softer here, thus harder to sleep in. He's always had this problem in strange beds, knowing he's going to wake up in unfamiliar surroundings and suffer a few seconds of ass-kicking disorientation before he remembers. It's worst in hospitals, but it's going to be weird here, too. He tosses and turns, jolting into gasping consciousness several times when he dreams of a bed surrounded by flames, and wakes as sweaty as if they were really there.

There's no daylight here, nothing to regulate any of them

except eagerness to keep going. He meets up with the others outside the gaming room a few minutes after seven, a wolfed breakfast sitting heavy in his belly.

"Ready?" he asks, bumping Nick's fist with his own. The dreams made him grumpy, and now he just wants to shoot something.

"Yo," says Josh. Grace is silent but moves toward the door. Leah nods.

Through the cache, through the overworld. They don't exactly have to retrace their steps through the sewers, they've established some of the dead ends, but they still wind up crisscrossing routes that look the same as the night before. "Status update: this is a pain in the ass," says Miguel. His earpiece bleeps. He's grateful they have a chance to warm up before running to or from something, but running at least feels like progress, and beneath his clothes, his skin itches against the sensor strips. Other teams might be so far ahead of them, it's difficult to tell. They're updating from different cities, different landscapes. Some may be too busy playing to update at all. He'd put money on some of them having played through the night, though there's only so long they'll be able to sustain that.

"What are we doing? This whole thing feels like one massive detour."

Water drips down the slimy walls and splashes under his

feet as he paces.

They're all looking at him.

"Let's split up. Update if anyone finds anything, then stay where you are. Find a hiding place if you have to, and the rest of us will come to you."

He picks a direction at random, turning his back on the others and walking down the tunnel. Soon his echoing footsteps are the only ones he can hear, and a strange feeling steals over him. Maybe the others are feeling it, too. He'll ask Nick later.

Never in his life has Miguel been inside Chimera truly and utterly alone. Not even an assemblage of pixels is gathered behind him, waiting for an order.

And the Storyteller is silent. She hasn't turned up once today, which means he's on the right path, totally on the wrong one, or she doesn't feel like stating the obvious.

The tunnel surrounds him, curved, echoing walls and damp, grimy floor. There is no sound except for the water.

But there is light. A light. There, at what looks like the end, though perspective is shit here. He moves toward it, one hand on his holster. It's one light, not two, which suggests it's *probably* not the eyes of a monster, but he's not going to wager his life on that.

And whatever it is, it wasn't there last night. He went down this tunnel with the others, not to the end but close enough that he would've seen it.

"Clever, Gamerunners," he says. They don't answer any more than the Storyteller ever does.

"Have you guys found your keypads?" he asks, voice picked up by the microphone on the visor his real-world body is wearing. Keypads that weren't there last night, that have only appeared once Miguel made the decision to separate.

"Yes." Nick's answer is loud in Miguel's ear.

"Yes."

"Almost there, I can see it."

"Yeah."

"There now."

Okay. They either need to press something at the same time or in some kind of order. He has no clue. "Any ideas?"

"Oldest to youngest?" Leah asks.

"Or the reverse?" That was Grace.

"Too simple," says Nick. "Expertise?"

"We're not all on different levels," says Miguel. "Josh and Grace both are on Fourteen. How do we decide which of them goes first?"

"Screw it," says Leah. "One, two, three . . . go."

He should be pissed at her, he's the leader, but at least it's a decision. He hits the keypad, and the floor beneath him drops away.

He doesn't have time to prepare, fill his lungs. Choking, he falls, lands on something soft enough to cushion, hard enough to hurt. Grass? No. He opens his eyes and tests the surface with his hands. A slightly padded, lightly sprung floor, not unlike the floor on which his real body is standing—actually lying—in the gaming room. Inside, Chimera, though, it means there's something on the wall he needs, the wall of an otherwise empty room.

You are in a room alone. Your teammates are nearby, but you cannot get to them until you find the exit, which you must locate without help. Inside this puzzle, your communication systems are inoperable.

Oh, excellent. He's happy to do this alone, but who knows what stupid decisions the others are making without him? Nick's the only one he has any faith in. Miguel's in charge, so what are the Gamerunners playing at, taking away his ability to lead his team?

Oh, well. His laugh bounces off the walls. If they were with him, he'd have to resist the urge. He isn't supposed to do this. He can picture the same expression on every one of dozens of faces, young and old, the doctors he's seen over his lifetime, all warning him not to.

But he can't stop himself, not for a million in-game credits and a save point every thirty seconds.

The floor bounces under him. A running start and he is

flying, tumbling over and over in the air before landing not quite right, soles of his feet burning as if pierced by hot knives.

He does it again.

And again.

The others might be waiting for him, but they can wait. Leader privileges. Only when his chest starts to hurt past *comfortable*—for a given value of *comfortable*—does he stop. Time to find the way out.

Leah probably has it easy, wherever she is. Won't even need the floor, she can just inspect every inch of wall by walking over it in her new boots. Miguel has to do it the old-fashioned way, jumping at likely spots and hammering with his fist. The tile, when it pops free, whacks him in the shoulder. Its somersaults aren't as good as Miguel's; he gives it a six out of ten for form, then climbs into the air duct.

This is . . . not good. Nobody knows about his dislike of enclosed spaces, not even Nick and Anna, who know pretty much everything else about him. *Claustrophobia* isn't the right word. If it had been, he could've had it dealt with years ago. One electrified probe later and boom, no fear.

But they don't know where all fears lurk inside a mass of neurons. Some are well hidden. Fear of being trapped—even in a wide open space under an infinite sky—is well hidden.

He can do this. He'll be out again soon. Voices, faint and muffled for sure, but voices, get louder as he crawls through a space an inch wider than he is. Elbows bruised, he pulls himself closer.

These are not his friends, his team.

So close, his face an inch from the outlet grate, he can see the room but not the people in it. He doesn't need to. He can hear them well enough.

"You're right," says his mother, clanking something. A dish maybe. A mug of her synthmint tea. "There isn't anything we can do about it now, but I'm not arguing."

"Don't get me wrong," says his father, "he's a good boy. It's just that we haven't been able to do any of the things we planned. It's always been this doctor, that doctor. Doctors who didn't catch the thing before he was born, doctors who can't fix it now."

"Remember all the dreams we had? Travel, you taking time to write a book . . ."

"Now look." His father gestures around. "We just have this."

Miguel's vision blurs, scattering the various input sectors on his visor to raindrops of light.

Is the rest of his team facing everything they fear, or is he the lucky winner?

It can't really be them. They'd never say that.

Would they?

No. Not out loud. But maybe they thought it sometimes.

The walls squeeze tighter.

The grate falls at his shove, doesn't bounce this time. When Miguel drops into the room, it's empty.

He has always been alone. Even his closest friends, his family, don't understand what it's like to be him, though he doesn't blame them for that. He doesn't always understand what it's like to be him either. He tries his best not to think about it, to immerse himself in Chimera and hope that if he's in an empty room when his heart craps out, someone will find him.

He checks his pulse with his biomech. Whatever. He's okay. What's next.

Cockroaches. He should have guessed. Gross. But it's not difficult physically to cross the room, it's only impossible to do without the sickening crunch-splat under every footstep. Killing them, he's fine with, he just doesn't know why something so small has to be so disgustingly loud.

He must be done because there's nothing else he can think of. Being trapped, his parents wishing he'd never been born, cockroaches. That's the list.

He opens the door and steps into an operating room. Nurses move around. A doctor stands next to the table. Only her eyes are visible above the mask, and they're familiar but unidentifiable.

Cold sweat beads across his chest, over the back of his neck. "So you know what I'm afraid of," he mutters. The Storyteller isn't listening, never listens. "So what? This isn't Chimera. Where's the game? What am I doing here?"

"Life is a game," says the doctor. Dr. Spencer.

"Are you real?" he asks her. She wavers, flickers, pixelating in the air.

"Nothing is real."

The nurses fade away with her, and he is alone again.

Too bad he can't do surgery on himself. All the equipment is here. Along one wall, a glass-fronted cabinet displays its temptations in beautiful, temperature-controlled sterility. Hearts, lungs, eyes, kidneys, all jacked into a central hub and glowing with function lights. He could turn himself into a proper cyborg in here, but not with only one pair of hands.

Several more pairs sit on the bottom shelf of the cabinet.

Nope. He's here to defeat monsters, not turn himself into one. There'd be something kind of awesomely Frankenstein about doing the operation on himself, complete with terrible stitching job.

Nah, he'll wait. This is probably what the Storyteller was talking about, traps set for him to choose between personal gain and the larger aim.

He's not that stupid.

But he will take that knife. It sits on a tray of surgical

equipment, but it is not a knife for cutting someone open unless you don't care whether they live. A long dagger with a carved handle, out of place among the sterile steel. He lifts it, feels the motif of apples and vine leaves etched into the brass.

Object number one. His com system still doesn't work, he has to wait until he finds the rest of the team before he can tell them he found it. He might be wrong, but he doesn't think the map counts. Normal Chimera has those. And okay, it has knives, too, but not like this one.

The next room contains a table, five chairs, four other doors, no windows, a spotlight reflecting off polished wood. A blue button shines in the center; he'll save when everyone else gets here. His fingernails click against the tabletop, next to the knife. Waiting. His clock glows in the corner of his visor.

"Status update: I am in a room," he says because he hasn't updated in a while. He wants the other teams to know he's making progress without telling them anything helpful, and the Storyteller's taught him well. He won't broadcast to the outside world that he's alone and has no clue where his team is. It doesn't matter how safe he is inside this private Cube, that just feels like an admission of weakness. Of vulnerability.

And he doesn't trust the game.

He blinks. Is that true? This Chimera is different, but he's always felt safe inside a gaming room, the only true risk lurking inside him, not around a corner.

This Chimera is different.

When the others arrive—and where the hell are they anyway?—he won't tell them this. Maybe when they've given up for the day and gone back to their cushy suites, he'll talk to Nick, but there's a problem with that, too.

He doesn't trust the Gamerunners. They could be listening to anything and everything. Miguel would be surprised if they weren't.

"I get it," he whispers. "I'm alone." The four other chairs stay empty as the minutes tick by. Rhythmic, hypnotic.

He startles awake. Grace steps slowly into the room, her face etched with fear and tears. Her chair scrapes against the floor as she sits down, eyes darting to every corner. She apparently decides Miguel isn't a threat, and her shoulders relax slightly.

"You okay?" he asks. Someone waiting for an eye upgrade could see she isn't.

"Fine."

"Do you want to—"

"Nope. But you seem okay. Are you that good at Chimera? You've been waiting for us for so long you've calmed down? Or aren't you afraid of anything?"

"I'm a pretty Zen guy."

A hint of a smile. "You're so bottled up, if I cut your head off, you'd bleed champagne."

"Bad vintage, though."

Her smile widens just enough to make her look almost nice, almost friendly. Another door opens, and Josh appears. Grace's mask slips back into place, matching Josh's expression of determined fear, doubt that the horrors are over.

"I guess you don't want to talk about it either," says Miguel. Josh doesn't even answer.

Nick arrives next, paler than Miguel's ever seen him. Miguel's stomach does a slow, uneasy somersault. He doesn't know what could scare his friend that much.

The final door opens with a crash. Leah bursts in, a gun waving wildly on the end of a shaking arm. "It's okay!" Miguel shouts, his chair falling back, the thud echoing around the room. "Don't shoot. Leah, it's us!"

Frantic, she looks at each of them. Miguel approaches her, cautious, hands up, and from the corner of his eye he spots Nick edging around behind her. "We're your team, Leah. We won't hurt you. Whatever it was, it's over."

"It was . . . They said . . . I—"

"Just put the gun down."

He doesn't trust this game. Doesn't trust the bullets.

She draws a juddering breath. "Oh." Her hand drops. Nick clears his throat as a warning and swiftly disarms her. "Sorry," she says.

"It's okay. Come on, sit down."

She's in no shape to talk now, and the others probably aren't ready. Miguel could, but he doesn't want to. Something tells him it's necessary for the game that he know what scared his team members so much, but that would mean reciprocating.

Compared to what they seem to have experienced, his own fears seem . . . small. Or maybe not small exactly, but things he can easily pack into boxes and put away on the back shelves of his mind. Boxes of fears. If he dreams of a box of cockroaches tonight, he's not going to be happy.

"It's almost midnight," he says. "I vote we call it quits, get some food, some sleep, and talk about this in the morning." The others nod.

"Hold on." Nick leans over the table and slaps the blue button.

"Thank god that's there," says Leah.

"Yeah," Nick says. "Look, we can talk about this tomorrow, but does anyone have any idea what the fuck that was about? That doesn't fit with Chimera at all. I don't get it."

"I do," says Miguel. It's only fair, he's had more time to think. "It's the game telling us it knows us better than we know it. The Storyteller told us to expect demons. It didn't say what kind."

"So the first ones we had to face—" Nick begins.

"Were our own."

FEED • 2

[Terry Schulemann] That first level is weird.

[Avril Anaya] Weird and *boring*. What's the point in that? I want to see them kill something.

[Olivia Sellers] I'll bet it wasn't boring for the players. Would you want to face your greatest fears?

[Brian Bochenek] You can learn a lot about a person by finding out what they're afraid of. Maybe the Gamerunners want us to get to know them before we decide who to root for.

[Catherine Carr] I'll root for whoever causes the most bloodshed. It's coming for sure, between them finding these objects they're supposed to collect.

[Terry Schulemann] Yeah, what's up with that? You think once this beta test/competition is over, we'll all have to do that in the game? That sounds kinda cool, actually.

[Anselm Lokuta] Ha, you go on your treasure hunts all you want, give me a boss to fight any day.

[Avril Anaya] Anyone have a favorite team yet?

[Olivia Sellers] Too soon to tell. There's a team in London that's looking pretty good.

[Avril Anaya] We can all see your geoloc.

[Olivia Sellers] Whatever.

LEVEL NINE

It's good to be alone. A few hours ago, when he was sitting at that table under the spotlight, it had been weirdly disorienting—weird because he's used to playing Chimera with digital assistants he can never shake but who also never speak. Somehow, quickly, he's become accustomed to having his team of real people around him.

Now it's good to be alone because he's getting the hell out of here.

There's no rule about their not being able to leave, and if there was he wouldn't mind breaking it anyway, but he didn't expect to leave this soon, after just a couple of days.

Okay, they know about the heart, he took their medical, and they can even be forgiven for guessing the fears that go along with it. And he's been trapped in the game before, so maybe they've noticed his heart rate go up.

But he's never seen a cockroach in the game before that he

can remember.

Which is why he needs to go home. If anyone asks, he'll say he wanted to see his parents. If the Gamerunners asked, they'd probably believe that, knowing what he saw on his path of fears.

No one stops him on his way out of the Cube. His code works just fine to get him a hoverboard. His front door unlocks the same as ever.

It's the middle of the night. His parents are asleep. His Chimera sim, though, wakes up at the touch of a button.

The sky is lightening when he sneaks out again, retracing his route through the air. A few hours of sleep and he'll be ready to go again, the itch of an idea lodged in the back of his brain. He's not sure yet, can't grasp the full shape of the thing, but it's coming.

Maybe.

"Hello."

He jumps. Leah doesn't move from his couch, only her eyes, catching what little illumination there is, giving signs of life.

"How did you get in here?"

"Why did you leave?"

"I think, seeing as you're in my room, you should answer first," he says. "Code duello, or . . . something."

"I bring the duel, you choose the weapon? Ha-ha. Clever.

I couldn't sleep."

"That's a *why*."

"Is it?" she asks, all innocence in the near dark.

"I went to see my parents." The lie is easy because it isn't one exactly. He had opened their bedroom door an inch. Just his luck he got a faulty heart and not their joint ability to sleep through anything.

"Oh."

He joins her on the couch, carefully measuring the distance between them.

"You're still treating us like we're a regular team," she says. "Random renderings who only exist to have your back."

"Funny. I was thinking earlier how surprised I am that I've gotten used to you so quickly."

"We've played exactly one competition level together, and half of that we all were split up, plus a few days of training."

He shifts. "Then I don't understand your point. How can you say I'm still treating you like anything?"

"A feeling. You have . . . a wall."

"Last I checked, this was a competition, not a friendship-building exercise." He's arguing for the sake of arguing, knows she's right.

"Does it feel like a competition to you?"

"Not yet, but as you said, we've played one level."

"Yeah, it just feels like we're missing something. Already."

He opens his mouth, hesitates, but maybe this is the first step. "No," he says. "I think I've got it."

Her eyes light up, almost transforming her, and for a second he regrets her disappointment when he says he'll explain later, to everyone. But he doesn't want to go through it twice, not before he's thought some more and not before some sleep. His brain feels like porridge. He won't get much, but even an hour will help.

In fact, after she leaves, he doesn't get any rest at all. The pillows are soft, exactly the way he likes them because the bed was designed for him, but his mind races as fast as his heart. Trying to get to the end of a thought.

There's a big difference between *how* and *why*. He doesn't know why the Gamerunners invented the competition, or Chimera at all, for that matter, and there's a good chance he never will. The *how* of the competition is a different story, and the answer to that was in his sim, sort of. The end of a tangled thread was in there, and it had never occurred to him to pull it before. It had never mattered, until someone had tied the end of the string around a cockroach. What he hadn't told Leah was that it was a good thing he'd been thinking of them as a digital team these past few days. That was the key.

Eventually he gives up on sleep. Through his lenses, he watches all of their statuses switch to green. Awake, online. Leah first—he doubts she went to sleep either. Josh, Grace,

Nick. A cold shower is a crap substitute for a good seven hours, but it'll have to do. Teeth chattering, he dresses in more new comfortable gaming clothes from his stocked closet. But they won't really be playing, not yet.

The breakfast that arrives a few minutes after he pushes the button on the wall is, predictably, porridge.

"Okay," he says when they've all gathered in the gaming room. "Suit up." Leah nudges his shoulder with hers as they walk to the cabinets, and he nods. He hasn't forgotten. He puts his visor on last, selects start, calls up the overworld. A new spot glows on the globe, linked by a path to the city they were in yesterday, but he ignores its temptations for now. Yesterday's level has become a series of tiny, linked dots, the save points they hit.

"What are you doing?" Nick asks as Miguel reaches to touch his biomech to the last one.

"We need to talk."

The room changes. There's the table and chairs.

"We could have talked outside."

You are in a room.

"One we've seen before, thanks, Storyteller. Yeah," he says, addressing Nick, "but if we're being listened to, I feel better knowing it's because we were in the game and not because nowhere is safe. We're being broadcast, sure, but people can't hear us unless we update. That might not be the same outside." He has no illusions about their being watched, overheard. There's likely not a square inch of the Cube that isn't covered. They could be anywhere, and so the *where* doesn't matter except in his own head.

"What the hell are you talking about?" Grace demands.

"Sit, everyone," he says. Nick is curious, Josh confused, Grace outright incredulous that they're not immediately going to investigate the next challenge. Part of him thinks they should be, if only because he's almost certain that what will be there now, and what will be there after this conversation, aren't the same thing.

Miguel isn't just sure the Gamerunners are listening, he's counting on it.

Quickly he scrolls through updates from other teams. Every one of them has started the second level; he has to hope that some, if not all, haven't found the real one yet. If he's right. If he's right, they'll spend the day running around in circles on some bullshit landscape and achieve absolutely nothing. Random treasure hunts aren't the point of Chimera.

"What's up, Mig?"

Miguel takes a deep breath. "I think we're all agreed yesterday was weird, right? Not just for us, for all the teams? Has anyone encountered anything like that in Chimera before?"

"Well, it's a different kind of Chimera," says Grace.

"Right, but why that? Like I said, the first demons we had to face were our own. The game is telling us it knows us. Why?"

"It wanted to scare us, but they're just getting us warmed up, so they didn't want to throw us in with a boss right away?"

offers Josh.

"Well, maybe. I can see them giving us an easy time of it in the beginning, even after our training levels together. Lull us into a false sense of security, give us a chance to learn to function as a team." *Team.* That was it. That's what he'd spent all night looking at, going back over the notes he'd made about his virtual bodyguards in all the levels he's ever played. The ones who'd been with him for years, the ones who'd flickered out thanks to his own mistakes, only to be replaced by others.

That wouldn't happen this time. *What's damaged stays damaged.*

"We need to talk about what happened to each of us yesterday, the things we saw," he says. "We need to talk about ourselves."

"What the hell for?" Grace demands. "I signed up to game, not for some stupid group therapy session. I've been through that already, thanks very much."

"It's not about that." Miguel looks at Leah. She's about to get the answer she wanted in the middle of the night, and for some reason it matters that she be the one to understand this. To think he's right.

"What do you guys know about alignment?"

"That it's good for your spine?" Josh says. Miguel cracks a smile.

"Gaming alignment." He might get some of these wrong,

but he can guess. "Lawful good," he says, pointing at Nick. "Good," he says to Leah. *He hopes.* "Neutral." He taps his chest. "Evil." That's Josh.

"Chaotic evil," says Grace. She doesn't seem unhappy about it. Proud, if anything.

"Necessary," says Miguel. "I'm not saying you're horrible people in real life or anything, but you play a character in Chimera, right? Even if that character is you. You know that what you're doing isn't real, so you can do whatever you want, within the limits of the game. The visor is a mask, if you want it to be."

"I never looked at it like that," says Leah.

"I hadn't either, but I started to wonder when the Storyteller placed such an emphasis on choices and then the thing with the fears. I haven't told anyone I'm afraid of cockroaches in years. Shut it," he says to a sniggering Nick. "The game is saying it knows us better than we think, it knows who we are and what choices we'll make. I've noticed that before, like needing codes in the game that mean something to me in real life, as if it's scouring our Presences or something to find information to use against us. Now it's—it's trying to get inside our heads."

"Hasn't Chimera always been about choices?" asks Josh. "Choose to go right, go left, whatever."

"Sure, but in the normal game, your team has to follow you no matter what, even though"—he looks pointedly at Nick, the only other person alive who knows about the secret in Miguel's bedroom— "I'm pretty sure our digital assistants follow the same alignment pattern. When it's just you and a bunch of pixels, that doesn't matter. You can overrule what they're programmed to do. I might be the leader here, but I can't overrule you guys unless you let me. There's literally nothing stopping you from shooting me in the game and taking your chances without your leader."

Grace's expression is as clear as a status update: *don't tempt me*. Miguel fights back a smile.

"All right," says Leah. "Why?"

The eternal question, applicable to almost everything. Often there's an answer, but Miguel doesn't have one now, at least not on a grand scale. On a smaller one . . .

"Because whatever's coming, however we win this game, it's going to require us to play to our natural strengths and instincts. That has to be why we're all aligned differently. To win, we have to work as a team even when we disagree."

Nick will want to do whatever is the right thing, the best thing for the whole team, every time. Leah will try the same, but context will matter more. Josh will watch out for himself if he has to. Grace will do whatever is right for her, regardless of the wider effects, to get what she wants. She might actively sabotage just for fun.

Miguel can go either way. Left or right. Up . . . or down.

He doesn't say any of that aloud, but he can tell from their faces that they're all putting it together, coming to the same conclusions. That is *if* he's right in his guesses about them, and mostly he thinks he has to be. If he's wrong, he'll find out soon enough.

None of them especially want to talk about their experiences from the day before. He could make it slightly easier on them and go first, but what's the good in being the leader if he doesn't take his privileges?

Up . . . or down.

Nick starts instead, with the simple stuff. His life, his family, and Miguel tunes out. He knows all this already. Leah's eyes are on him, have been ever since they first sat down. He shifts in his seat. Either she's so astonished by his idiocy she can't bring herself to argue with his ideas, or she agrees and, like him, is trying to figure out the point.

In the original Chimera, the little hints that it knew him had just felt like the Gamerunners showing off. *Look at us. We can provide such a personalized gaming experience that the code you need to open that door is your girlfriend's birthday.* That still might be all there is to it. It's not like all of this information about him isn't searchable online. Find out what clothes he's been looking at, put them in an in-game closet. Look up who his girlfriend is, check her birthday. Almost his whole life is there. Almost all of his hopes, dreams, fears.

"Anna."

Miguel blinks and glances sharply at Nick. His friend's face is pale, lips thinned.

"So you had to save a girl and you couldn't? That's what you're afraid of?" The scorn in Grace's voice makes Miguel's hands itch. She doesn't know how Nick feels about Anna.

But he didn't either, not how serious it was.

"Guess I'm next," says Leah. Miguel sits up a little straighter. She talks about her four sisters, which he knew, and being the youngest, which he also knew, but he hadn't done much digging on her family. She's about to be older than the one who died, frozen permanently at seventeen. They never caught the guy, and so it was a nameless, faceless dude in a mask who had chased her through a warped Chimera landscape, calling to her that she was next.

"I wonder what would've happened if I'd managed to get off a good shot. It's why I have these," she says, pointing to the scars behind her ears. "I like to hear what's coming." She's pale now, too, and Miguel can't reach to touch her across the table.

But he wants to.

"I was in a room full of snakes."

"That's it?" Nick eyes Josh doubtfully.

"That's it." Josh leans back in his chair, looking at all of them in turn, his expression a dare.

"This is dumb." Grace folds her arms across her chest. "I'm not talking about it. Your turn, oh, esteemed leader."

He opens his mouth to object, stops himself because it makes sense. They have to learn to cooperate while accommodating one another's instincts, meaning he has to trust her choice even if he doesn't trust *her*.

That's okay. He knows the game she's playing, and he can play it, too.

That doesn't make it easy; first he needs to spot the line he has to walk. The major advantage of a life lived in carefully chosen status updates or alone in a Cube is not having to talk about yourself much. A scroll through his feed would show only Miguel: The Highlights, hardly any of the stuff he'd rather keep to himself.

"I'm an only child," he begins, "and I worry my parents wanted someone . . . different. That I'm not enough for them, you know? There's an upgrade I want," he says, feeling Nick's gaze and forging ahead, "and I think part of me feels like if I get it, I'll be who I always should've been. So I play Chimera all the time, trying to get far enough to earn it, even though the actual surgery part scares me to death."

"Touching," says Grace.

"Oh, shut up," Leah snaps. Surprisingly Grace falls silent. Leah's good, depending on context. He needs to remember that. Stay on the right side of her.

"If Grace still refuses to talk, we're done here," he says, standing, waiting for the rest to follow suit. "Overworld," he says when they have, barely waiting for the violet globe to come into focus before calling up the cache, the room changing around them again.

"Get whatever you can carry," he says. It's a good chance to get Nick alone as he chooses from a range of guns. "Hey, man," he says, "I didn't realize."

"I know," says Nick. "It's okay. She and I are good, we talked again last night once we were done playing."

"Good."

Nick lowers his voice. "Notice you left out some key details there. Not to mention letting Grace get away with not saying anything, and I'm positive Josh lied."

"Me too. But I think this is the way it's supposed to happen. If I'm wrong, then maybe we don't win, and I have as much to lose as anyone, at least, if we don't. I'll tell them when I'm ready."

"You'd better."

"I said I will!"

"You guys okay over here?" Leah approaches, a rifle slung over her shoulder, grenades bulging in her pockets.

"Totally fine." Miguel meets her eyes. She has nice ones. Nick moves away to inspect another shelf. "Are you?"

She smiles faintly. "Yeah. Thanks. I get what you're saying about the alignment thing, and it makes sense, but why is it such a big deal that we know about it?"

"Because the increased human element is what makes this Chimera different from the regular one. If who we are as people doesn't matter, the competition would be one-on-one like normal play. Why they've done it, I'm not sure yet, but you were right, what you said in my room." His face warms a degree, a display on his visor alerting him to the change. "We need to see each other as people. It's important."

"You think any of the other teams have figured it out?"

He's checked his feed every few minutes, automatically, without thinking. He hasn't seen anything that indicates they have, but he's not planning on broadcasting it either. The people who need to know what he thinks were listening to him in that room, that much he is sure of.

"I don't know. Are you ready?"

"Ready."

She's real. He could reach out and touch her and she'd feel warm, human. Behind her smooth forehead, shielded by an invisible visor, are feelings and thoughts of her own, not like the teammates he's used to. He could kiss her and she might kiss him back.

He knows for a fact that's not true of the digital versions. He was thirteen once.

"Let's go," he says, loud enough for everyone to hear.

Back to the overworld. The new level glows. Leader privileges, Miguel reaches out to touch it. The air changes.

"Holy shit," says Josh behind him.

"Well," says Miguel, "this is how the game really begins."

■CUTSCENE: LUCIUS

To the outside world, Lucius and Blake are seen as the owners, inventors, masterminds of Chimera, and that's true so far as it goes, which isn't nearly far enough.

They only chose the method.

Lucius's bosses had been demanding results. What was the point of all this glorious technology, they asked, if not put to good use? Until the end of days he and Blake will argue over whose idea the whole thing was, and that's fine. Lucius knows it was his, and Blake will always claim otherwise.

Lucius steps into an office building, an elevator, a boardroom. All the chairs are already occupied, but he's not expected to sit. Sunlight streams in through the windows, blinding him to their faces.

"Things are progressing well?" one asks.

"Very well. We're on the brink. One team has already discovered their balance, speed will only increase from here."

"We don't understand why there had to be such balance at all," says a different voice. "You insisted upon it, but why not simply fill the teams with the competitors you desired?"

Lucius fights the urge to roll his artificially enhanced eyes. Just because he can't see them doesn't mean they can't see him, but really, he's been over all of this with them before. First, it is unfair, and second . . . There isn't really a *second*. He wasn't supposed to be unfair, none of them were.

Couldn't and shouldn't are different things, but that's a debate for another day.

"We can't predict the decisions people will make until they actually make them," he says instead. "What if we guess wrongly? Better to watch and see what happens. If you were unhappy with the numbers in the data banks, I presume you would have summoned me before now."

"We are pleased thus far. Be careful to keep things moving in the right direction."

"I'll do my best," Lucius says, firing off a salute. None of them really understand sarcasm. Or humor. They care only about their bottom line, a tightrope they'd fall off if they laughed.

He understands that they're impatient, and why. As he leaves, he passes beneath the same clock he did when he arrived, if it can be said to be the same when it now displays slightly different numbers. Are things the same if they remain static in essence while their details change? He'd had a long argument about that with Blake once, every Friday afternoon for most of the eighteenth century. He blames the humans for that. They'd done a lot of thinking back then, and it was contagious.

The clock isn't actually a clock exactly. It's a timer, and Lucius remembers a time when most of the numbers weren't zeros. Only the last two are still counting down. That the *number* of numbers has never changed can mean only one thing.

They've always known how long it would take, exactly how long they would need.

▮LEVEL TEN

Standing in a circle, they stare at the place around them. It is at once unfamiliar and the way Chimera always should have been. The graphics are so good they make them, the humans, look fuzzy and pixelated. Like they've stepped into the next evolutionary stage but haven't caught up with it yet. Like the gods were just practicing with them and got it right with version 2.0.

Miguel doesn't believe in any of that stuff, but he can't think of another way to describe what he's seeing, and spending years in ChimeraCubes has definitely affected the way he thinks. "Let's go be gods," Nick had said.

But even through his visor, it almost hurts to look at.

Reality—with extra everything. Lights are brighter, and he can see every color in the white. Lines are sharper, as if they'd cut skin. Sounds are loud, clear. Traffic, people, music, the endless hum of a city. It doesn't matter that it's not one he recognizes: the strangeness cannot be ascribed to that. He glances over his shoulder; Leah is right there, close. Her open mouth seems blurred at the edges.

"Are we all seeing the same thing?" she asks. "Is it just me, or does it look—"

"More real than real does?" Josh says.

"Yeah, that."

Miguel takes a step. A careful one, he's not too proud to admit. The street feels as if it could shatter any second. It doesn't. The sidewalk is solid, every atom sparkling individually but fusing to form dull stone.

Chimera delights in reminding you that you never know what's around the corner, under that rock, on the other side of a doorway. Mountaintops to skyscrapers, deserts to oceans, skies to depths.

He's never left his city, but he's seen the world. Maybe that's part of the appeal or part of the point. Show the players the planet they're trying to survive on.

"This makes no sense," he says. "The Storyteller said we're playing on a damaged world, we're supposed to save it by passing these twelve levels. Does any of this look damaged to you guys? The last level didn't either, until the earth split open. It all looks perfect." The road is completely smooth. Trees are lushly green. Mirrored buildings catch and hold the light.

"Does ours? The real world? No, and we know it is," Grace

answers. "We know the damage is there, in the sun and the rain and the soil, but we can't see it. All they do is build more sheltered parks and erect more composite trees and clean more junk off the streets."

"That's true, but—"

"It's human nature to cover up anything broken, anything ugly. Leah, you wake up in the morning with a zit or something, what do you do?"

Leah's eyes narrow. "Put on makeup."

"Right. And then you catch your reflection an hour later and you can pretend the problem isn't there. You know it is, but the pretense makes you feel better about yourself. Stronger, more confident. If it didn't, you wouldn't cover it up in the first place."

"But the whole world does it," says Miguel. "The real one. Who are we showing off for?"

Grace holds up her hands. "I'm here to game, not philosophize. All I'm saying is that something's lurking beneath the veneer."

"Okay," he says. "Let's see what's waiting for us." He moves further into the brilliance, the team following. He assumes from the height of the buildings that they're downtown, but he knows the city only as a place on a map. He can't see any landmarks he's heard of or seen pictures of online.

A station sits across the street, too obvious to be coincidence among the towering buildings. Every time he's ever seen one inside Chimera, he's needed it.

"I think we're supposed to find out where we are, or be up high for something."

That's why Nick's his best friend.

"Yeah," he says. "Everyone, grab a board."

They don't need to enter codes for these; they're meant to have them. Grace is the slowest to get hers from its dock, and when her fingers curl around the curved edge, her knuckles pop from her thin hands.

"You got a problem? You think we should be doing something else?" Miguel asks, already standing on his.

Her lips thin, and she shakes her head, turning so she can sit on the thing.

You are rising rapidly in the center of a cluster of buildings. From this height you can see most of the city.

All of them can, except Grace anyway, who can see only the backs of her eyelids.

"Heights!" shouts Miguel over the wind, stronger than it was on the ground. "That's what you wouldn't share with the rest of the class?"

She manages to sneer while keeping her mouth decidedly closed, which is probably a wise move. Puke from up here could do some damage, albeit only to a collection of tightly packed pixels below. In real life Miguel had dented the hood of a car once, but that hadn't been out of fear.

They spread out in a circle again, about ten feet apart. Miguel has a better sense of where they are now than the overworld gave. A real city, just not his. The needle of glass and concrete in the middle distance beyond Nick is famous.

He yells. Nick, Josh, and Leah follow his pointing finger. Grace still has her eyes squeezed shut, and Josh swoops over to touch her on the shoulder. She jolts, only her iron grip on the hoverboard keeping her from falling.

What would take an hour or more on foot takes a few minutes in the air, the city whizzing by underneath them. Computer-generated people walk up and down the streets, go in and out of stores and offices like nanobots moving through veins to and from a pulsing heart.

They land on an observation deck so high it would be abandoned in the real world, the atmosphere too close. Grace grips the railing, knees knocking together. This probably isn't much of an improvement for her, though she must be glad to be off the board that is now a bullet shooting back to its dock.

"Are you okay?" he asks her. "Look, I didn't mean to . . . We're all scared of stuff."

"I'll be better if we get inside," she says, shaken enough to sound like a real person for once. Nick pushes open the door, and inside, the silence rings without the wind to fill it. The curved couches follow the lines of the walls and windows, because climbing halfway to the moon to sit around like the way you could do at home is everyone's idea of a good time.

There's even a fruit bowl on a glass table.

With a golden apple in it. Nick and Miguel spot it at the same time and Nick dives, claiming the out-of-place thing. He caches it and turns to Miguel, grinning. "Well, we found the item. Any idea what else we're doing here, oh, Chimera expert?"

Leah snickers.

"No," he says, mock scowling, "but landmarks are kind of the *point* of cities, you know? They define them. Take away the thing in every picture, and it's just . . . a place that could be anywhere. People like something to focus on. Icons."

"So now you're our leader *and* resident psychologist?"

Oh, good. Grace is back to herself.

"You were the one who said we cover up the broken things. Follow that thought. What do we preserve for as long as we can? What outlasts the people who built it?"

"I got stuck in a pyramid for a week once, playing every day," Josh says.

"Exactly."

"But things like that are ruins, and we don't cover them up," says Nick.

"No, because ruining something you made is easier to accept than ruining something you've been given. You can always make another one." His heart thuds a reminder. "But none of that matters now anyway. My point is . . . there is a point." The more real than real detail of this level has wormed its way into his brain. "It makes sense that we're here, that's all. No matter where you are in the game, there's a goal, and a path to follow. It's never aimless, even if it sometimes feels that way. Ask me how I'm sure."

"How are you sure?"

He grins at Leah. For now he can pretend that he realized this is the moment he laid eyes on the building and that it hadn't been a lucky guess borne of more game experience than he should really have. In fact, he hadn't known until midway through the flight.

"Because," he says, blinking several times to bring the right image up on his visor, letting it draw itself in violet lines on his field of vision, "we have a map."

The thing about being on top of the world is it makes you feel on top of the world, as long as you're not scared of heights. He blinks again to send the image to all the others, and together they inspect it. The path is marked from room to room, but there's no indication of what's waiting for them in each. That'd be way too easy.

"First one is on the thirty-second floor," says Nick. "We're on the thirty-third."

"Does he always state the obvious?" Grace asks.

"Almost, yes," says Miguel. "Ready?" This landmark is old enough to have an elevator instead of a tile, he leads the way to doors that open at the push of a button.

The other thing about being on top of the world is that it's a long way down.

Nobody ever complains about treasure hunts, but he's not going to lie, he was expecting something more exciting.

It's harder to be democratic in an enclosed space; last time they were out on the street and with more real estate, opportunity felt correspondingly more expansive. After the first couple of rooms and Grace being what he is rapidly learning is *Grace*, he makes a choice.

"We can take turns. Leah, take the next one."

"It's another map," she says a moment later, emerging from some kind of storage room. "Not sure where to, doesn't look like a building."

"Keep it," he says.

"Don't you mean she should send it to you?" Grace asks.

"Oh. Yeah. Send it to me," he tells Leah, silently and probably unfairly cursing Grace. Between them—to put it democratically—they've found the map, a bulletproof vest, another gun, and a parachute. "Nick, you good with the elevator shaft?"

"Hell yeah. Gonna need a rope, though, unless you want I

should just parachute down and hope I get lucky."

"I've got a rope," says Leah, rummaging in the backpack she brought with her from their cache. "What? Never know when it might be useful."

He helps Nick rig a harness while Josh sends the elevator to another floor and pries the outer doors open, muscles bulging. "Don't look, Grace," Josh says.

"Don't you dare fall, I don't know how I'd explain that to Anna."

"Three simple words: I dropped him."

Miguel laughs. "Get down there."

Nick lowers his voice. "You okay?"

"I got you. Go."

The rope burns Miguel's hands. He holds it as tightly as he can, and it's not so bad with Josh and Leah taking some of the weight. They're almost up against the opposite wall, unable to see Nick after his head disappears below the floor. Clangs echo up and down the shaft as Nick's boots strike metal. The rope stretches tight, Miguel leans back, knees bent, toes curling inside his socks like that will help his feet grip better.

"Damn," pants Leah. "Why'd they have to hide something down there?"

"It's not like this is an office building or some shit," says Grace, leaning easily against the wall beside them. "It's a giant phallic 'look what humanity can do, look how special we are' piece of crap with no actual use. It doesn't need to be filled with convenient rooms to hide things in. It only needs to be tall."

She might not be wrong, but Miguel is too breathless to agree with her even if he wants to. Something sharper than a blade is stabbing his chest, the pain searing all the way up to his jaw, cracking like electricity between his gritted teeth.

"Got it! Let go!"

"What?"

"I can drop down to the top of the elevator from here." The echo sounds like several Nicks. "Take the stairs and meet me on, uh, fifteen."

"Roger that," says Miguel, dropping the rope.

"Who's Roger?" The laughter of many Nicks fills the air.

"Your friend has a terrible sense of humor," says Grace, just in front of him on the stairs.

"He knows. It's kind of intentional."

"Oh, well, that's all right then."

Nick has the stairwell door open, waiting. "A first-aid kit," he says, preempting the question. "Filled with all kinds of stuff."

"So any damage is real but can be healed?" Leah takes the kit from Nick, rummages through it.

"Good to know," says Miguel. He bets he can test that theory, and for a second the walls of the building close in, narrow and narrower, to squash his thudding heart. Keep playing and maybe die. Don't play and definitely die. Black spots burst across his eyes, he gulps the air quietly as he can. Don't panic.

"I am curious how this game even works, like, the code parts. In the normal game, you get hurt or die, you wake up just fine with LEVEL FAILED flashing at you, and I get that. It's never game over. Now they're saying the injury or whatever goes with us, if we make it out alive, but we can be healed inside the game. And outside of it, I guess. I wonder what actually happens when one of us gets really hurt," Leah muses.

He suspects they're going to find out sooner rather than later, but he doesn't say so. For one thing, Leah's probably guessed the same, and for another, expecting it will only make it happen faster.

He blinks. The violet map flickers to life. The next thing is a dozen floors down.

Elevators are better than stairs, but Miguel still has to stand in the corner trying to hide the pain, the wheezing breaths that won't calm. Nick squints at him, one eyebrow raised, and Miguel shrugs. He's okay, it happens.

"There's no third floor on here," says Grace. "Goes from four down to ground."

"Ground," says Miguel, unsurprised to step into a huge, open atrium when the doors open. It's his turn, but he can't see anything obvious. The walls are flat, smooth. There are no nooks in which something could be hidden. Maybe a secret panel? But the map says the thing is on a nonexistent third floor.

He looks up. A giant chandelier glows despite the daylight flooding in through the windows. It looks like the twisted metal claw of some robotic god, something now wandering out in the wild, handless.

The bulb pulses. His mouth opens.

He found one once. Only once, and that was lucky. He's the only one he knows who ever has.

"I need those boots," he says.

"Will they fit?" Leah asks.

"They'll fit."

"I could get it for you," she says, but he shakes his head. No. He's going to claim it. It's his. He needs it most.

"Cache," she says, blinking. "Summon boots." They appear in her hand. "I still haven't used these," she says, passing them over without argument. They're tight, not as bad as they must've been for Josh. He can put up with it for a few minutes. Also, how big are her feet?

"Don't even. Buying shoes is a pain in the ass. I have most of them custom printed when I can."

Oops. He hadn't meant to be that obvious about it. Oh, well.

"Mig—"

"I'm fine," he tells Nick, walking to the wall. He just needs to walk up it and then hang upside down for a while. No problem at all.

The wall actually *isn't* a problem. It's a little weird, leaning forward and trying to pretend the laws of physics are just optional guidelines, but in Chimera they kind of *are* optional guidelines, and he's done stranger stuff in the game when he's had to. One foot in front of the other, one breath and another, one prayer that the soles will cling again every time he lifts his foot.

He stops with his face six inches from the wall. *Ceiling.* Now for the fun part. His arms automatically spread for balance, like that's important, but it's better than letting them hang down above his head. Or below. Whatever. No wonder bats use echolocation, this seriously fucks with perspective.

Each step is more careful now. One, two, three toward the middle of the ceiling that has become a floor. Cool air blows across an inch of belly; he tucks his shirt tighter before it can blindfold him and show his crisscross of scars to his team below. His head sways, and the claw blurs, reaching for him. Come, let me crush you in my fist.

Half expecting it to burn, he reaches carefully for the bulb. Far below, Nick says something indecipherable.

"Mine," he whispers under his breath, fingers closing around it.

As is always the case, the return journey is quicker, easier. Miguel barely notices the rising blood, the pounding in his head increasing with every beat.

Relief floods him, a better drug than oxygen, when he plants both feet on the actual floor.

"So *that's* what they look like," says Josh. "I always figured I'd know when I saw one." An orb of living light, swirling and shifting inside something that feels like glass but that compresses slightly under Miguel's thumb as he tightens his grip on it.

"You good?" Nick asks. Miguel nods.

"Small price to pay for ten minutes of invincibility."

"Damn it." Grace pouts. "Wish I'd found that one."

"Cache," he says, and it vanishes from his hand. "Status update: landmark achieved."

▌LEVEL ELEVEN

The darkened chandelier, looking even more like a claw without its bulb, glints in the daylight. It *feels* as if this Chimera, like the normal one, is operating on a standard clock. That could change anytime, but for now nobody's tired and they don't yet have to quit to get some sleep. Good thing because they haven't found a save point yet.

There are patterns everywhere, as a team they've fallen into some already. Miguel leads the way outside, the brilliant preciseness of the world not so overwhelming now that he's used to it.

But his senses are still heightened, maybe from the blood rush. And there's something—

"Run!"

The inhuman pixel people on the street don't hear his shout, don't respond. Thankfully his team does. In this world of insane detail, the seconds are crystalline, individual as time slows. The earth shakes, rumble to roar, and the explosion is deafening, a chasing hellhound of sound. All that glass, metal, concrete, not real but more than real, shattering. It fills the air around them, a razor shard misses his shoulder by a whistling breath.

Not real. More than real. It's more contained than it should be, would be in the real world, because they're meant to escape it. The building has fulfilled its purpose: to lure them in, reward them, keep them in one place.

He slows two blocks away. Whatever's behind them, they aren't going to outrun it, and he doesn't want to. They have to get rid of it to move on. As one the five of them turn around.

It stands where the tower did, a demon of metal and mirror, mouth bared in a toothless, soulless grin. Red eyed and angry, it fixes on the five and crushes the ground under its first step toward them. Humanlike, but clearly not. He was right about the hands—just the Gamerunners' little joke. Chimera is full of them.

"Get everything you have!" he shouts, scanning the monster. It will have a weakness. Somewhere, a critically weak spot.

"Don't we all?" he asks himself, raising his gun. Aiming.

Bullets ping off its shell, hailstones off a window. Not doing anything, but he has no other ideas except to keep shooting, looking through the sight for the right place. Nick is beside him, Leah just behind to his left. "Flank!" he shouts to Josh and Grace, but they already are, running in different directions to circle it.

The machine monster's head swivels, attempting to keep all of them in view at once. A faint glow seeps from the seams made by its joints.

"Cache! Summon pulse gun!" The weapon in his hand changes to an early, heavier version of one of his favorites in the normal game, one he wishes he had more excuse to use. It should still work even if it's not as good as his old one.

Or it would, if Josh wasn't about to be stupid.

"What the fuck are you doing? Move!" he screams at Josh, who ignores him and runs, leaps onto the monster's back, slipping and scrambling for a grip on the slick sculpted metal. Confused, enraged, the boss staggers, arms flailing. Miguel dives around a corner in a haze of searing red light, a fountain of sidewalk pluming up where he was just standing. He rolls to his back, gasping, hand still curled around the gun. Nick screams his name. Chest burning, fingers numb, he points it but doesn't shoot. "Get off! I can't shoot it while you're on it, I'm gonna fuck up your biomech!"

Josh pretends not to hear him, or actually doesn't hear him. Noise crashes everywhere, and Miguel doesn't know how loud he was, how much voice he squeezed from his burning chest. His eyes still work. Nick and Leah are a few feet away on either side of him, crouched, unable to do any more than he can. Grace is somewhere on the other side of the monster, which is still flailing, swatting at the irritating human on its back.

"What the hell does he think he's doing?" Miguel asks, not expecting the others to answer. Josh is going to get himself or the rest of them killed. He votes for the former, if he has a choice, but damn it, he doesn't want to lose a team member at the first boss.

It takes another heavy step forward, roaring, its eyes blazing fire in its silver skull. Josh is clinging to its neck with one arm, the other hidden behind its shoulder. What *is* he doing, besides pissing the damn thing off? Its clawed hands curl to fists and open again as its eyes focus with laser precision on Nick.

It reaches. Swipes.

"No!" Miguel screams as Nick is lifted in the air, the monster's twisted fingers closing around him. "Josh, you have five seconds to get off there or I'm shooting anyway and fuck your biomech!" But it's an empty threat now, and they both know it. He doesn't mind fusing out the inhuman parts of Josh, but he won't destroy the things Nick's spent years earning.

Seconds feel like minutes. Does he have time to summon the orb, use it so he can just plow the monster down?

Metal screams. So does the monster as its arm disconnects from its shoulder, falling, Nick with it. Josh releases his grip and jumps, landing hard but on his feet. "Now!" Miguel tells Leah, and they both raise their weapons, firing electromagnetic pulses at the roaring, angry robotic hulk. He has no idea how many times he fires, who gets off the kill shot. He doesn't care. The boss raises its remaining fist for a last furious swing and stops, staring curiously at its own hand as the light in its eyes fades to black.

Miguel scrambles out of the way just in time to avoid being crushed by the tumbling body. He doesn't stop moving, running to Nick, still on the ground. "Where's that first-aid kit? Cache!" He summons it, rifling through, ignoring the disintegrating boss behind him. "Nick? Can you hear me?"

"Yes," whispers Nick, blinking. "Jesus, stop shouting. I'm fine. Ow." He points at his ribs and winces. Miguel finds a preloaded syringe, places it against Nick's arm, and presses the button to send the painkillers flooding into his system. Only then does he turn, just in time to see the last metallic flash of the boss wink out of existence, leaving a glowing blue save point in its place. Grace runs over and stomps on it. Like she'd helped at all.

"He okay?"

"Yeah," Miguel tells Leah, standing. "Want to tell me what that was about?" he demands, advancing on Josh, who smiles, still holding the monster's disembodied arm.

"Quit out," Josh answers. "I'll show you."

They do, Nick grimacing as he pulls off his visor in the gaming room. Leah moves to help him with his sensor straps, Miguel follows Josh to his cabinet in the wall.

Inside is a gleaming new biomech arm, its hand a claw, hooked to a power hub, the nicest, most impressive one Miguel's ever seen. "When I got behind it, I saw a green light where it joined the shoulder. Green light all over it, actually, from the back."

Oh. "Meaning it could be taken out of the game." Sort of. Meaning that a replica would be waiting on the outside. "And you decided to risk the whole team without telling me? And not mention that maybe there was other stuff we could take?" Thoughts spark in his brain. *Chimera.* Until now biomech rewards have been selected at the end of certain levels, a restaurant menu of transhuman technology. Turning them all into cyborgs, piece by piece.

This is . . . different. *Rewards that will make your previous enhancements look like toys.* But not earned the same way. Of course the Gamerunners didn't tell them that.

"Sorry." Josh shrugs.

The doors open, two women in medical uniforms walk in. "We are ready for you," one says to Josh, gesturing at the open cabinet. "Does anyone else need assistance?"

"I should get checked out." Nick joins them. "So should you," he says to Miguel.

"I'm fine."

"Mig—"

"Seriously." He is. He didn't go into the gray zone for more than a few seconds.

"We'll be upstairs," says one of the doctors. Grace follows them out, leaving him and Leah alone. "Well," she says, "we beat our first level. Go us?"

"Ha. Yeah. Thanks for the help there."

"What I'm here for. Do you want to come eat with me? I'm starving."

He does, but— "I should actually go keep Nick company."

"Okay."

He waits for her to leave, walks over to a corner of the huge room. The sprung floor isn't uncomfortable to sit on. His bed or the couch in his suite would be nicer, but she's proven she can get in there, and while he doesn't think she'll check on him right away, he needs to be alone. Needs to think. He puts on his lenses, lighter than the visor he's been wearing for hours.

"Status update: first level passed," he says, giving no hint how or what was waiting at the end of it. Later he'll read through some updates, see where his competition is.

There's so much he needs to do. Lead his team, keep track of the others, find treasures, defeat bosses.

Find another metal demon.

And tear its heart out.

Ten minutes with the doctors upstairs, and Nick is healed because some things are easy to fix. Miguel's heart can't be healed like that; some things are beyond repair from the moment they begin to exist.

Well, he's one step closer, despite Josh's stupid stunt, which he'd resent a lot less if it didn't mean a delay. It'll be a couple of days before Josh can play again, and they have to wait for him. Miguel could go home, but it sort of defeats the point of proving his independence, his ability to do this, if he runs back every chance he gets, and the Gamerunners might think he doesn't have what it takes if he leaves again so soon. He's answered his parents' many messages, and Anna's, too, that's enough.

Anna. He's pretty sure that's what Nick's doing, talking to her. His geoloc tag on his last public message had him in his suite, then silence. Miguel's just enough of a masochist to imagine what she's saying to Nick, the same kinds of things she used to say to him, ages ago, but he's still not mad about it. Relieved, if anything, that they're happy and he doesn't need to worry anymore about what being with him did to her.

Which isn't to say there aren't some things he misses.

Leah's in her suite, too, also not saying much publicly online beyond a few vague comments about the level. Maybe she has someone she's talking to.

As with every night of his life that he hasn't been able to play Chimera and hasn't been forced out of the house to do something else, he winds up online, blinking to scroll through page after page on his lenses. Clothes he doesn't need, news he doesn't care about, video game history he's already trawled through too much of. He wouldn't call himself a scholar on the subject, but Chimera fascinates him, and not just the playing of it. The why, the endgame no one has reached. God, he can only imagine what'll happen when someone finishes the hundredth level: the cameras will be worse than the crowd outside his house when he was named to the competition. That person better enjoy their last Chimera experience because they're never going to get a moment's peace once they defeat it.

He envies them the fame he imagines and the surely completely metallic reflection in the mirror. A body built, small at first, fingers and toes, to spine and ribs and heart and kidneys. Plastic composite skin wouldn't look as cool as silver or black, but it would make them appear more human.

But how much humanity would they have left? They would be full, true . . . chimeras.

A message interrupts his thinking. From the one person he doesn't want to talk to.

[Zachary Chan] **Miguel Anderson** Congrats. I see you beat that boss.

[Miguel Anderson] What do you want?

[Zachary Chan] Nothing, man. Just saying, don't get too cocky. You aren't going to win.

[Miguel Anderson] Go away.

He blinks, sending the text off into nothingness, pulls off his lenses, stares at the ceiling of his suite. He should be thinking about how to do what Josh did. Not all bosses in Chimera are robotic, some are as much flesh as he is. More so, with wings and talons and tails. Even if he could take the heart of one of those, he doesn't want anything like it put inside his chest. He needs something like the boss they defeated today, another machine.

A sick feeling floods through him. He puts his lenses back on, opens a message to Nick.

[Miguel Anderson] You still talking to Anna?

[Nicholas Lee] Just finished. What's up?

[Miguel Anderson] Come to my suite?

[Nicholas Lee] Roger that.

The knock comes a minute later; Miguel lets him in, wanders over to the sofa, and waits for Nick to slouch down at the other end.

"She okay?" he asks.

"She's great. You haven't talked to her?"

"Not as much as you have."

Nick smiles. "Fair. She's great. Wanted to know all about the level."

"Yeah, about that . . ." He stands again, moving to a small fridge the Gamerunners had thoughtfully included among the many benefits of his room. He grabs two bottles of water, tosses one to Nick, who catches it easily. "Josh's new arm," he says, sitting back down.

"You think that's how you're going to get a new heart."

This is why they're friends.

"What if that was the only one and I missed it? Sure, the

rest of the bosses we have to face could be humanoid machines, but what if none of them are? I want to go back in. Fight it again. Crack it open and see what's inside."

Nick's eyes widen. "It's gonna be a couple of days before we can. And, uh, how do you plan on telling the others that we need to go back and repeat half a level we've already beaten without telling them why?"

He knew Nick was going to ask that. "I'm not going to tell them, and I don't want to wait."

"You mean—"

"Your ribs okay? Awesome. Let's go." He walks to the door, swings it open, and keeps moving down the corridor, giving Nick no choice but to follow him. If Nick wants to talk him out of this . . .

He does, and he does. "This is a bad idea, Mig," Nick says, jogging to catch up. Their boots echo on the stairs. "We need all five of us."

"Do we? We know how the level goes between the last save point and the boss. Simple treasure hunt." He opens the door to the gaming room, breathes in the dim light and air of expectation. "And we're not re-collecting any of the stuff we found, not even the arm. That never works, once you pass the next save point. If we could keep going back and collecting invincibility orbs over and over, that's all we'd do. We'd never get through the game. So we're just going to go to the building and see if we can trigger the monster."

"And if we can't? Or the arm was the only thing we could take?"

"Then we can't." Miguel turns away, opens his cabinet, takes out his visor and sensor strips. "But at least I tried," he says more quietly. He feels Nick's hand on his shoulder.

"Mig, man, no matter what, you're going to get it. Whether through the competition or out in the normal game when it's over, you're going to get what you need."

The gaming rooms always have their own special kind of hush, soundproofed, protected from the world outside and containing an entire world within. He doesn't want to tell the others what's wrong with him. Don't show your weakness to the world. Cover up your flaws. But this is Nick, who already knows most of it, and maybe it's the right time, the right place, for Nick to know everything. He closes the cabinet door, visor hanging from one hand, and leans against the glass. "I'm not going to make it in the normal game. I don't have enough time."

Nick visibly pales in the soft light. "Did a doctor tell you that?"

"Yes." He bows his head. He's been telling himself she was wrong and that's why they let him into the competition. He remembers the look of certainty on her face, and that was before he'd entered this Cube for two months of solid gaming. "But I think I knew anyway. I could feel it, and I was trying to ignore it. The game getting harder, me getting weaker. This competition is my last chance. I either have to find a new heart in the game, or I have to get one as a prize when we win. Or—"

The first time he told Nick he was sick, they both were too young to totally understand it, Miguel repeating stuff his parents and doctors had said without fully grasping what any of it meant.

Nick had nodded slowly, and then he'd walked away.

It seems they're both remembering that. "I don't have any rocks right now," he says, putting on his visor, "but I've got your back. Come on."

They grab pulse guns from the cache, hit the save point on the overworld. The level, the city, is different at night, the extreme detail blurred by the moon. Different digital people go about different businesses in the semidark. Lit up, the hoverboard station beckons more than it had the first time, waiting to release two of the disks into their hands. They don't need to wait for Grace's fear, for Leah or Josh, and so they speed through the sky, aiming for the landmark they'd seen explode a few hours ago. What's damaged stays damaged, but they have rewound time, gone back to the moments before the destruction. They land on the observation deck and don't linger in the weird living room in the sky or stop on their way down to the ground floor. It's a good thing they're not repeating the treasure hunt, no way could he hold Nick down that elevator shaft alone.

Under the chandelier, Miguel pauses, shrugs. A clue, in

hindsight, but just because he hasn't seen anything to indicate a heart, that doesn't mean he's not supposed to take it.

He exchanges a glance with Nick. They're both ready. The ground had started to shake just after they stepped outside the first time. He pushes open the door and strides out, into the empty square surrounding the building. Far enough to avoid the explosion, but this time he's not running.

He waits.

Stillness. A perfectly rendered cloud drifts across a hand-drawn moon.

The weapon is heavy in his hand. "Come on!" he screams, stomping the concrete with a steel-capped boot. "Come and get me!"

Nothing happens. He looks helplessly at Nick. He's so close to getting it. Josh said it was full of green light. He wants to live. "Come on!" he screams again.

"It's not going to work," Nick says, softly to counter Miguel's panicked volume. "Either because we don't have everyone here or because we just can't repeat ourselves. Let's get out, get some sleep, wait for Josh to recover."

Numb, Miguel nods. A sound is building in his ears, mixed with rushing blood, and it's not until the second he quits out that he thinks he identifies it. He stands in the gaming room, visor still over his eyes, with the Storyteller's laughter echoing through his mind.

CUTSCENE:
BLAKE

"Nice try, Mr. Anderson," says Blake, watching one of many monitors. The outside world might have to wait for a status update to know where their favorite team is, but Blake and Lucius can see what's happening whenever they wish. Creator benefits. Several other screens are active, too, teams in various parts of the world obeying biological imperatives of day and night in their respective time zones.

Not much surprises Blake these days, his eyebrow had raised only a fraction at the sight of his favorite player reentering a level he'd already played. He knew instantly why the boy had done it, but he wasn't going to make it so easy. The boy knows now how he might get himself a new heart even before he crosses the finish line, he will simply have to wait and see if there are any more opportunities to do so.

Blake smiles and gives the monitors a final, cursory glance before he stands. He's hungry. Perhaps Lucius could go for a bite, there's that all-night place downtown that does the incredible shrimp thing. He spent part of the evening double-checking the coding on the water level, he could just go for some seafood, artificially farmed though it may be.

Nothing's the same as it once was. That thought might cause Blake some sadness if it weren't for the far happier one that things are heading in exactly the right direction.

He fetches Lucius, and they hoverboard to the restaurant. Nobody knows who they are, but they have no trouble getting a table in the corner where they can talk without being overheard.

"Horses for everyone next," says Lucius between bites of shrimp.

"We need to test them."

"Oh, agreed. A handful of teams have progressed to the third level already, I notice, but they're all still in the early stages. And Eighteen, of course, has been delayed."

Blake's lips twitch. "I wouldn't call it delayed, Lucius. All he teams will experience off-line time while one or more of their numbers are undergoing surgery. You're trying to provoke me."

"I would never," says Lucius, the very picture of innocence.

The lie doesn't really count since they're both aware of it. "If I haven't said so before," Blake says, "your choice of story was inspired. I have of course told my superiors it was my idea, but between us . . ."

"Well, it's a good story," Lucius replies, pleased. "The fact that it's complete lunacy doesn't change its creative appeal. Besides, we didn't steal the whole thing, just what we needed. We're not"—he waves a hand and lowers his voice as if about to curse— "*plagiarists* or anything. More of an homage, really, when you think about it."

"Are you trying to convince me or the people you visited the other day?"

"Should've known you knew about that. Both, I suppose."

"You're fine," Blake assures him. "Dessert?"

FEED · 3

[Jacques Vernier] Come on, **Eighteen**, you were looking good, now you've just stopped.

[Leonardo Pereira] Right? **Eighteen** rocked that boss they met on the second level, way better than some of the other teams.

[Jacques Vernier] Ha, yeah, did you see **Twenty-six**? I could've beaten that thing faster than they did. Hurry up and get your dude back, **Eighteen.** I wanna see what he looks like with that new arm.

[Hona Ojima] And what he can do with it. Nine hundred ninety-nine other teams to beat, **Eighteen.** Get on with it.

▪LEVEL TWELVE

The next destination glows on the overworld. Two levels down, two items collected. A knife, an apple. No idea yet what they're for.

Miguel pulls off his visor. Going in alone would be dumber than going in with only Nick, and probably even less effective. It's been three days, and he's tired of waiting. No wonder the Gamerunners said the competition would take two months if half the time is going to be spent doing nothing while team members are busy getting upgrades. It's not just Josh, several other teams are a member down now, and so Eighteen isn't the only one whose tag is filled with messages from people who for whatever reason have decided to cheer for them but are getting almost as impatient as Miguel.

He doesn't care much about the spectators; he's been reading the messages only out of boredom. He doesn't need fans to win, but he does need his team, and at this point it feels like Josh is just enjoying lying in a hospital bed upstairs and having his every whim catered to.

The door opens behind him. *The door opens behind you,* says the imagined voice of the Storyteller inside his head, narrating his life. He needs to get back into the game.

"Hey," says Leah.

"You're back." She had disappeared the morning after Josh's surgery, after Miguel and Nick had so fruitlessly sneaked back into the game.

"Yeah, I went to visit my family. They worry, you know. Typical overprotective parents."

"Oh, believe me, I get that," he says, though given what happened to her sister, he guesses her parents' protectiveness isn't typical. He still gets it. "Look, I don't think I ever said I'm sorry about what happened to her."

She shrugs, steps toward him, her large eyes shadowed for a moment, clearing again. "Thanks. How've you been?"

"Fine. Ready to get back in there."

"Me too. He's still lazing around in bed, right? Where are Nick and Grace?"

"Nick's probably talking to his girlfriend. Grace, I don't know. She hasn't made an effort to be sociable."

"Something tells me that's normal for her. Nick's girlfriend . . . who used to be your girlfriend."

"He tell you that?"

Leah shakes her head. "You're not the only one who can use a computer."

"Ah."

"That's not a problem for you?" she asks, eyeing him curiously.

"That you can use a computer? No. No, I'm okay with that."

He gets the distinct impression that it's a good thing the gaming room is empty, their visors and sensors locked in their cabinets, because there's nothing handy to throw at him. But he also doesn't think she'd throw anything that'd hurt too much. "You know what I mean."

"It's not a problem." He walks past her to the door but holds it open, invitation more than chivalry. She doesn't actually need anyone to hold the door for her, she could probably rip it off its hinges. She's slim, but there's a poised strength to her that makes him glad she's on his side. Like she's just waiting for the right target to let loose.

He's doing better, he thinks, at treating her like a person and not a digital helper. He's even treating her like a friend, albeit not a close one. She knows as much about him as Seb or Taz or Amanda. Man, he hasn't thought about those guys in ages. He should ask Nick how they're doing. Check in. They've probably been following the status updates he's posted about the game, but he hasn't followed theirs about whatever they've been eating for breakfast. He doesn't care, but he should still say hi.

Leah is just behind his shoulder, where she'd be in the game. She still has questions for him, an idiot would guess that. He's not ready to answer them, but he'll have to at some point, after the competition is over, if not sooner.

"There are sixty-four bones in the human arm, starting from the shoulder," she says. He stops, the doors to the medical bay visible ahead, decorated with a stylized *C*.

"What?"

"Just thinking about Josh and what he had replaced."

"Um. Okay."

"I like weird facts."

"Good to know." The doors open with a hiss. It doesn't matter what Josh lost, it matters what he gained. That biomech is guaranteed to be stronger than what he had before, and strength is never a bad thing in Chimera. If it ends up helping them, he might forgive Josh both the delay and the stupid stunt he pulled to get the thing in the first place. Whether he'll ever forgive Josh for not telling him about the arm while the boss was still alive, not giving him a chance to check— Miguel's not thinking about that. It's easier that way.

The arm looks good. Josh is in a secluded room, eating cake with it. His bed is half shielded by green curtains, two shades lighter than the walls. Chimera's designers take this whole color theme business seriously. "You ready to put that thing to the test?" Miguel asks from the doorway.

"Dude, I've been ready since yesterday morning, it was those damn doctors." Yeah. Another thing Miguel knows about. "They said I could go once I'd eaten something, though."

"You're never going to put a shirt on again, are you?" Leah asks.

"Nope."

"Oh, good."

"And you won't believe what I can lift now. It's awesome."

"Can you find Nick and Grace?" Miguel asks Leah. She nods and jogs back toward the exit, excitement lighting her eyes in the brief look she gave him before taking off. They're all ready to keep playing, catch up with the teams who have overtaken them, run ahead, *win*.

Josh has figured out—or been taught—how to use the claw pretty well; he moves it easily as he dresses. Miguel looks down at his own finger, his singular piece of biomech. There are other things he could have earned along the way, most people he knows are more chimera than he is, but surgery for things he doesn't need hasn't been worth the risk. Despite their skill, that the game's doctors can take someone's arm off and have them up and running again in a couple of days, his unpredictable body can't handle the stress. The next time he goes under a laser knife, it will be for the thing he wants. *Needs*. Anything else can come after that.

Tiny lights flicker around Josh's bicep and in a line from elbow to wrist. It is functioning properly, receiving signals from his brain. Josh reaches up to scratch at his hair, the silver arm gleaming. It's made of tough stuff, but it won't stay so pristine forever.

A tiny part of Miguel hopes that Josh will struggle with lacing his boots, curses internally when they present no challenge. Oh, well. There'll be enough challenges in the game. Nobody stops them as they go, Miguel doesn't see any doctors at all, so either Josh picked his moment or he was telling the truth about being allowed to leave. Miguel doesn't really care which. He wants to get back inside.

Nick, Leah, and Grace are in the gaming room when he and Josh get there. Their sensor strips on, visors in their hands, they almost look more impatient than he feels. Almost. He posts a quick status update—that Eighteen is about to enter the third level—straps on his sensors, and swaps his lenses for his visor. They have no idea what they might need from the cache. A supply of weapons, the first-aid kit. Leah grabs a length of rope. Miguel's invincibility orb beckons from a shelf. It will make any challenge easier, but only for ten minutes. He's not going to use it until he has to.

In the overworld, the save point he'd returned to with Nick catches his eye, but this time he touches the new glowing spot, halfway across the green globe from the first one. He is expecting the air change, the scenery, but with any new level there is always an instant of held breath, of anticipation, of not knowing what he's about to see. A lake of fire or the top of a skyscraper? A mountainside or an empty gray room?

You are on an old dirt road. Fields and woods surround you. To the west, there is a village. It is raining.

He remembers her laughter. Miguel grits his teeth as a particularly fat drop of rain splats on his head. "Can you get that thing wet yet?" he asks Josh.

"Fully waterproof."

"Then let's go."

"Wait," says Leah, holding out her arm. "I hear something."

Miguel holds his breath as she cocks her head to listen. The others stop moving.

"What is it?" he finally asks in a low whisper.

She shakes her head. "Like . . . thunder? I think."

"Makes sense," says Grace. "It's raining."

She's like a physical manifestation of the Storyteller. Stating the obvious and mostly unhelpful.

"Yeah," Leah agrees. "Okay. Do we know which way west is?"

Miguel calls up a compass on his visor, checks it, points. The road is washed out, slick with mud, but it is a path to follow. The sky darkens, the rain falls heavier. Somewhere, in a gaming room, his body is warm and dry, walking in place on a sprung floor. He shivers as the water seeps down to his skin. Nick summons coats and hands them out; Josh can barely get his claw through the sleeve. A pulse of envy beats Miguel's heart, and he touches his biomech to his wrist. He's fine, just walking. He likes to walk. But he'd prefer it if it felt like they were actually getting somewhere. The village still hasn't come into view, no lights or buildings to indicate any signs of life. The trees are pointed shadows, the fields patches of deep gray fading to black.

He has the feeling that they should be spending this time bonding . . . or something. Talking at least.

He falls into step beside Leah. "What are you hoping to get out of this?" he asks, voice low, covered by the sound of rain hitting the road. She can hear him.

"Rewards, you mean?"

He has to lean in to catch her answer. He doesn't have her hearing. "Yeah."

"Whatever I can pick up, whatever I can find. But at the end, if I can get it, there's a procedure I want."

He turns his face to her, raises his eyebrows in question.

And she shakes her head. "I'll tell you mine if you tell me yours, and I'm guessing you don't want to."

"What makes you say that?" Years of pain and secrets, of not showing his weakness, have given him a very good straight face.

"There's something about you. You're super private, even your Presence doesn't reveal much about you except that you play Chimera a lot. So either that's all there is to you, or you're careful about what you share."

"Maybe that's all there is to me." It does feel like that, sometimes. Wake up, go to school, play. On and on and on, for all the time he has left.

She laughs, the sound swallowed by a rumble of thunder. "I doubt that. Either I'll figure it out or you'll tell me when you've decided you can trust me."

Another pulse, guilt this time. A familiar emotion, but a strange one to feel inside Chimera.

"You know what this reminds me of?" Josh asks, stopping in the middle of the road and turning to face Miguel and Leah. Up ahead, Nick stops, too. "That part of Seven where you have to walk through the city for ages, not finding anything, and I mean there weren't even any weapons or a damn piece of rope, because the point was that by the time you got to the boss you'd be too tired to fight it. It took me weeks to get past that, I kept not being rested enough."

Miguel's mouth opens. Josh is right. Another of Chimera's clever tricks.

"Yeah, but there was a shortcut," says Miguel.

"Was there?"

"Through the shopping mall. Don't worry, it took me a while to find it, too."

"So where's the shortcut here?" Grace looks around. Nothing but fields and woods and darkness.

"I have no idea. Cache: summon flashlights."

It takes an hour of searching, a black night fully drawing in around an increasingly heavier storm. They haven't found a save point, they can't stop or they'll have to do this all over again. There are tents in the cache, but he doesn't love the idea of putting them up in the rain.

Finally a path, splitting off the road and heading through the trees. A few minutes later a village appears through the leaves.

"Good thinking," he says to Josh, clapping him on the new arm. Ow.

They're tired, but not too tired to keep going. Hungry more than anything, and the lights of a tavern on the edge of a main square beckon them.

"Let me," Nick says, pushing around Miguel to open the door, as if there might be some boss lurking behind it. Which, okay, there might be, but Nick going in first won't make much of a difference.

No demons, but no people. Not regular Chimera people. Those . . . can't be called people, can they?

And yet, when he thinks about it, that's what they're all

looking to become. Humanoid robots, sitting at tables, drinking god knows what from steel mugs.

Miguel doesn't think they can eat here, and there's no green light.

"Hello?" he says. None of them look up. Well, that makes them more like regular Chimera people.

Okay. They need to find out why they're here, what the point is. There are always signs, in every level, every challenge. He looks around the tavern. The incongruity of the brick and wood and fireplaces with the gleaming metal is both startling and familiar. All worlds are a blend of history and future, of the impossible and the certain.

"Can we spend the night in here?" Leah asks. "The storm's getting worse."

He trusts her hearing. He doesn't know. Putting up a tent in the rain is suddenly a more appealing prospect than bedding down around these guys. They're not looking at anything with their glowing eyes, not speaking to one another with their metal mouths. He shivers again, and not from the cold, wet clothes fused to his skin. He's used to seeing people who are part machine—he can't remember the last time he saw anyone over the age of twelve who wasn't. He's never thought of them as creepy before.

"There are pictures on the walls," says Grace. He should give her more—grudging—credit for being observant, and he isn't surprised that she's the one who notices. His mother is the same biomech eyes ready to capture the smallest detail.

The pictures are of horses, animals that Miguel has only ever seen in pictures. There are still some in the real world, in zoos or kept by rich private owners like every other animal.

And he's sure they don't look exactly like this. They can't. He moves along the wall, from frame to frame, each image a running beast, every one a different color, all perfectly formed machines.

"The hell are we?" Nick asks.

"The future?" Miguel answers, amused despite the situation. He's wet, cold, tired, hungry, but he gets to say he's been in the weirdest Chimera level he's ever seen, so that's something. "Let's check out the rest of the village. There's no save point here."

"I think we should stay in here," says Leah, covering her ears and grimacing. He hears the thunder now, too, growing, roaring. It's just a storm, and the rain here can't hurt them, burn their skin. Lightning might be a problem for those robot dudes at the tables and maybe for Josh.

He opens the door. The square spreads out before him, cobbles wet and slick, glistening in the lights from windows. The rain has stopped, but the thunder hasn't. It's still getting louder, closer.

And it doesn't sound like thunder anymore. He steps into

the square, the other four in the tavern doorway obeying his raised hand. His team, his choices.

Sometimes you just know when you've made a mistake.

Sparks shouldn't fly from the wet stone, but they do as hooves strike, and he looks up, frozen. They are terrible, and beautiful, and there is no time for anything but diving out the way. He slides between legs of sinuous, rippling metal, gasping for breath. One lands a bruising kick to his back, and he thinks he screams. It could be one of them, shrieking. He rolls for what must be an eternity, comes to a stop as the thunder disappears into the distance, leaving him curled on the ground. The stone is cool, wet from the storm. He blinks hated words into focus.

LEVEL FAILED.

▊LEVEL THIRTEEN

"**S**o we're not supposed to kill them," says Nick as they walk along the road a third time, in sunlight now.

The two-day-old bruise on Miguel's back twinges, but it's healing. He hadn't gone to the medical wing about it, though it's the same attractive shade of green as ChimeraCube Chartreuse. He is nothing if not stylish. "And we still need to collect something. I haven't seen anything," he says.

They'd come back after sleep and food, armed with pulse guns. Everything but the weather had been the same: the road, the tavern, the thunder, the end result. It had felt . . . wrong? To kill something like that, the destruction of something so beautiful. But it hadn't worked anyway, they'd just kept running, so his conscience is clear.

"We skip the tavern this time," says Miguel. "It's useless. There must be something else in the village that tells us what we need to do."

Grace and Josh walk ahead, Leah just behind them. Nick falls back, slowing his steps in time with Miguel's. "You okay?" Nick asks, not as quietly as he thinks he does. Leah's head cocks slightly.

"I'm fine. You don't need to ask."

"But I'm going to. Fancy that. Hey, Mig . . . they're biomech."

Miguel gives Nick a sideways glance. "They're *horses*. I'll wait."

"Okay, but it'd be pretty cool."

"Sure." Miguel laughs, and Leah fully turns, walking backward as if that will bring her into the joke. Miguel shakes his head, rolls his eyes for her benefit. She heard every word, but she'd have to be even smarter than she is to guess what they're talking about.

The village is as quiet as it's been the previous two times. He's sure the same robots are inside the tavern, the houses, but sees nothing through the curtained windows. Narrow roads snake off the square, and he picks one at random. Both times so far the horses haven't turned up until nightfall, and it's still the middle of the day; they got an early start. He walks quickly. He's not failing this level again.

A save point would be useful. It wouldn't be whatever they have to do with the horses or the object they're supposed to collect, but it'd be something. Then they could just start here in the village instead of walking . . . again.

At the end of the road the village turns into more fields. Next. They return to the square, start down another. It's Grace who spots it, and if she keeps being helpful, he's going to have to start liking her a little. Mistrust still scratches at the back of his neck, but she has warmed up, contributed more in the past couple of days.

Maybe it's all part of some cunning plan. He'll take it as long as it works in his favor.

"What is this place?" Josh asks.

"I think it's where they live," says Grace. "Or used to." She points at the broken chains hanging from the walls. "Before they escaped."

"And I think we're supposed to catch them," adds Leah. She moves deeper into the stone building, runs a hand over empty wooden troughs.

"What? I've never had to catch anything in Chimera before," says Grace. "It's just bosses, puzzles. I know we've figured out we can't kill them, or not with pulse guns, but—"

Miguel glances between them. He wouldn't have thought of catching the horses either. But they gave him a team to lead, they gave him a human one so they'd have brains.

"Okay," he says. "We try it. If catching them doesn't make something happen, at least we'll have them while we figure out what else to do."

"Easy," says Nick, and Miguel grins at him.

"Easy."

All the other times the horses had come through the square. They have several hours until nightfall, enough for him to come up with some kind of plan, a plan that needs to involve those broken chains on the wall, if not start with them. He remembers the horses bearing down on him, their eyes, their hooves, the pain.

Strong. Terrible. Beautiful.

Angry.

Nick's hand on his shoulder brings him back to *now*. He nods at the question. Yeah, he's fine. Just thinking.

Unfortunately what he's thinking isn't what he wants to do. And it might not be the only way, but it's the fastest way out of a level they've been stuck on for too long.

He touches his wrist. Yellow. Fine. No bets on what it might be like later, okay for now.

They make themselves as comfortable as possible, and he resists the urge to check his feeds. He should apologize to their viewers for being so boring; they should be running around, shooting things. But then, they're not the only team on this level, he knows that much, and either everyone else has been through this delay or he doesn't want to know if they haven't.

He's being unfair. Lots of Chimera—lots of all video games, as far as he's been able to learn—have periods of downtime. It's just that usually nobody's watching this intently.

Leah sits, close enough for him to feel the heat off her bare arms. "Still thinking?" she asks.

"Yeah." Still thinking of a way that isn't the one he's already thought of. "Have any random facts about horses?"

She laughs. "Fresh out. I can look some up?"

He shakes his head, smiling. She shifts, closer still, stretching out her legs. Something clinks, knocked by the toe of her boot. An empty vial, small enough to fit in the palm of her hand.

"What's this?" She turns it over with her fingers, holds it up so Nick, Josh, and Grace can see.

"No idea," says Miguel. "Keep it. Okay, let's go. The sun is setting."

Nobody disturbs them as they arrive in the square, the villagers remaining hidden, silent. Miguel takes a deep breath. "Okay. Leah, I need you to walk out onto the road. Take Nick. Tell me when you hear them, when they're getting near."

"Okay."

"Josh, you get to use that arm, and those chains. I'm gonna slow them if I can, but you've got to lasso them quick."

"Sweet." Josh nods.

"How do you plan to slow them?" Grace asks. "They nearly trampled you to death once."

He wishes he didn't have to use it for this. Maybe this is what it's for, but he wishes he could keep it.

"Cache," he says. "Summon orb."

The ball of living light appears in his hand. The others come closer, gazing at it with envy and awe.

"You sure, Mig?"

"I want to get out of here."

The past few nights the horses have come through the square, gone down the narrow road on the left of the square, past the stone building, disappeared. Narrow is key. If he stands, invincible, at its mouth, he can hit them one at a time. Hopefully. Break their pace enough that Josh, behind him, can trap each one.

He tells Leah and Nick to go, Grace to stand by the building's open door, slam it shut when the last one is inside.

The wait for Leah to get into position is too long, for her warning to come even longer. Josh is at his back, and Miguel prays he has it. They have only one chance at this.

Soon he hears the hooves himself. Loud. Angry. He grips the orb, its glow illuminating his skin. Pinpoints of a red appear on the road on the other side of the square, larger with every second.

Wait.

Wait.

Be sure they're coming this way. He's not wasting this. If for some reason they turn down one of the other roads that run like cracks off the square, they'll have to try again tomorrow.

No. Come this way.

Now he sees their sinuous metal, black and red, white and gold in a line across the open space.

Now.

"Activate," he whispers.

The warmth is instant, so is the strength, the sensation of power. He has just enough time to glance at his hand, see the glow from under his skin as the orb disappears, used up, empty, gone.

They can't hurt you. Remember that.

He throws himself at the first, the golden one, as it enters the narrow road, sparks flying on the cobbles. His fingers close around the formed metal of its mane. He drags it to a crawl and shouts for Josh. The others, behind it, scream in fear and confusion, but he's too fast for them, too invincible. He runs between their heaving flanks and kicking hooves, knocking them off-balance long enough for one chain, two, three, four to loop around their necks. Heaving, straining, but strong enough to pull them the rest of the way, Josh drags the horses down to the open door, shielded from their rage and fear by Miguel's impervious body.

Grace slams the door shut. Together Miguel and Josh fix the chains to their bolts on the walls.

A sound of rushing. Not water, something slick, oily. The troughs fill and the horses still, in an instant as calm as they were angry a moment ago. The building turns blue, lit by a save point that appears on the wall.

Footsteps outside, running.

"You did it!" Leah says, breathless, Nick just behind her. Miguel grins and is so happy he could kiss her.

"You okay?" asks Nick.

"Yes. Where's that vial?"

"Oh. Here." Leah pulls it from her pocket. She steps carefully to the trough in front of the black horse, the one Miguel's pretty sure kicked him, fills it, sends it to the cache. Three objects down. Seven more. The horses are docile now, calm, but he isn't sure they are as beautiful. Nick punches the save point. Time to get out of here.

"That was," Miguel says, collapsing on the floor of the gaming room and tearing his visor off, "the weirdest Chimera level I've ever played, and I've battled that dragon thing on Fifteen."

"There's a dragon on Fifteen?" Grace scowls. "Damn it."

"Big one. I'm going to bed. Meet here in the morning."

"Nice one," Josh says, raising his claw.

"Yeah. Not high-fiving that. Night."

Leah follows him to his suite. "Good job," she says, stepping inside uninvited, but he won't tell her to leave. "I should ask you if you're okay."

"You don't have to if you don't care."

"I care, I just don't want to annoy you by asking a question you've already answered a bunch of times today." She pauses. "Why does Nick keep asking you that?"

His heart beats. "Nick's a worrier."

"Yeah, sure." She is inches away. He can smell sweat—not unpleasant—and something nice that he's sure isn't perfume. Lingering soap maybe. She's not the perfume type.

"Is it just me?" she asks quietly.

He shakes his head.

He hasn't kissed anyone since Anna. He hadn't kissed anyone before Anna either. Stop thinking about Anna, she isn't part of this. It's different. Better or worse requires more research. Her hair is thicker than it looks, her body stronger.

He feels invincible again.

There's diving gear in the cache the next morning. Leah moves up beside him as he inspects it, touches the back of his hand with a finger. She doesn't seem shy or nervous or regretful. He could kiss her a second time, right here in front of the rest of the team, but he doesn't. Some secrets are good ones.

He's going to have to tell her soon, isn't he? Before he kisses her again. He got away with the horses because of the orb, that won't happen a second time. The spot in his private cache where it sat is empty, and he's unlikely to find another.

In fifteen levels of normal Chimera, he'd only ever found one.

"Can you swim?" he asks her.

"Like a fish. Although, did you know fish don't actually exist?"

He stares at her. "What?" There aren't very many in the oceans these days, but he's pretty sure they are a thing. That would be a very complex mass hallucination.

"There's nothing that can categorically be called a fish, never has been. It's a name for a group of very disparate things that all happen to swim. It's like thinking frogs and kangaroos and rabbits are the same because they all hop."

"I . . . did not know that."

She grins. "Stick with me, kiddo."

The others come to inspect the gear. "No heights, Gracie," says Nick. "Just depths."

"Call me Gracie again and you won't make it back to the surface."

"Got it."

"We'll leave it here," says Miguel. "I don't think we're going to pop up in the middle of the ocean."

They don't. The overworld lands them on a beach. The Storyteller helpfully informs them of this.

It's a pretty beach, made of the same pure detail that Miguel thinks he's gotten used to in this new Chimera until the sand blinds him. Each grain of white glints in the whole. Behind them, tall mountains rise from green to frosted snowcaps. Large boulders are scattered around, carelessly tossed by a giant hand. An arm of rock juts out into the water.

"Boat." Grace points to the end of the jetty.

None of them know how to pilot one, but they get it started after a few attempts and circle around, jagged teeth of stone scraping against the bottom. It's so real, every aspect. The sky is endless, almost cloudless. It's hard for Miguel to remember that there's actually a ceiling above his head, pinpoints of light on the walls, a huge visor covering half his face. Perspective is everything. That feels like the dream, and this the real world.

Grace screams. Miguel drops his hands from wheel. "What?"

He follows her finger.

"What are those?"

He's never seen one. No one alive has seen one. But he goes to school and reads online. "I think it's a dolphin. It's a kind of fish, which I've recently learned don't exist."

"Wrong and right," says Leah. "It's not a fish, if there was such a thing. It's a water mammal."

"They're pretty," says Grace, calming down. "Will they hurt us?"

"Not likely," says Leah. "In fact they're very intelligent. There were experiments on them for a long time. It was thought they could think like humans. There are a lot of old stories about their guiding fishermen away from storms or out of trouble." She looks out at the expanding circle of dolphins, all watching the boat with squeaky, chittering interest. "Maybe we're supposed to follow them. Go closer and see what happens."

He's trying, but the boat isn't cooperating, and he relinquishes control to Josh with relief. Josh steers away from the rocks, speeding toward the dolphins with a roar before figuring out how to slow down.

Back in the gaming room, Miguel is wearing a long-sleeved shirt, but here his arms are bare and warm under the sun. A safe sun, presumably—he wouldn't sit out in it in real life. Leah's dark skin glows with sweat, and Nick's hair shines impossibly blond. The dolphins gather around, close enough now to touch. He doesn't. Grace squeezes her hands between her thighs, but Leah reaches out, lays her palm on a smooth, silvery nose.

"Are you here to show us where to go?" she asks. It squeaks and bobs its head as though it understood her, pulls away, and turns in unison with the others.

Speed and wind pick up, ruffling Miguel's hair. He is alive and in the sun.

Who cares if it's a game?

Grace is the first to spot the flag, rippling in the distance. The dolphins race ahead to circle around it.

"Cache," says Miguel when the boat has stopped and he can speak normally. He summons the diving gear, it lands in a pile at their feet. Large pieces of biomech, like lungs but clearly meant to be worn on the outside, are attached to a hose and mouthpiece.

"Should one of us stay up here with the boat?" Nick asks. "We don't know what's down there."

"Good plan. Any takers?"

"I will," says Josh.

"Cool."

The rest of them get ready. He can't remember the last time he went swimming, though it was definitely in the game, and not like this. The water laps around his shoulders, cool and wet, the dolphins have moved away. Nick, Leah, and Grace bob around him.

The world changes to greens and blues and rainbows of fish—or whatever—that swarm a dazzling reef. If ever he needed a reminder that Chimera was the product of two imaginations, this is it. Nothing is both easier and harder to imagine than history.

"Can we talk down here?" Nick wonders aloud. "Yeah? Sweet."

They aren't here for the reef. They are here for the ship wrecked upon it, a few hundred feet away through the crystal-clear water. It's like flying, weightless and free. Breath comes easily through the diving lungs. Laughter bubbles like air. Leah does a somersault, grinning, then gives Miguel a look that can mean only one thing.

He kicks, outpacing her but not by enough. She's right there, keeping up with him as he races through the blue, the ship looming larger and larger, its skeleton like the hulking carcass of a dead sea creature.

He wins only because his arms are longer, fingertips stretched to touch rotting wood and rusted metal. "Ha!" he says victoriously, chest aching with the effort. Worth it for the look on her face.

Together they wait for Nick and Grace to catch up, the four of them swim through a gap in the hull.

As always, they don't know what they're looking for, so they spread out to explore, Grace taking what's left of the top deck, Nick the galleys, Leah the lifeboats that saved no one.

Miguel goes down, deeper, following broken pipes and skirting sheets of jagged steel.

You come to a sealed room. The lever is rusted shut.

"I think it's here," he says, "Down at the bottom.

"I think it's the old engine room," he tells them when they arrive. "Any bright ideas?"

"Cache. Axe," says Nick. It appears in his hand, and they all stand back. Miguel's flinches at the first strike, is more prepared for the second, the third. Chimera follows the laws of physics when it suits; the water slows the movement, dulls the assault. The ax slips from Nick's grip, spins through the water, heads for Miguel's face. Leah catches it an instant before impact, overcompensates, smashes it against the wall behind her. The head breaks free and, unbuoyed by its handle, crashes to their feet.

"Uh. Maybe not that then," says Nick.

Miguel moves closer to the door, wraps his gloved hands around the lever. It's an effort, even when Nick moves close behind him and adds his own strength, but not an inhuman effort.

Disturbed rust billows, clouds the water in front of them. Metal grinds against itself. Tiny increment by tiny increment, the lever shifts, and the door finally opens with a screech.

Black water rushes out, the crystal blue of the reef long gone, stained by inky darkness. By feel, not sight, they enter the room, bumping into one another and the unseen engine.

But there is a light, not the swirling, living light of an orb, but the faint dull glow of a save point. Beside it a glass bottle hovers. It's not surprising that the bottle is full, but it's surprising that it's corked.

A bottle of water, probably salt water. A vial of oil. A knife. An apple. Miguel caches it and blocks Nick's hand from the save point. He weighs the pros and cons of getting Josh down here. Five would be better than four, but he doesn't know what will happen once they hit the save point. If they have to get back to the boat, they need Josh keeping it where it is.

If they're sent somewhere else, they'll go without him.

"Josh, you there?"

"Yep. Find anything?"

"Get your gear on and dive. You'll see a ship."

"On it."

Once they hit the save point, they can log out and return here whenever they want. Better to do that together.

Even if it means killing a boss twice.

He hears Nick giving Josh directions. He hears Josh cursing that he can't see shit, and several loud bangs. Finally Josh's voice comes from nearby, and Miguel slams his hand down on the button.

Nothing happens.

"Just wait," Miguel tells himself. Something will come. Patterns repeat. He's never been here before, but he's been *here* before.

Water is everywhere, but from somewhere out in the blackness a current rushes. The ship tilts and shifts as if it were on the surface. The dark lessens, water flooding out of every gap in the hull and not returning.

"We're going up," says Grace.

"Get out of here and onto the deck," Miguel tells them, leading the way. The water is at his forehead now. He has to time this right, pull off his lungs at the perfect moment. It happens on the ladder; he tears them away and breathes clean air. Behind him, the others do the same. He races up the last few rungs and lands on the rotten deck, eyes on the vanishing sea.

He grins as he spots the thing in the distance. The horses were fun and all, definitely different, but this is the kind of boss he's used to: something he can kill.

"Let me guess!" he shouts to Leah. "That's not a fucking fish either!"

Her laughter rings across the water, across the visible bones of ships and sea creatures. But the one coming is alive, flesh, blue-black with scales and spines. Huge wet eyes drip slime and rage. It wants them as badly as he wants it. He scans the area, ducks past Nick to the broken railings that run around the deck. One wrenches free with a scream of rust.

Just for this moment he is in the old Chimera, the one he knows. No rooms of fears, no horses to tame. Just this.

And he is good at this.

"You're mine, you bastard!" he screams as it rises over the deck and swipes a disgusting tentacle at them. The others jump out of the way, but Miguel stands his ground on the slippery deck.

"What are—" Leah shouts as he runs at it, right into the path of another oozing swipe.

"Leading!" he shouts back. Help and cooperation are all fine and good, but this one, this one is his. It isn't a machine, and he can't take its heart, but he can take its computer-generated life.

It swipes again. The sharp, pointed tentacle curls around his waist, crushing the air from him. Weak point. Weak point . . . where?

There.

He sights, aims, lets the makeshift spear soar from his hand. Watches its flight through the air.

Doesn't see the boss make a last, desperate strike.

Until it's too late. The orb that could save him is gone now, used up.

Searing pain explodes in his chest like a bomb. His own weak point. He hears screams that aren't his, his breath is gone. He touches his wrist, an automatic movement. The information will be useless. The number flashes in black. Shit.

"Got you," he says as he falls.

LEVEL FOURTEEN

Everything is too bright. Miguel can't see; it's that blinding kind of light that obscures instead of illuminates.

But he's thinking very clearly. Too clearly? Maybe he's still in the game, where everything is detailed, precise. His chest hurts. It's a different kind of pain, though. Focused, not spreading in rippling waves to his fingertips. A sharp, tight line of ow.

He hears voices but not words. His eyes are open but could close so easily, blot out the brightness, and just sleep forever. Temptation drags at his brain and his eyelids, pulling them down, under. He forces his eyes back open. The brightness is thinning, shapes now discernible. The source of the voices. Lots of them.

"God damn it, Mig, wake up."

Someone is crying and trying not to.

He *is* awake. He can see them.

Can't he?

In the morning before school, sometimes, he'd be sure he was awake, up, getting dressed, only to have his mom come in and shake him.

He opens his eyes again. Anna's face swims in front of him. What the hell is she doing here? Wherever here is. He turns his head toward a green wall.

Oh.

"He's awake!"

"And his ears still work," Miguel whispers. "Shhhh."

"Sorry." Her voice drops several notches. "How are you feeling?" Other faces join hers. His parents, Nick, Leah. One he doesn't recognize except in the way all doctors are immediately identifiable to someone who has seen too many of them.

"How are you feeling?" The doctor this time.

"Um."

"Good answer," he says. "We won't know everything for a day or two, but for the moment it looks like the transplant was a success. It's been switched on and is fully operational. Ha-ha."

"Ha," says Miguel. There is literally nothing worse than a funny doctor. Every one he has ever met needs a humor transplant. Wait. "Transplant? I—"

"All biomeched up, dude," says Nick, raising his hand for a high five. "You finally got it."

"How?"

Nick's eyes dart to Mr. and Mrs. Anderson. Miguel nods. They can hear whatever it is.

"So you got hit right when you took down the boss. Do you remember that?"

Maybe. Some of it. "Yeah," he says so Nick will get to the point.

"Right, so there was a save point in its skull, if you can believe that. Josh hit it with that badass arm of his, and we got you out of there, called for the medics from the gaming room. They brought you up here, and some dude turned up with a really hot doctor—not you, sorry, man—and told them to give you the transplant."

"But . . . I thought I'd have to find it, or wait until we won—"

Nick shrugs. "Apparently not."

"You should have told us," Leah says, scowling. "I've been wondering for ages what's wrong with you. Why Nick asks you if you're okay every time we have to run for a minute. You try to cover it but you can't, not always. It would've been nice to know our leader could kick it anytime. What if something random had happened earlier?"

"Sorry." He's not sure if he is, though judging from the look on his mother's face, she's going to do her best to make him feel sorry later. But Mrs. Anderson has a sense of privacy, and he inherited it from her. Leah's not completely wrong that it was kind of the team's business, but she's a little bit wrong. It's his thing. His problem.

Was.

Still, it's hard not to feel indebted to a girl who's torn a demon's head off with her bare hands for you. He should get her a present.

"Am I on drugs?" he asks.

"We did a few neuro tweaks to ease the pain while you heal," says the doctor. "They'll wear off soon. In the meantime you should rest. Your heart may be the best it's ever been, but the rest of you isn't. You need to heal. You need sleep."

"We want to talk to you," says his mom, "but we'll come back in a bit. Everyone out."

As soon as the door closes on the last of them, Miguel pulls aside the papery cloth covering his chest. A fine, fresh scar slashes across flesh, already knitting together and almost healed. From under a shroud of skin and muscle, faint lights flash.

He stares at them for so long his neck starts to ache.

So this is it.

He doesn't know what he expected, whether he ever truly let himself think this far. For years, in dreams both asleep and awake, he's thought of what it would be like to reach the end of a level and know that what waited for him on the other side of a quit command was this, a new life. None of this has happened the right way. He's not complaining, but he always imagined that he'd know, be prepared, not that he'd just wake up truly alive for the first time in his life.

It won't fail. Ever. Something else could take him out, but as the doctor said, his heart is now the healthiest part of him.

He feels like he's back in the first level of the competition, on the ceiling, about to grab the orb. Flipped upside down and closing his fingers around invincibility.

Sleep, the doctor had also said. Yeah, that's likely. But Miguel closes his eyes, sees the blinking lights on the inside of his eyelids and counts each flash the way he used to count his heartbeats.

How long does it take to count to infinity?

He smiles. This is going to change everything.

"You're not rejoining the competition."

The way his mother says it, it could be a statement or a question. Either way, he hasn't thought about it yet, so he does now.

He actually doesn't have to. Keep going, that is. Another thing he'd never considered. Even if the competition had never come up, what exactly was he planning to do? He always had a vague idea that he'd still play, gather up some other biomech rewards more in line with the actual point of Chimera: to protect them from the sun, the rain, the air. Replace weak, vulnerable human flesh with impenetrable metal. Be the first to ever beat the game. But would he play as seriously? Would he care as much?

Yes. He hasn't spent this long getting good at the game to throw it away.

"I don't know," he says. His father sits on the edge of the slim bed, too high, as all hospital beds are, his toes barely touching the floor.

"We've been following it. Not only your team, all of them. Something else could hurt you."

"And we just got you back."

"I never went anywhere," Miguel protests. "I was here, downstairs. Twenty minutes away from home." But he knows what they mean. They haven't got him *back*, they suddenly have the healthy son they never had before.

"We know," she answers. "But think of all the things we can do now. Take a trip somewhere, maybe?"

Only in Chimera has Miguel ever left the city, seen an approximation of the world. They'd never wanted to go too far from the doctors.

"I'll take some time off work," his father says. "Might as well see some of the world while we can."

Before it ends. Now that it's likely to end before his heart quits, Miguel can think about that. Nobody knows when it will happen or how. Gradually or so fast nobody on the planet will even realize. Miguel votes for long and agonizing, if history is an accurate prediction of the future. But it's close, everybody knows it. It's why everybody acts like it isn't happening. Maybe in his lifetime, maybe not. That requires different math now anyway.

"We'll let you rest," says his mother, and like an alarm falling into silence, it's only now that the worry is gone from her face that he realizes how loud it was.

He's still not going to sleep. His lenses are folded on the bedside table.

Cubes are a lot of things; they're especially good bubbles. Sure, he's checked on the feeds now and then, but mostly he's been focused on getting his own team ahead. A message from Zack blinks.

[Zachary Chan] **Miguel Anderson** Aww, did little baby Mig stop to get an upgrade?

He doesn't bother answering, blinks it away, and checks the team feeds instead.

Just rescued the horses. That was Team Nine, this morning. Bunch of old guys with experience and slowness. They might catch up while he's lying in this bed.

Stuck in the woods. Can't find the village. Don't worry, we'll figure it out. Ha. Sucks to be you, Twenty-one.

Found the ashes.

What? Where is that? Miguel's brand-new and fancy heart

sinks. Zack's team. Great.

It's harder with just four of us. We really miss you, Liat. Team Seven lost a member? Miguel blinks back through their updates. So that's what his father meant, and his parents aren't used to not having to be careful about upsetting him anymore. Oh, damn. There was always the possibility she'd just given up, but . . . no. He blinks again to read the reactions, outpourings of sympathy from around the world, cheers from those who are supporting other teams. Some questions about why the competition is being allowed if it's that dangerous. Arguments that it isn't dangerous, she hadn't died inside the game, she'd been injured and not called in the medics until the infection was too advanced.

A sound jolts him away from the scrolling feed. "Yeah?" he calls, hoping it's Nick or—maybe better?—Leah. It's probably one of the doctors, though. He assumes from the green walls and the lack of anyone's correcting him that he's still in ChimeraCube Chartreuse, in the medical wing, but he isn't actually sure of that.

"Good afternoon, Mr. Anderson," says a voice, familiar and strange. "It's a pleasure to meet you."

Miguel turns his head.

"Hi? Do I know you?" Doctors don't usually dress all in black, and he *thinks* he's free of needing a mortician, at least for the time being.

The man shrugs and nods at once, somehow. "In a manner of speaking, yes. I wish I could say I'm sorry to meet under these circumstances, but in fact I'm not. Do you mind if we speak?"

"I guess not," says Miguel. Instinct itches like his rapidly healing scar. "You're one of the Gamerunners." He's inherited something from his mother; the man takes it as a statement, comes closer.

"Well done. Yes, I am. How are you feeling?"

"Fine, thank you."

"You're welcome. Are you enjoying your new heart?"

"Kind of wish I'd known it was coming," says Miguel. "Waking up like that was, uh, surprising?"

The man laughs. "I would imagine. However, there was no possibility of warning you, as we didn't know ourselves."

The words hang between them in the sterile hospital room, all smooth surfaces and that shade of green that's starting to make Miguel vaguely nauseated. Outside the window, if it's a real window, the sun is on a gentle slide downward but nowhere near setting. Miguel takes it in while his brain absorbs the words. "I wasn't supposed to get my heart after that level."

"I *am* glad I chose you. No, though I have no doubt you would have found it eventually, if your bioheart had been up to the challenge. When you collapsed, I made a decision."

"Um. Thanks." What a weird thing to say to the person

who held your life in his hands and the choice that saved you.

"Again, you're welcome. I see something in you, Miguel, but I wonder if it's gone now? You're a very good player, always have been. I wasn't aware of you until you entered the competition, because even I cannot keep track of everyone, but I did my research, and of course I've been watching along with the rest of the world. Do you still want to play, or is that fire extinguished?"

"Are you kidding? I want to keep playing."

The man smiles widely. "Well, that is good news. This is easier than I expected. I was prepared for you to be tempted to return home to your family."

"I was," Miguel admits, "but not for long."

"Good. It would be a shame to lose you."

"Out of curiosity, what would happen to my team if I just stopped?"

The man wanders over to the window, looks out. "That . . . has been a subject of some debate, if I'm honest. But we have agreed that if the leader retires or is . . . otherwise indisposed, the team must withdraw. Losing any other member is not such a problem."

"Because you made the best people the leaders?"

Laughter. It's dry, rasping. *Old,* though the man is young enough. Then again, lots of people have lung damage from the air. "It's good to see your ego is as healthy as your heart," he says. "That is a consideration, but it's more, too. Think. I know you have figured it out."

Miguel shifts under the Gamerunner's gaze. It'd be easier to think if he wasn't being stared at. He closes his eyes. "Our alignments," he says. So they have been watching, listening. He'd never posted a status about that. It's not surprising, but it's useful to know that nothing in the game is safe. Or sacred.

"Well done. There aren't that many of you. I mean, millions, of course, but fewer than any of the other types. Only a small percentage of those are entertaining to watch, only some of *those* have talent, et cetera, et cetera."

"So you need me," says Miguel, a smile beginning to form. The man laughs again.

"Don't get too cocky, Mr. Anderson. I've already given you the thing you wanted most in the world."

That's true. Maybe Miguel would be more grateful if he could really believe it.

"I want you to think about how limitless your chances will be if you return. Until now, you have played Chimera—and well—under a constant threat. Out of fear, you have never pushed yourself to your limits, and of course that fear wasn't unjustified." He gestures at Miguel in the bed. "But it isn't a worry anymore. Think of how good you could be. Think of how far you could go."

"Is this about that girl who died? You don't want the

publicity."

The man's good humor slips just enough for Miguel to see that while it isn't a mask, it could be. Something else lurks behind it, ready to be summoned at will. "I can absolutely assure you that you'll never guess at my motives," he says, "but I promise you they are not publicity. I didn't give you a new heart so that you could skip off into the sunset to enjoy it. At least not yet. Yes, we need you. The competition is about testing new material, and we need good players to do that."

"There are tons of people better than I am," says Miguel. Painful to admit, but true. He's just arguing for the sake of it now; knowing he's not going to die anytime soon is a shot of adrenaline.

"An honorable thing to say." The man's eyes narrow in the fading light. "And true, but we need players at as many levels and with as many skill sets as possible. You are *very* good for your age, particularly when you consider the unique obstacles with which you have had to contend."

"Do I really have a chance to win?" That's the real question, the one he's wanted to ask since he guessed who the man was.

"A better than average one, and you can do it just because you want it. For the love of the game and your own skill, without this cloud hanging over your head. The game is about choices, it always has been. Left or right? But you've never truly had one, have you? I am curious how well you'll play when you do.

I think, Mr. Anderson, that the game can teach you who you are. That is, no longer someone sick, so who is it?" He pauses, mouth still open as if he isn't quite finished speaking.

Miguel jumps at the knock on the door. The man doesn't. Both look.

"Hey," says Nick, not waiting for an invitation. "You okay? Hello," he says, nodding at the man.

"Hello. I'll be going now. Think about what I said, Miguel."

He and Nick wait until the room is empty. "Who was that?"

"Just another doctor." Miguel lies.

"Gotcha."

He talks to Nick without really listening, a stilted half conversation that can be attributed to the painkilling neuro tweaks and exhaustion, but he's relieved when Nick goes to find dinner and Anna. Let them spend as much time together as they can if they're going to disappear back into Chimera in a few days. The sunset that blazed behind the Gamerunner's back is gone now, the view from the window now a cloudless moonscape. He still doesn't know if it's real or fake, or if that matters. All that matters is that he's alive, and he can keep playing.

FEED · 4

[Cassandra Burns] He needed a new *heart*?

[Danilo Viviani] That's crazy. A friend of mine failed his medical for having a bad back.

[Danilo Viviani] Wonder what makes **Miguel Anderson** so special.

[Lika Sergeyeva] He is pretty good. Using that orb on the horses was sweet.

[Thea Johansen] Waste of an orb, if you ask me. He should've kept it to save his life. He could've made his team take the risks with the horses. Who cares if one of them dies?

[Cassandra Burns] You seriously don't care if someone dies playing?

[Thea Johansen] Hey, no one forced them to sign up for this.

LEVEL FIFTEEN

Obligation. That's what he tells his parents: that he can't let his team down, he has to honor his commitment or whatever. The game will end for the rest of his team if he stops, he'll be ruining their chances. Parents are big on that stuff, they buy it even though he can tell they want to argue with him some more, tell him how pale and tired he looks. To Nick, he pretends there was never any doubt that he'd come back, and Nick runs off to find the others while Miguel paces the green room, waiting for official permission to leave. He wants to get downstairs. He wants to climb back into the bed and sleep. Time is curiously disjointed, both limitless and too short.

Discharged, he counts his steps down to the gaming room like he used to count heartbeats. Before he opens the doors, he stops, straightens his shoulders.

Chimera is fun. He would always have played it whether he needed a new heart or not. Everyone plays it. He would always have entered the competition just to prove how good he is. Focus on that. Don't think about anything else.

The others are waiting inside. "I'm sorry," he says, preempting them. "I should have told you all before." He's still not sure be believes that, but it's what they want to hear, and he needs them to forgive him enough to keep playing.

"'Sokay, man," Josh says. Grace shrugs. Leah gives him a stare that could nail two planks together. She hadn't visited him in the medical wing after that first day, when she had either decided not to yell at him or was forbidden to. He's fair game now. She turns away.

"What happens when you die?" Grace asks.

"Well, there are different theories . . ."

"No, you jackass, *you*. What happens to us?"

The Gamerunner had told him to keep his mouth shut, but Miguel thinks he can share this. They need to know. "The game ends for you guys. Leaders have to live for the team to play."

"Then do you maybe want to warn us the next time you do something stupid that might kill you, so we can back you up? I don't give a damn what happens to you, but I'd like to keep playing, thanks."

"I wonder why they didn't tell us that at the beginning."

He looks at Josh. "Probably because if they had, we'd let you take more risks for us. Like, if you're replaceable, and I'm not, I'd hide behind you. Not much of a victory at the end for me if you've done all the work. I'll warn you," he assures Grace.

"Thanks so much."

Sarcasm fits her like a tailored shirt. Whatever. He doesn't have to give her anything, but he will if the situation allows for it.

And if it doesn't, and things go badly, at least he won't ever have to hear her complain.

Might almost be worth it.

He had to study geography, so he's pretty sure he knows what's waiting under his fingertip, pressed to the fourth glowing spot on the overworld's globe. He's expecting the heat when the air changes and the room dissolves around him, but it hits him like a punch from Josh's metal arm.

Oh, *goody*. A desert. They haven't had one of those yet. He was hoping they wouldn't. These are bastard levels, he's hated every one he's ever played. Storms whip up with no warning, mirages fuck with your head, and the answer is never obvious. Plus while the sand doesn't leave the game with you, it feels like it does. Grainy, gritty, itchy. He always has to shower at least three times to wash off the illusion.

You are standing on top of a dune. The desert stretches as far as you can see in every direction. Footsteps lead to the north.

With the exception of that first day of the competition, in the overworld, and the laughter he doesn't want to think about,

Miguel has only ever heard the Storyteller speak the obvious truth, but that doesn't mean her implications can be trusted. Some truths mean: *Run the other way, as fast as you can. Leave your shoes if you have to.*

And some lies invite you in for a cup of tea. They give good hugs and offer you a place to sleep for the night.

"What do we think?" he asks. Grace is annoying, possibly evil, but he's mindful of what he said to her, and she's not the only one whose good side he needs to find again. He's not likely to find a map for that anywhere in the sand. Leah is several feet away, her back turned.

"We could split up," Josh suggests. "Shout if one of us finds something."

They could. Miguel hesitates. That doesn't *feel* right, and they're already behind a whole bunch of the other teams. Have to make up the time Miguel spent in the hospital wing.

"We follow them," he decides. What the hell. The footprints look human, and they have guns. *What the hell, if we're wrong, we're wrong.* He can play like that now.

Chimera thirst isn't real thirst—or it never used to be. Miguel isn't so sure anymore, the lines between the game and reality shimmer like mirages on the endless sand. It doesn't make sense that injuries sustained in the game can follow them outside and back again, but things like thirst and hunger don't. Either way, the scratching, clawing dryness at his throat is as real as any thirst he's ever known. None of them speak as they trek through the desert, watched over by a sun glued to its highest point. It takes him an hour to confirm it is actually moving. No blue save points rise up from the dunes.

The desert is mesmeric. The sands, uniformity made of infinite difference, the repetitive motion of stepping across it. Lulled into contemplation, the Gamerunner's face ripples across Miguel's mind. To say there was something weird about him is to say Chimera's coding is sort of clever.

The problem is that Miguel is sure the Gamerunner is exactly who he claimed to be, that he was telling at least part of a truth, and that he is terrifyingly sane. Sometimes you hear about those companies run by reclusive madmen who go barefoot all the time, even in winter, and will drink only water with live grasshoppers in it. Whatever. Crap like that. But the Gamerunner didn't give off that "humor me, I'm a little warped" vibe.

He gave off that "excuse me while I look into your mind and see the thoughts you can't" vibe instead.

Heat is slowly baking him, but Miguel shivers.

What *is* the point of this game, this trek through endless sand? To make them all live another few decades. Money for the Gamerunner—both of them? Is it like climbing a mountain, and they did it just because they could, because a Chimera-shaped hole was there and they decided to fill it?

Despite the heat, the sweat running down his back, and the stink of it reaching his nostrils, the sand in his shoes and his hair, Miguel smiles. It doesn't *matter.* He can finally play the way he's always wanted to. He can run to see how far he'll go not because he's being chased.

"What the hell are you doing?" Grace asks as he sprints down this dune, up the next. At the top he faces them, spreading his arms, daring them to catch up. Nick is the first to scramble to his side.

"What's that?" Nick gasps, pointing. A square shimmers on top of the next dune. Miguel shrugs, leaves Nick to wait for the others, and runs again, half expecting it to be a mirage when he gets there, but it's solid. A wooden crate, full of food and water. A collection of welcome pixels. And firewood. The next breath of wind carries the faintest thread of cold.

The footprints they've followed stretch into the distance. Sometimes the path is clear.

"Cache," he says. "Summon tents." And sleeping bags, ropes, anything else he can remember seeing in the cache that might be helpful. Josh and Grace build a fire as the first stars appear in a four-color sky, the reds, purples, oranges, blues of sunset.

"Let me help you with that." He jogs across the sand to Leah, who needs no help with the tent. Wordlessly she hands him a pole. It probably takes longer with two of them than it would with one. Anger seethes off her and touches him like the cold fingers of the settling night.

They eat, clustered around the fire, convincing the body in the gaming room it is fed and warm. Grace drops her plate and disappears into one of the tents, Josh following her a moment later. Miguel raises his eyebrows, Leah shrugs, Nick clears his throat and says he's going for a walk. Good friend.

Miguel tilts his head up. "I know it's a game, but look at that." The sky is astonishing, a million pinpoints of light, as if the whole world is a gaming room and the stars are the sensors tracking his every move.

The silence is absolute.

"Are you going to talk to me?" Miguel asks.

"Maybe one day."

"But not tonight."

She laughs without a trace of humor. "No."

Unreasonable anger warms him from the inside as the fire warms his skin. He gets it, sure, but it's not like he didn't have a reason.

"Let me know when you want to," he says, standing, feet slipping on the sand as he climbs into one of the remaining empty tents. Shirt off, he watches the lights glow through his skin. Right now it is fusing with his flesh, taking him over.

He doesn't remember falling asleep, but he is awake when the sun comes up, as quickly and spectacularly as it has gone down. The others get up, he sends the gear they don't need back to the cache, finds the trail of footprints.

More hours of walking. Of sweat and thirst and sand. Another square ripples on a faraway dune, and he thinks it's more food at first, but it's too big.

The lines of reality blur even more. They're already inside the game, they can't enter it again. A mirage, must be. First sign of madness: hallucinating ChimeraCubes where there are none.

Usually the people around you don't hallucinate the same thing.

"That's . . . meta. Or something. Makes my head hurt," says Josh.

"It's not really possible, is it?" Leah asks.

Honestly, it probably is—at least possible to make them *feel* like they've gone into the game from within the game. Miguel's never set up that kind of loop in his sim, there's never been a reason to, but lines of code write themselves across his mind; he can see how it could be done.

The Cube doesn't waver and dissipate as they near, it's truly there. Still, when they reach the last of the footprints, Miguel closes his fingers around the door's handle to check. Solid.

Inside, coolness and shade are so absolute, so relieving, they can do nothing but stand in the entrance to relish it. That's not helping them catch up. He focuses on one last breath of chilled air.

"Let's look around."

As in other Cubes, at least the ones which haven't been altered for the competition, a second set of doors opens onto the corridors lined with gaming rooms, stairs at every corner. A map on the wall of the lobby usually shows which ones are free. Here, they all are. But every door he tries is locked. He presses his ear to one of them but can't hear anything. Rolling her eyes, Leah cocks her head, then shakes it. There's no one inside.

"Split up," he says, pointing to the closest stairwell. "This could be like the fears, we have to be apart to work together. Message if you find an open one."

Half an hour later he tells them to meet back in the entrance hall. He stomps there himself and leans against the wall, enjoying the cool concrete on his back. Time to think. He doesn't have many more half hours to waste. They're assuming that they're here to enter the gaming rooms and play. What else could it be?

The others join him, talk, wonder aloud. He ignores them, pushes their voices to background noise.

Way, way back during that long first summer after he started the game . . . It hadn't looked like this, but the principle could still apply.

"Do you remember that puzzle section on Two? In the original game?" he asks, scanning their faces for signs of recollection. Leah's eyes are the first to widen.

"You think it's a labyrinth?"

"It could be."

"Actually"—she corrects herself—"that was a maze, not a labyrinth, but I see your point."

"Aren't they the same thing?" asks Grace. Miguel remembers the fish. Grace is about to be sorry she wondered.

"No, a maze has several possible paths to the center, or wherever the end point is. A labyrinth has only one."

"A-maze-ing." Nick laughs. Leah flicks his shoulder, and envy twists Miguel's stomach. Sure, she's fine with Nick, even though he'd known Miguel's secret and kept it.

With no other ideas, the best—only—assumption is that the beginning is where they are, at the building's main entrance. He has no clue where to go from here, how the puzzle is unlocked to take them to the middle of this weird Cube in the middle of the desert. Chimera puzzles are always solved with some kind of code, but it could be numbers, names, anything. The best the others can come up with are the things he's already thought of: their birthdays, people important to them.

Sometimes they need maps. Have they found any more? "Yes," says Grace reluctantly. "I found one when I was alone on that fear thing, but it's to something outside, I think. No straight lines, and this place is all straight lines."

Now she tells them. He wonders how many times they're allowed to get it wrong and how obvious it should be. A quick check of his feed tells him all teams but one, apart from his, have made it through, which was to be expected. He knows that they're behind. That healing from a heart transplant takes longer than someone's having an arm or a finger or a patch of skin replaced.

He grits his teeth. It doesn't look as if the other teams spent too long solving the problem. Much to Miguel's dismay, the other team still stuck isn't Zack's.

"There has to be a hint here somewhere," Miguel says, pressing random spots on the walls, looking for hidden panels.

"Maybe we missed something outside, or in another level."

"God, Josh, don't say that. We'll never find it," says Leah.

"Sorry."

"Okay, let's say you're right that we need to split up," says Nick. When Miguel had done his first maze, years ago, his digitized team had come with him because they'd had to. This time they have five real people, five working brains. At least in theory. His isn't helping him much right now.

"Hold on." Grace is out the front doors before she's finished speaking and back a few seconds later. "We did miss something. This Cube is smaller."

"What?"

"It *looks* huge because the desert fucks with perspective, and it's the only thing for miles, and we were so glad to see it, right? But it has only five floors. Normal Cubes have seven. You think that's a coincidence?"

Hell no.

Five floors. Things keep coming in fives. The first, five underground tunnels.

He's been an *idiot.* "The last time we were faced with something like this, what happened?"

"The fears," says Nick right away.

"And what did we learn from that?" This means the other teams have figured it out, too.

"Oh, shit. Our alignments."

"Right."

Leah pushes herself away from the wall. "Took you long enough." Miguel turns on her.

"You knew?"

"I guessed."

"And you didn't say anything?"

"Oh, look at who thinks he has a right to say anything about *that,*" she spits. "If you're not going to treat us like actual people, why should we help?"

"If you're not going to help, why are you here?"

"None of your business. Something else you know all about."

"I said I was sorry!"

Nick, Josh, and Grace back away. "You should be!" Leah yells, the sound too loud in the small space. "Look at you! You're the most instinctual Chimera player I've ever seen. I've checked your feed, I've watched you since we started. You *get* this game. You make decisions and you trust them. You trust Chimera. But you didn't trust us."

"I don't trust Chimera," he retorts. He doesn't realize it's true until the words come out of his mouth. That meeting with the Gamerunner left an unsettled feeling he's been trying to ignore. Maybe that was the point. The game—and Gamerunners—know everything else about him, why wouldn't they know how good he is at ignoring discomfort?

But his words surprise her. "What?"

"I don't trust the game," he says. "I trust me. I don't understand this competition the way I thought I understood the regular one. I don't know what's going on here or why we're doing this. I only know we have to win. We have to keep going. Nick, go to the room above this one on the fifth floor. Leah, you're on four, and Josh, you're on two. Grace, stay here. And everyone, message on your com when you're in position."

"I have questions," Leah says, following him up the stairs.

"And I'll answer them when I have answers. Not now, not here."

Behind him, her feet pause. "Okay," she says, frustration

echoing up the walls.

He opens the door onto a third-floor corridor, she keeps climbing.

Hand over the doorknob, he hesitates. Breathes.

It opens, and this one isn't empty.

"What was that?" Grace asks through her com link. "The entrance hall just totally changed around me. It looks pretty much like an ordinary gaming room now. I think the lights mean something."

"That was success."

"Damn." Josh chimes in.

An ordinary gaming room, almost. Pinpoints of light dot only one wall. In normal Cubes they're all over, rendering his image from every angle. His sim at home is two dimensional, more of an out-of-body experience. He watches himself on a screen.

"How many gaming rooms along each outside edge of this Cube?" he asks.

"Ten," says Leah swiftly. "Fourteen in real ones."

He counts the dots, lit and unlit. The one in the center at the bottom of the grid glows slightly brighter than the rest. That always means something. It does in the overworld. Okay. That's where he is now. To get to the next one, he has to go out again, turn left, then right down one of the corridors that cut through the grid. Four rooms along on the left side.

"I need to go left," says Josh. So they're not all tracing the same route. Interesting.

"Go. Check in at the next room." Miguel runs down the hallways, doesn't pause this time. The door opens. Score. It works for everyone else, too.

Three right, two left. He finds his little bright light. Only one more. Left, right, left.

"Um," says Leah, looking at him. "How did that happen?"

"I didn't feel the building move. And we were all on different floors." Grace purses her lips. "Weird."

You are in a large room. Along one wall are two doors. Behind the first is a save point you may use at any available time that will allow you to progress to the next level undeterred, with the item you seek. Behind the second is a prisoner you have five minutes to save. If you do, you may also continue on to your next challenge. If you do not, you must restart from your last save point.

The beginning of the level. They hadn't found a single one in the desert. Still . . .

"Actual information," says Josh. "That's useful."

Yeah. That aside . . .

"We save the prisoner," says Nick. Leah nods.

"Oh, come on." Grace protests. "Who cares? Whether we save them or not, we still get to go to the next level. Why waste the time?"

It's the wrong question for her to ask because it's the one that gives Miguel pause. Time.

"I'm with Grace. In an ideal world, sure, but we're behind as it is," says Josh.

Miguel's would be the deciding vote even if it weren't the last. He looks at the doors, as if they'll tell him the right choice to make. There's a reason the prisoner is there—maybe there's other stuff behind that door: gear they can use, a shortcut, anything.

Sometimes you think you're prepared for what you're going to see. Sometimes you think you know the game you're playing. He doesn't think that about Chimera anymore.

Miguel opens the second door. His hands drop to his sides, his mouth opens. Over his shoulder

Nick lets out a strangled gasp at the room, the seamless glass cage within it.

Anna.

LEVEL SIXTEEN

In the corner of Miguel's visor, a countdown timer begins. Four fifty-nine. Four fifty-eight. There is only one thing in the cell apart from her: a small fire in the farthest corner. She fills the box with soundless screams, the glass too thick to hear her. Mouth bared, showing all her teeth. Fists clenched, she beats against her prison, knuckles landing bruising blows an inch from their faces.

"She can't breathe, there's no vents! She's going to burn to death! How the hell do we get her out?" Nick screams. "Cache! Summon ax!"

But he doesn't have it anymore. It broke on the ship, right before Miguel woke up in a hospital bed. Leah summons hers and throws it to him. The glass doesn't even chip under the blade.

"I'm using the save point," says Grace over the noise. "She's not even real."

Nick wheels on her. "You . . . don't . . . k now . . . that."

Miguel is frozen. Potential choices cartwheel through his mind. He hears the other door open, two sets of feet stomp through it.

Fuck them.

This game will teach you who you are.

He doesn't know what's real anymore, doesn't know who he is, but he knows there is no world, anywhere, where he will leave Anna to die.

Like so many of Chimera's rooms, this one is empty, gray, windowless. There is nothing in it but the cell, and nothing in that but Anna and the fire.

Three forty-seven. "Your boots," he says to Leah. "Can you climb the walls? Maybe there's something on top of it?"

Her mouth twists in pain. "I think we'll find out soon anyway. It's shrinking," she says, though she doesn't need to. He can see it.

Wasted time, spent watching the glass box. Tears run down Nick's face. "Stop screaming." He begs the caged Anna. "You're using up the air. Move away from the flames." But she doesn't seem to hear him. "Please, Anna. Please."

Three-fifteen. "Cache!" Miguel says. Maybe a laser gun? He has no idea. "Summon!" He motions to Anna to move to one side of the box. Shards of light bounce around them and inside the cell, Anna's mouth closes. Her face is as wet as Nick's, the blaze in her eyes turning from rage to pure fear.

Two thirty-one. The cell is half the size it was. The fire starts to lick at her skin, and she screams again.

"Do we have anything else?" Nick begs. As the cell shrinks, the room around it grows. "Is there anything else here? There has to be something else. Come on. Please."

Nothing. An otherwise empty room. Miguel doesn't need the Storyteller to tell him that.

At two minutes, he can nearly reach the top of the glass. The outside is cool. He feels along the edges for cracks, weak points. Places to land a critical hit.

Still nothing.

"Hold on, Anna, please." He pleads under his breath.

At a minute and a half, she can almost touch both sides of the cell. The door behind them is still open. Beyond that, another room and another door. Safety for all three of them.

No.

Miguel swaps out his gun, laser for bullets, hefting its increased weight.

"What the hell are you doing?" Nick screams. "You're going to kill her!"

"Gunshot wounds can be fixed!" Miguel shouts, but it's a moot point. The bullet ricochets off the glass, orange with flames now, spins out into the gray oblivion.

At fifty-nine seconds, Anna is locked inside a perfect glass coffin of fire. Together, Miguel, Nick, and Leah kick, punch, push at it, anything to break it or tip it over. "Okay," Miguel says, panting. Fifteen seconds. Not enough time to get to the save point, probably. He'll do the fucking level over again, because he's not leaving. "Stop." He and Leah manage to pull Nick away, struggling, arms flailing. "Don't look."

Miguel can't either. He turns his head, watches the timer count down.

Three. Two. One.

Slowly they raise their heads. On the floor, in what was the middle of the cell, a blue button flashes. Atop it sits a box of ashes. They were meant to lose. It was never about saving her. Miguel caches the box, whatever the fuck that's for, and stomps on the button hard enough to break it, though it doesn't break. The outcome was always going to be the same. He quits out, tears off his visor, replaces it with his lenses from his locker. Nick does the same thing, faster even, is already sending a message to Anna when Miguel starts talking into his mic.

Surprisingly, she answers him first, in seconds, but she probably has less to say to him.

"Yeah? What's up?"

Thank god.

Miguel's voice shakes, but the mic on his lenses translates to text just fine. "Talk to Nick. He'll explain. But you're okay?"

"Dude, I'm fine. Watching the feeds. You're getting your

asses kicked."

He knows.

"Gotta go, Nick's messaging. Talk later.".

A hand touches his shoulder. "You okay?" Leah asks.

"Yeah." He tears off his sensor strips. No, not okay. "Yeah. I need to . . . I need to go."

He should talk to her. He should find Josh and Grace and give them unholy amounts of shit for flaking out. He should eat to counteract the adrenaline still coursing through his veins.

Alone in his suite, he does none of those things. For the first time, he opens up the special inbox he was given as a team leader in case he needed to communicate with the Gamerunners.

"You're listening," he says to the empty room, watching the words translate to text. "I need to talk to you."

Nothing happens. He washes his face and gets a bottle of water, throat still dry with memories of desert and fire. Dry as ashes. If the game is about choices, he should feel good that he made the right one, the one that will let him sleep tonight. Except he won't, he'll be wondering what the hell to do about having two team members he can't rely on and whether he needed that five minutes more than a box of ashes.

He's researched Chimera before, but that was out of curiosity for a game he loved and needed, a game that had never made him watch something like that. He's wondered about imaginations before, not sick minds. "Search: Chimera, Gamerunners, benefits." What are they getting out of this?

Article after article. "Organize by date."

The first, a tiny piece from years ago about a pair of unnamed tech geniuses preparing to launch an "experience" they claimed would revolutionize not just the gaming industry, but the world.

Well, they'd kept their promise on that front. The skeptical reporter probably feels like an idiot now.

Next, quotes from world leaders about the sneak preview they'd been permitted, lots of platitudes about how the game will be of untold benefit to humanity. In return, of course, the Gamerunners would be granted certain allowances to ensure their success. Details are scarce, but Miguel knows what those are, it's hard to keep that kind of secret. News of tax breaks and access to special resources gets out because that's the kind of thing that pisses people off.

But nobody was mad, or at least the few dissenting voices were quickly silenced by a swelling roar of approval for the game. Chimera is fun! It's cool! The biomech is awesome!

He flicks through the screens. More of the same: excitement, feedback from the first players. Interesting, but not really what he's looking for, and he read most of it years ago.

The first real criticisms come a few years later, from a direction with which he is all too familiar. Yes, it's a positive thing that everyone, not just the rich, suddenly has the opportunity to earn top-notch medical care, necessary in these dangerous times, but the divide hasn't vanished, simply shifted. The world's best doctors have been lured to Chimera with astronomical salaries, state-of-the-art equipment, and, there are rumors, faster progression through the game for themselves. Soon enough, Chimera didn't need to bribe existing doctors, they merely trained their own, offering free training to anyone who agreed to work for the game.

He blinks.

From medical debates to environmental ones: people questioning the resources Chimera uses. But those had pretty much stopped eventually, too. He knows all this already.

He skims through more search results. Nothing else jumps out. An online forum is populated with theories about why the Gamerunners invented Chimera, but it's just an excuse to talk about money and power, and there aren't many new posts since the last time he checked. The game must make them a fortune from product placement alone; the clothes that appear on Miguel's body, on anyone's, when he enters the game come from a large, popular retailer who have paid to put them there. He has real-world versions them, too, earned in the game. A dot of green light spotted a shirt or jacket or new pair of boots in the glass cabinet in his gaming room when he quits out.

Money is usually a good reason for most things, be it

incentive or deterrent, obstacle or what smooths the path. When talking to the Gamerunner, though, Miguel hadn't gotten the impression that Chimera is just some giant coin quest for him and his partner.

The game will teach you who you are.

You are in a bed. People are coming at you with strange objects in their hands. They wish to make you bleed, take part of you away and replace it with a machine. You want to move, but you are paralyzed. The light above you is bright, blinding if you look at it for more than a second. You thrash and scream, but you cannot stop them from coming, coming, coming . . .

There is no bright light this time when Miguel's eyes snap open. It's the middle of the night, and everything has been dimmed to some scientifically determined optimum level for restful sleep.

He was not sleeping peacefully. He has to hand it to the biomech designers; his heart hammers just as the old one did, pounding in time with his gasping breaths. It feels real. He touches his artificial finger to his wrist, a habit he'll probably never lose, and counts.

He was dreaming about Anna until the light of the blazing fire became the light above an operating table.

"Can't sleep?"

"God!" Miguel sits bolt upright and stares into the darkest

corner of the room. A pair of eyes glimmer in a pool of black. "Are you trying to give me another heart attack?"

"Can't happen, not now."

"I beg to differ."

"No need to beg."

"What are you doing here?"

"You called for me."

Miguel blinks. "That was hours ago. Wasn't it?" The curtains are closed; even if they weren't, the window wouldn't necessarily tell him the truth about the sky.

"If you expect that people are simply sitting around waiting for you to beckon them, I'm not surprised your last relationship failed." The Gamerunner smiles. "Apologies, that was cruel. Better luck with the next one."

"There isn't a next one."

"Oh? Shame. Now, what was it you wished to discuss? I assume there was something."

There was. "Yeah," says Miguel, swallowing. "What the hell was that about today?"

The man's face is the picture of innocence. "You mean, what you found at the end of the maze?"

"Yes, that!" Miguel pushes himself off the pillows, sitting up. "Did everyone see someone they love in that box?"

"Does it matter?"

"Yes, it matters."

The Gamerunner shrugs. "It was part of the game. A choice you had to make."

"Did I make the right one?" He had, of course he had.

"Again, does it matter? You want to stop now," the Gamerunner says, the last part not a question.

"I don't ever want to see anything like that again." Miguel shudders. "I'll go back and take my chances with the normal game. I know it doesn't pull crap like that."

"Oh, no, I think you'll stay in the competition."

Until this moment Miguel had been prepared to be convinced. It's the Gamerunner's absolute certainty that cements his resolve. He climbs out of bed, the lush, thick carpet squishing under his toes. Living here had been nice.

"You know, I realize I didn't introduce myself before, and because you are doing me a favor, continuing to play, you should possibly know who you're doing it for." The man steps away from the wall, moves to the end of Miguel's bed, long-fingered hands curling around the bar at the foot.

"You seem pretty sure I'm going to keep playing," says Miguel, finding a clean shirt. "I told you, I'm leaving."

"Oh, I am certain you'll stay. Well, Miguel, my name is Blake, and you are one of only a handful of people who know that. Tell me, is there anything else you need here?" Blake gestures around the suite. "Anything you'd like?"

Tons of stuff. Better breakfasts, more books, help inside

the game. The best weapons, invincibility orbs around every corner, easy bosses, not to see someone he loves burn alive. "Answers. Before I go."

"That depends on the questions."

"Why?"

"Because I can't tell you everything."

Miguel clenches his jaw. "You're not stupid. Don't pretend to be."

Blake—if that is truly his name. Miguel's not a hundred percent sure he believes it—smiles widely. "Ah. Good boy. I suppose the answer is because someone has to, and as it turns out, that's me and my . . . business partner. Governments are utterly incapable of repairing the damage that people have caused for thousands of years. Humanity needs to feel as if it is fighting for something. Survival. Rewards in Chimera give people a real chance outside the Cubes. It's a public service really."

"Why don't I believe that?"

"Because you don't trust me. Which is probably the smartest thing I've seen from you."

The uneasy feeling that has curled through Miguel's belly and up to his heart since the moment he first met Blake squeezes painfully, reminding him it's there. Blake walks to the window, parting the curtains an inch to look outside. Admiring the view, if it's real, or inspecting his handiwork, if it isn't?

Choices. Right ones, wrong ones, ones that fall on both sides of the line at the same time. Miguel closes his eyes.

"I'm not going back," he says. His team is going to be pissed, but Nick will forgive him, Leah he can try to talk to if she'll let him, Grace and Josh he doesn't care as much about. It's not worth the risk, something else could happen. *What's damaged stays damaged.*

His parents will get their son back, for the first time. Maybe they will take a trip somewhere, let him see the world outside Chimera when he has only ever seen it through the lens of a visor. He can always go back to playing Chimera like normal, when he's ready.

"That is . . . a shame," says Blake, turning to face Miguel. "I did not want to have to do this."

"Do what?"

Blake raises a hand, points one of those long fingers at Miguel's chest. "The heart you were given is not the one you would have earned had everything gone according to your plans. And mine. It is programmed with a virus and is degrading as surely as your bioheart was. You are no longer in any danger if you exert yourself, but it will kill you regardless."

"You can't do that." He can't breathe. He finds the nearest wall, leans on it.

"I invented Chimera. Do you really think I couldn't make this happen?"

"No— But—"

"But finish the game, Miguel. Don't speak a word of this to anyone, win the competition, and you'll have what you want. I promise you."

"You said you'd already given me what I wanted. Before. Why should I trust you now, when you've told me I shouldn't?"

"Because I had no need to tell you the truth before. You wanted to keep playing, so why tip my hand?"

"Because you're killing me!" When it'd been his own heart, he couldn't do anything. Now the betrayal is outside his body, and Blake's game taught him to hit things. He crosses the room in seconds, fist raised. Blake steps neatly out of the way.

"I don't think you want to do that."

"You know," Miguel says, panting, "I really do."

"Calm down, Miguel. There's no reason this has to change anything. Just keep playing. I can even make it easier for you if you like."

The best weapons, invincibility orbs around every corner, easy bosses, not to see someone he loves burn alive. "I won't cheat."

"Not even with your clever simulation?"

Who *is* this guy? Black spots pop across Miguel's eyes. He gulps the filtered air.

"Why? Why are you doing this?"

"Because I can. Because you intrigue me. Because I want

to. Mostly because my partner and I have what you might call
. . . a bet. One I wish to win."

Miguel swallows dryly. "If you're so big on choices, do I
have one?"

"Of course. You may choose to die."

"You're insane. Nobody would choose that."

Blake smiles, a knowing smirk that Miguel wants to slap
off his face. He guesses that wouldn't end well, though. "You
already did, once before. I saved you from yourself then, too."

The room starts to spin. "How do you know about that?"

"It doesn't matter."

"And if I say fuck you and go home anyway?"

Blake moves swiftly to the door. "Then you have a few
weeks, perhaps a month, to live. Enjoy it."

CUTSCENE:
BLAKE

Lucius is going to be furious. Blake smiles. It's a certainty that Lucius already knows what he's done but for his own reasons has chosen not to intervene. Divine. The boy will return to the game to play harder than ever.

Lucius angry is a rare but highly enjoyable sight.

Dawn is breaking as Blake leaves ChimeraCube Chartreuse, departing silently from the roof on his hoverboard. The city awakes beneath him, those foolish electric cars humans still insist on coming to life and moving around like so many vividly colored little beetles. His grin widens as he spots his . . . friend, standing in the doorway atop Chimera headquarters, artificial eyes sparking with righteous indignation.

"That was *cheating!* And cruel!"

"So?" Blake asks mildly.

"So!"

"Your eloquence astounds me." Blake laughs, claps Lucius

on the shoulder. "I'd like you to point out where I ever promised to play either fairly or nicely. Don't tell me nature should have taken its course; we both know that's a myth. Every aspect of Chimera is designed to defy that."

"That is completely beside the point."

"It's really not. Coffee?" Blake asks, sliding inside and waiting for Lucius to follow. "I picked up some of the good stuff you like. It's getting more difficult to find. Not for me, but, you know, in general."

"You're too kind."

"Sarcasm doesn't become you."

"What can I say," says Lucius. "I am . . . perturbed."

That's exactly the word, too. Only Lucius would use a word like that. They step onto a tile and descend to an office that doesn't belong to either of them but does have a coffee machine on neutral territory. Neither of them wants to imagine the wars that would break out if they kept it anywhere else. Of course they could each have one, but this gives them a place to meet.

Lucius's mug has a bunny on it, an actual bunny. Sometimes Blake completely despairs of him.

"I'm not saying we should have let him die," says Lucius. "I was against his inclusion from the beginning for that very reason."

"Not enough for us to forbid people with such handicaps

from playing at all. It could have happened anywhere at any time. Inside a Cube or on the street. Lucky it happened now; the resources were close by, and response was quick. He might not have been so fortunate otherwise."

"Right," Lucius agrees, "but if he wanted to stop, that's his choice."

"And he can still make it. He wants to play. He doesn't know how badly yet, but he wants to win."

"Do you think he can?"

"Yes. And there is nothing stopping you from taking your chosen and giving them advantages, you know." Except they both know there is everything stopping Lucius from doing precisely that. Lucius takes his coffee and sits on a chair designed to look comfortable without actually being comfortable. Blake's never known how humans manage that, or why they'd want to, but there you are. "If it makes you feel better, he refused to let me help him. That *should* make you feel better."

They sit in silence, which means the debate is over. Lucius knows when he's beaten, and soon, very soon, he and his employers will know just how beaten.

Blake told Miguel the truth about how much longer he has, how long the competition has left to run. All he and Lucius needed was enough time to—briefly—unite the population, get them focused on one thing and voicing their opinions about it. Millions of messages scroll by every second, each one an indication of the personality of the human who sent it. The competition won't last long enough to give them time to reconsider their choices. The first indication is always the purest, the right one. Which isn't to say the world will end the moment they crown their victor, but it will dictate the start of the next phase.

Blake knows what his plans are. Lucius does not. And the other way around.

LEVEL SEVENTEEN

"Mig? What's wrong?" Leah sees his face and his hands gripping the door frame, but not the sweat slicking his palms. "Sorry, is only Nick allowed to call you that?"

"What? No. No, it's fine. Did I wake you up?" He doesn't know why he stumbled here instead of to Nick's room when Blake left. He'd only known he couldn't be alone, now here he is.

"I couldn't sleep." She shrugs.

Can't sleep?

He shakes Blake's voice from his head; it does nothing to quell the rest of his racing thoughts. Blake *can't* be doing this. Breath tight in his chest, he focuses on the details around him. Leah's suite is identical to his, though less messy. "Seriously, are you okay?" she asks. "You don't look so good."

"Yeah, well, you're beautiful."

"Now I *know* there's something wrong." A smile tugs at

her lips. C'mon, sit." She leads him to her couch. An empty plate and a half-full water glass sit on the table in front of it.

"Am I interrupting?"

"No."

"I had a nightmare." It's not the right truth, but it's not a lie. He can't tell her the truth. He can't tell anyone. This can't be happening. The tips of his fingers are numb.

"About what happened today?"

And other things. "Yeah."

She nods. "Man, that was intense, huh? I take it she really is okay?"

Understatement. "Yeah. Are you?"

"I'm fine. I mean, that was awful, but worse for you and Nick. Listen," she says, taking his hand, "it wasn't real. She's okay. You're okay."

He almost believes the lie she doesn't know she's telling. In this room he feels okay. Her voice is soothing, her hand warm. His next breath comes a little easier. Blake will keep him alive as long as he stays, plays, wins. He's safe . . . for now.

"I'm glad you're here," Leah says. Miguel raises his eyebrows, and she continues. "You seemed to need some time alone, but I think—I think I need to talk to you about something."

"Are you going to yell at me again? Because I probably do deserve it, but let me get comfortable."

She laughs, a single huff of air. "No. After today, I forgive you for not trusting Josh and Grace, and it's not like you know me much better. I don't like it, but I get it."

"Thanks. So, you know now what I wanted. What are you trying to get?"

"You can still get comfortable if you want."

He shifts on the couch, drawing his knees up to sit cross-legged, facing her. Waits. Her lips twist as she thinks, decides where to begin or what to say. He has no idea what it is. He has no idea about a lot of things lately.

"I want to find out what happened to my sister. There's a procedure they can do. Implanted memories."

"Oh." He's heard of that. As the world disintegrates, learning where dangers lurk from people who didn't have time or skill to survive them could be important.

"I think I know the point of the competition," she says.

He leans forward so suddenly she jumps. "Sorry," he says, pulling back. "But . . . what?"

"Maybe not the *point*, exactly. It's . . . something. We said, from the first level, that there being a story is new, right? Normally Chimera's just a collection of levels, there isn't a common thread. I think I know what the thread is. How much history have you done at school?"

"Enough, why?"

"Myths and legends?"

"Not a lot. Some."

"Twelve levels," she says. "Twelve labors."

He thinks, combs through a brain that for years now has mostly regarded school as something to do between Chimera sessions. A vague spark of recollection ignites. Hercules? "The twelve tasks all were completely different," he says. "Weren't they?"

"Mostly, yeah. But there are a couple of weird similarities. Golden apples, those horses, which . . . I've never seen anything like them in Chimera before. And there was a sea monster, I think, though that was a hydra, not a leviathan. But the point of all the labors was that at the end of them, he would be made immortal. A god."

"You think they're trying to make us immortal?" Miguel laughs.

She frowns again. "I don't know. I think maybe they're testing something. They said they're beta testing, but what if it isn't the game, what if it's the parts they're giving us as rewards? I know this sounds crazy, okay? But *can* they actually give us so much biomech we'll live forever? Giving different parts, different things to different players. They could've done it in the normal game, but this gives them an excuse to watch us really closely. Even after the competition ends. Maybe their plan is to eventually combine everything into one person, who will barely be a person anymore."

He's had the same thought—about the one person at least. He should tell her about Blake.

When he doesn't answer, she shrugs. "Maybe I am crazy. Maybe they're just not very original. They knew the story and stole the idea."

"You really believe that?"

"No—"

You will never guess at my motivations.

"So, the girl today."

"Anna."

"Anna," Leah says, drawing her knees up to her chin. He knows a little about body language. "You sure she's your *ex*-girlfriend? The way you looked at her wasn't the way guys usually look at their best friends' girlfriends. If they do, pretty soon they're doing it out of a couple of black eyes."

He knows what she's asking; she's hinted at it once already, but that was before she found out he'd lied to her. He won't assume he knows what she's thinking, feeling now.

"Anna's been one of my best friends since we were little. Me, her, and Nick. She was my girlfriend until a little while ago, but it's complicated. She stayed with me because of my . . . issues," he says, gesturing at where his human heart once was. Now a scar, a machine, twinkling lights, a ticking bomb. "I stayed with her because . . . I'm seventeen and I like girls. She deserved better, and she always liked Nick. It just took me a while to realize it. And that I was being a selfish jackass."

Her knees drop to the side. "In that case, good."

"What's good?"

She smiles. "I wouldn't consider kissing a guy again if I knew he'd ditched someone he cared about and left her to be squashed and burned to death in some freaky glass box of doom, whether it turned out to be real or not."

"So you are considering it." His stomach flips, in that good way. "A few hours ago you hated me."

"Signs look favorable. I'm a complicated girl." She inches closer. "And now I'm mad at other people. Grace and Josh," she adds.

Oh. Them. Yes. Anger he'd been too afraid and then too shocked to feel simmers up from somewhere, lava finding a crack in the crust.

"Yeah," he says through gritted teeth. It's too late to ask the Gamerunners to replace them, even if he wanted to ask Blake for anything. And if he did, and they did, it would just be with people with the same alignment. What's that phrase?

Better the devil you know.

"Any ideas?"

She shrugs. "Watch them. Don't give them any tasks unless you have to. Don't trust them."

He'd gotten that far already, which isn't to say he doesn't appreciate the advice. It's good to know he's thinking straight and that Leah has his back again. According to their geolocs, they're both in Grace's suite, but Miguel will wait for Nick before confronting them and trying to figure out how they can continue to work as a team.

Nick can spend as long as he wants with Anna. Leah's suite is quiet, peaceful, and has her in it. He knows what his task is, what he's been ordered to do, blackmailed into doing. He knows what will happen if he doesn't. But for only the second time he can remember, the real world holds more appeal than the game does.

[Self: Miguel Anderson] **Nicholas Lee** where are you?

[Self: Miguel Anderson] Come on, we're all ready to play. We're waiting for you.

[Self: Miguel Anderson] Are you okay???

[Self: Miguel Anderson] **Anna Kasperek** Have you seen Nick?

[Self: Miguel Anderson] Okay, I get that you need time together, but answer me.

[Self: Miguel Anderson] That's it.

He doesn't have time to wait for the rain to stop. Here's hoping that they actually are right, that the chemicals aren't too damaging. The green edges of the Cube glow brighter in the gloom. Hoverboarding in the rain *sucks*, but he doesn't have time to walk either, or to be recognized.

Droplets fall on his gritted teeth. Of all the times for Nick to disappear, when the biomech in Miguel's chest has turned to a ticking bomb and the only way to diffuse it is to stay inside the Cube and keep playing.

Some things don't change, at least not for long.

And some things do. The first time he'd been able to tell Nick what was wrong, the first time he'd ever told anyone who didn't already know. God, they'd just been kids then. Nick had been feeling bad about Miguel's beating Level One before him, even though Nick had started earlier, his birthday a few months before.

So Miguel had explained why he needed to play so much, get ahead so fast. Speeding through the air, he pictures Nick's expression, remembers its changing from one frown to another then to determination. He'd walked away, leaving Miguel terrified that he'd lost his best friend and that his best friend would tell everyone his secret. But Nick had come back a minute later, a blue rock in his hand. Miguel's trophy, he'd said, because he wouldn't be able to collect many in the game if he was only waiting for a heart at the end of Twenty-five.

It wasn't the last one. In his room at home, a shelf holds a line of stones, all different shapes, sizes, colors. Twenty of them.

The board descends, landing in front of Anna's building.

Officially there's a security lock. Unofficially, if he hits the door just *there*, it pops open.

Not that he's ever used that before, of course. He runs up two flights of stairs, skids to a halt outside her door.

"Guys, let me in," he says, knocking. "Please."

Footsteps. Voices. Creaking hinges and Anna's frustrated but smiling face. "You guys are gonna need to figure this out yourselves." Nick's behind her, sitting on the couch, scowling.

"Figure *what* out? What's your problem?" he demands, staring at Nick. "Hey," he says more quietly, kissing Anna's cheek but not taking his eyes from his friend, "glad you're okay."

"Are you?" Nick asks. "I saw you look at that door. You were going to leave, too."

"Oh, come on. I was not." Anger bubbles. A single glance in the wrong direction isn't in the top ten of his list of problems right now. "Yeah, I looked and I didn't leave. I'd never let anything happen to her. She knows that."

"I do know that," she says, sighing. "I told him that. Nick, come on. I get it was scary, and I'm not, like, superimpressed that they used me, but it makes a sick kind of sense. I don't understand the pair of you. You're somehow both cool with knowing the other's kissed me, but you're going to fight over me for this?"

"More than kissed," Nick mumbles. Miguel suppresses a

smile.

"We don't need to get into that," says Anna. "Are you going to grow up now?"

"Please," Miguel says, stepping closer to the couch. "I need you. We've got to get back in there and play." He hopes Nick can hear the undercurrent in his voice, even if he can't explain it.

"What about Grace and Josh?"

"We need them, too."

"Nick," says Anna, "I'm fine. Look at me."

Nick takes a deep breath. "I still don't trust them."

"You don't have to."

"Okay."

"Excellent," says Anna. "Get out of here, both of you. Go make me proud."

They hoverboard back together, Miguel sitting, Nick standing behind him. Inside Cube Chartreuse, they head first for Leah's suite.

"I'm glad she's okay," says Leah softly when she answers her door. Nick blinks, half smiles, strides over to her, and kisses her swiftly on the cheek.

"Thank you."

"Anytime."

Three of five. A majority at least. Good against evil, if you're going to look at it that way. Josh and Grace answer Miguel's knocks, which are hard enough to bruise his knuckles. Too much time playing; he forgets when he's not wearing gloves. Their joint defiance and self-assurance make him want to slam his fist against something else.

His team, his choices. "We're not going to talk about it," he says. "Either of you pull anything like that again, you're out. I don't care what it does to our chances."

Or to his own.

"Whatever you say, boss." Grace slides neatly past him. "We going back in now?"

They have to. The moon will rise in a few hours, but they've got to keep catching up. A quick trip to the cache, where the golden apple gleams on its shelf, and into the next level. It's a relief to be back in a city. All cities, known or unknown, are familiar landscapes. People, stores, museums, restaurants, offices, *life*. It doesn't matter if it's fake.

Every step is one forward, and for the moment he can walk without pain, breathlessness. He doesn't know how the virus will manifest, and so he sets a pace the others complain about. Whatever. He's not taking a leisurely stroll from one object to the next. Get them, get out. If they make it to the next save point soon, they can grab a few hours' sleep and keep going at dawn. Maybe they can catch up.

He doesn't feel any different, can't feel the virus, but apparently that means nothing. Funny how this has never occurred to him before. He always assumed all biomech was safe, if the given value of *safe* is that they do their recipients no harm.

Turns out that's a hell of an assumption to make.

Democracy rules again; they trade off gathering the rewards, though Miguel winces every time one goes to Josh or Grace. They'll both have to do something miraculous to worm their way back onto Miguel's gracious side, and given the type of players they are, that doesn't seem likely.

His fingers close around a new gun. Shooting them would be a bad idea, one he entertains for only a second. Leah catches his eye and shakes her head with a slight smirk. She knows that he wouldn't, that everyone has thoughts not meant to see the light of day. Yeah, he doesn't like them, but he's becoming more and more sure that maybe that's the point. Working as a team would be too easy if they all were sitting around singing songs together at the end of every level. Josh and Grace are here for balance.

They're here to make the decisions the rest of them can't. To show him who he is by showing him who he isn't.

So far he's mostly made the right calls.

He grips the gun.

So far.

CUTSCENE:
BLAKE

Blake had underestimated Miguel's love for the girl; he had stayed to save her. It's not an enormous setback, but it's a good thing to know.

It feels like the old days—not the *very* old days, when the most exciting things Blake had to look forward to were watching grunting men and women invent fire and the wheel on a predetermined schedule—but the early days of Chimera. Good coffee, darkness, an unending stream of code on the monitors before him. Elsewhere in the building, Lucius is almost certainly doing roughly the same thing, setting up rewards, putting glowing green dots on things, and dropping random invincibility orbs around the place like the angel of immortality.

Eh, close enough. He should have T-shirts made. He'd only have to drop the first *t* in *immortality* for his own.

"You're not as far behind as you think, Mr. Anderson,"

Blake says to himself. He won't give Miguel a pass to catch up, that would be far too simple.

He wants him hungry. He wants him desperate. But in Blake's experience, humans are desperate only when they think there's a way out, however small the crack they have to squeeze through. Seal it off completely and they give up.

It won't take much, a tweak here, a tweak there. He's been doing this for a long time, but it's still almost impossible not to laugh when he hears people say computers were invented by the forces of evil.

They weren't, but some of the code was.

Quickly Blake makes the necessary changes and stands, draining the last of his coffee. The tile takes him to the middle floor of Chimera headquarters, roughly halfway between his office and Lucius's. Extra security measures are in place here. His retinas can't be scanned by normal means, nor his fingerprints. The equipment won't even recognize a human, but that's not who they're trying to keep out. It's rare that their respective superiors drop by for a visit, but it's happened occasionally. He and Lucius aren't ready to show off their handiwork yet.

Their superiors are quite happy for Blake and Lucius to work together when it suits them. So it is written, they say. And if it's written down, in proper letters and everything, that's the way it must happen. So make it happen.

The enormous room is scrupulously clean, dust sucked away by huge vents. At various times it has been home to many inventions, including the first model of the heart currently in Miguel Anderson's chest. All that is gone now, however, the medical advancements relegated to hospital labs.

He and Lucius needed the space.

"Please tell me you're not making adjustments without me," says Lucius. He can be incredibly light-footed when he wishes.

"Would I do that?"

"Yes."

"You're probably right," Blake concedes. "I'm not, though."

"Good."

The four cells in the room are very like the cell that held the girl, but these don't shrink, and their occupants have long since stopped screaming or trying to escape. Nobody knows they exist, and for now it will stay that way. Blake and Lucius have been very careful to erase any hints, any signs that anyone has completed all one hundred levels of Chimera, let alone four people. Their families think they perished in various tragic, real-world accidents long before they reached the hundredth level. They were given dedicated gaming rooms in another anonymous Chimera building, cut off from the rest of the world. Four early players, talented enough to rise above the hordes and progress rapidly through the game. It had still taken them many years, years in which they have become testaments to biomechanical engineering and innovation.

They thought that they were being rewarded.

Nobody looking at them now would guess that they had ever been human. Hearts and lungs, limbs and torsos and skin all the innovations that have so benefited the world. Their brains came last, a delicate balance between human enough to be cruel and machine enough to act on it.

In deference to tradition—their bosses are the very epitome of traditional—Blake and Lucius have customized the colors. The usual silver of biomech is stylish but makes it difficult to tell them apart. Instead, they are red, black, gray, and the off-white of a nuclear mushroom cloud.

They aren't ready yet.

They will be soon.

LEVEL EIGHTEEN

In the morning Team Eighteen is four levels behind the leading group, if status updates can be trusted. A quick, easy demon guarding a bell, and by lunchtime it's only three. Miguel assesses the spoils of another treasure hunt and decides not to question his luck.

It isn't luck, is it? This is what Blake wanted. Him desperate enough to play quickly, recklessly. His feed is full of people cheering him on. *Status update: I'm being blackmailed. The Gamerunners aren't who you think they are. I'm playing for my fucking life here.*

They quit out; he eats lunch with Leah while Nick takes off to see Anna for an hour, to remind himself again that she really didn't die in that glass box. Anna will put up with that for another day, maybe two, then tell Nick to stop being such an overprotective idiot and get back in the game.

Grace and Josh disappear . . . somewhere. It's been like

that in the game, too. No conversation or input from either of them unless absolutely necessary, which suits Miguel just fine. He won't do anything to hurt them, but he's not about to become best friends. He has best friends, and they don't run away when things get tough.

Besides, he's not complaining about more time alone with Leah. They haven't done anything except kiss yet, but he's hopeful.

He likes her. He likes that she collects bizarre facts the way he used to collect heartbeats. It's kind of cute, really—if *cute* can be a euphemism for *She's so much smarter it's slightly intimidating*. Intimidating because it's not just the morsels of information but the way she links them when they talk over lunch, waving her hands to illustrate why this random thing affects that random thing.

How it's all connected. She's the one who put together the twelve labors thing, if she's right about that. He doesn't know how helpful it is, but any insight into the Gamerunners is a good thing to have. Are they really looking for immortality? And if so, why would Blake threaten to kill Miguel to achieve it?

He forces food down his dry throat, feels the heart in his chest, watches Leah as she explains something else. And listens, because she's the kind of girl who might quiz him later.

They all meet in the gaming room after lunch, go back in.

The overworld leads them to a maze of old, cobbled streets, their narrowness providing shade from a baking sun. Every door handle they try is locked. The windows of closed shops display objects he's never seen before, though some look like ancient precursors to modern-day things. All are covered with dust.

An expanse of brick wall greets them at the end of the lane, blocking their exit. The first twinges of frustration pinch at the base of Miguel's neck, and he checks his feed, not expecting to find anything helpful. The other teams have been as cagey as Eighteen about what they reveal, not wanting to give their rivals any hints. But geoloc tags can help a little, and they're not the only ones playing this level, though—he blinks—they do seem to be the farthest ahead.

"Where are we supposed to go?" Nick asks. The words are still hanging in the air when the wall begins to crack, a neat doorway carving itself in the brick.

"In there, I guess," says Miguel. Yeah, there's a door, but there's no handle. Thanks, Blake, he adds silently.

He could ask Josh for help, but he doesn't want to. The toes of Miguel's boots are capped with steel. Good enough.

Brick dust billows up at his kick, rubble falls to the ground. The hole is big enough for his hand, and he peels bricks away, throwing them behind him, until there's a gap big enough to step through.

You have entered a library.

As usual, the Storyteller is truthful without being helpful. He can see that, but it still takes his breath away. Libraries are mostly online these days, though the Library of Congress still stands, along with some others across the world. Anything can exist in Chimera, and anything can be made beautiful. Even time travel is possible, and that's what this feels like as he stands in the middle of a polished floor.

He's read a lot, mostly while lying in bed, too sick to do anything else, but he's never held many books, felt their weight, and smelled their thin, crackling pages. Trees are precious, too valuable to chop down and pulp when everything can be stored electronically instead. This whole place is a memorial to forests long gone: not only the books themselves but the gleaming wood. The floor, the tables lit by green glass lamps, the railings around the upper floors that rise in circles above them, the shelves creaking under the weight of human knowledge. The books fill the still air with a scent of snow and calm and the feeling of possibility, that he has to read to discover their secrets. More than the oceans and the deserts, the wind, rain, earthquakes, fire, this is an impressive collection of pixels. Grudging respect for the Gamerunners mixes with his hatred for one of them. Miguel has his sim, isn't bad with programming, but this is something else. They must have worked for years to achieve it.

"Okay," says Nick finally, breaking the spell. "Why are we here?"

Good question. "Books . . . knowledge . . . information . . ." Miguel begins.

"Logic. A puzzle?" Leah asks.

"Better not be like the last one." Panic crosses Nick's face. Miguel agrees, but he doesn't think it is.

"Codes, maybe?" he says. "Books were used for that a lot, right?" He didn't completely check out of his history classes, even if he didn't always pay as much attention as he should have. He liked learning about wars won and lost, spies, the way messages were passed.

Leah nods. "Absolutely. But we need a key. It'll tell us what books we're looking for."

"Could this be it?" Wow, Grace actually said something. Nick ignores her, but Miguel walks across the room to the chalkboard Grace is studying, the numbers scrawled on it faded, smudged. Legible enough.

"It looks like a computer address," he says. "But those are usually four sets of numbers, not three."

"Well, this is three."

He grits his teeth. "I can see that."

"Page, line, word," calls Leah. "But that doesn't tell us which book."

"Right." There are tens of thousands here. He could lose

himself for days, weeks, years. Shame he can't take any of them out of the game. Can he? He glances over the nearest shelf, sees no glints of green light.

He doesn't have time to lose himself. He doesn't have time to lose.

The first book he grabs is an encyclopedia of plant life. The word, according to the code on the chalkboard, is in a language he doesn't speak. A few rows down, he grabs a car maintenance manual. Then a romance novel. Then something about aliens. He discards each one as he did the bricks, tossing them behind him and moving on to the next.

It has to be here somewhere. He just needs to find it.

"Stop!" Nick yells over the sound of breaking glass. Miguel turns. "What the hell is wrong with you?" Nick demands. "You're playing like Zack! Slow down! Think. We'll find it."

Miguel looks at the confetti of glittering green fragments on the floor. Leah, Grace, and Josh are staring at him.

He inhales. "Okay. Sorry. Let's think."

"Famous books?" Nick turns his head sideways to read a line of spines. "One that's out of place?"

"Would we ever find it in here?" Impressive. Josh is talking, too. Defeatist and grumpy, sure, but talking.

"Never mind that the code there gives us only one word." Leah folds her arms, thinking. Methodical, not diving in without a goal. "I guess when we find the right book, there'll be something to tell us the next one.".

Grace picks up a volume at random and flips through it, more gently than Miguel had. "How long will it take us to get through, like, a million books?"

Miguel feels every second passing. He blinks down his feed: they're still only five levels behind Zack. He doesn't want it to go back up to six—or more. Think smart. Work, brain.

"What's the most famous book in the world?"

"That unofficial instruction manual for Chimera," says Nick. "The one the dude got sued for."

"I doubt it's that."

Think. There are always clues. What has the whole level so far made him think of?

Age. History. Ancient things.

"What's the oldest book?" he asks, knowing the answer, needing the others to scoff at him.

Leah gazes at him for a split second and runs off, her footsteps echoing through the hush. He follows her, hears her muttering under her breath but can't make out the words.

Her *aha* is audible.

"Ever read it?" she asks, holding up a massive tome, withered and crumbling.

"No."

"Me neither." She strides back to the middle of the library to read the numbers on the board, turns the pages carefully.

"It's the right one. First word, *Your*. There's another code here. Two numbers, so same book."

She flips quickly through the pages now. A look of disgust creases her face, and Miguel sees the effort with which she pushes it away. "Well. Congrats." She raises her head. *"Your turn, Grace."*

Grace smiles widely, the first time he's ever seen her truly happy. She takes the book from Leah, reads the words, caches it.

Great.

More delays. It's unfair to begrudge them, but not difficult. Immediately after they quit out, two doctors, the Chimera emblem emblazoned on their white coats, come for Grace. Nick seethes quietly, watching them go. Miguel's not any happier.

"Wonder what she's going to get," Leah says, coming up behind them. "This isn't like Josh's arm, which he found, or your heart, which you needed."

Yeah, he really needed a biomech heart infected with a virus that's going to kill him soon. Definitely going to kill him, because now he can't keep playing, catching up. He needs to wait for Grace.

"I don't care," he says. Whatever it is, he hopes it won't take too long to implant and heal.

"Come on," she says.

"Where are we going?"

"Outside. Let's go remember there's a world beyond this fucking game. Nick, look at the bright side. Go see Anna again."

Nick manages a smile. "She's going to get sick of me."

"Probably," Miguel says. "Ow."

The sun is blinding; he can't remember when he last saw it, the real one.

"We shouldn't stay out in this for too long," says Leah. "Follow me."

Food cooked by someone other than a Chimera hireling is a good choice—at first thought. He's barely sat down when someone comes up to him: a girl maybe a few years older than he is. Her biomech is obvious: arm, eyes, patches of skin. Things he could have earned if less necessary surgeries would have been worth the risk to his heart.

"Oh, my god, you're Miguel Anderson. And you're Leah!"

"Do we know you?"

"I'm Thea Johansen, Eighteen's biggest fan. Gotta root for the underdog, you know. The way you took down that leviathan and solving the maze in the desert . . . Pretty cool. What's going on? I've been following all your feeds." Behind her lenses, her eyelids flicker. "Why aren't you playing now? What happened?"

"Oh." Miguel shifts in his seat. Across the table, Leah is trying very hard not to laugh. The temptation to kick her in the shin is almost overwhelming. Everyone in the restaurant is watching them now. The girl's name is familiar, but he can't place it. "Grace is getting a reward." Reward for what, Miguel doesn't know. She's barely done anything to help. Whatever. "We'll be back in there soon."

"You'd better be! I mean, you have so much catching up to do if you want to beat that asshole Zack. Have you been watching him? He sucks."

Her loyalty is appreciated, but the lie isn't. Zack is good. Not as good as Miguel, but good. He's ahead now only because of luck. Because he's lucky enough not to have anything Blake can blackmail him with.

When Miguel loses, he won't just die, he'll die knowing Zack probably won. Fantastic.

"No charge," says the waitress, setting down their food. Miguel pushes his away.

He feels the gazes of everyone in the restaurant like heat. Fusions of human and machine, staring. He's been sheltered from this so far and wishes now he hadn't left the Cube. Leah was wrong for once: there is no life outside Chimera. She sees his face and isn't laughing now.

Not all biomech is visible. Miguel knows that as well as anyone. Blake and his partner—and all the doctors, scientists, engineers they employ—haven't figured out how to make working brains yet, but they know how to alter them.

Grace is on the Cube's roof. Miguel doesn't care how she got up there, though he can guess why. She's not afraid of heights anymore. "Get her down," he tells Josh. "Carry her if you have to. It's time to play." Another couple of days lost, and he doesn't yet know whether a fearless Grace is a blessing or a curse. It may have been the only thing holding her back from her true in-game nature.

Which may have been the point. Balance the teams, but give them the ability to use their fears against one another.

The point. He's been thinking a lot about that the past few days, at least when he hasn't been with Leah. The point of Chimera, the point of Blake's blackmailing him, the point of everything.

All he'd need to do is open a new status update: *Dear viewers, I'm being threatened with my life into playing Chimera. What game is worth this?*

He can guess how that would go down. Jeers from people who think he's bitter that he's losing. General mocking and disbelief.

And Blake, with his hand on a button, who was right about several things, but one in particular. Miguel would have died anyway. Somewhere, somehow. He is living on borrowed time, an unpayable debt. Blake gave Miguel an extension on his life that he wouldn't have had otherwise. What right does he have to claim the gift isn't good enough?

Every right. This is wrong. This is his *life*.

But none of that changes the fact that there's no one he can tell.

"You okay?" Nick asks as they gather in the gaming room and open their cabinets. "Sorry, I don't know why I keep asking you that. Habit. You're fine now. It's working, right?"

"Yeah." Miguel forces a smile.

He just wants to finish this.

Visor on.

It's midnight when they quit out, another two objects in the display cabinet in the cache: a wooden staff Miguel had wrested from among the otherwise iron bars of a gate and a flame Nick had cached, desperate to claim it, as if that will give him power over the fire that still burns Anna in his mind. As their cabinets fill, he tries again to imagine what the final level might hold and why they need these particular things. If he knew, or could guess, they might have a prayer. Or he could go home, put them in his sim, experiment.

Bad idea. Blake knows about the sim, although how, Miguel still has no idea. He knows, absolutely knows, that Nick wouldn't tell a soul, which means he, Miguel, slipped up somehow. Progressed through the normal game too fast and caught their attention. Maybe it isn't as protected on his computer as he thought.

Anyway, even if he could, that would definitely be cheating. He won't do that. He told Blake not to help him.

"Tell me something?" Nick asks, his voice low. "Why are you playing like such a demon when you've already gotten your heart? It's all the rest of us can do to keep up with you."

Miguel stops in the corridor near his suite. He's had to use his practiced blank face on Nick more in the past few days than in the entire time they've known each other.

"It's what I do," he says, shrugging. "You've never been able to watch me play before this. I guess I don't know how to do it any other way."

"You weren't like this when it first started."

"Nothing's holding me back now."

Nick's shoulders relax. "Yeah," he agrees. "That makes sense. Well, keep doing it, I guess. We're getting so close. Probably the last couple of levels will be killers."

"Ha. Probably."

Nick stops at his door. "I'm gonna go say good night to Anna. See you in the morning."

"Say hi for me."

"Will do."

In his suite, he showers, washing off the sweat of levels where he didn't have to run but ran anyway. The feeling of not knowing how much time he has left is familiar, but knowing it could only be days is strange. He didn't believe Dr. Spencer, but he believes Blake. He should check his feed, see how far along his rivals are.

He doesn't want to know. It wouldn't change anything. He will still do the same things, make the same choices, one step after another.

He checks his mother's feed, though. Likes a photo she's shared. She'll see the notification, know he's still okay. Like Nick, she thinks there's nothing to worry about anymore, and her images are filled with light, with beauty.

He stands shirtless in front of the mirror. One more scar, neater than the others, in a tangle of them. The best that can be said is that they didn't kill him. He blinks to open a window on his lenses and looks up the exact definition of *irony*.

"Nobody seems to be able to articulate that," says a voice. Miguel whirls around, sees Blake silhouetted in the doorway. Blake taps his own lenses. "I can see what you're searching for when you're in here."

Just because it's not a surprise doesn't mean it's not an intrusion. Or that Miguel doesn't recall the other things he's searched for. Information on Blake, for one.

Miguel blinks away a private message from Leah: she'd seen him and Nick talking, left them alone, wanted to say good night. He fights a smile.

"I thought it might be a good idea to check on you, see how

you're doing," says Blake, closing the door. "You are making good progress."

"People run fast when they're being chased."

"Of course. I'm curious about what you think of the new features. The improved graphics, the heightened story aspects."

"I didn't like seeing my friend being squashed and burned in a glass box, but then, you knew that."

Blake raises his eyebrows. "Please feel free to say it again if it makes you feel better."

It doesn't, much, but it's over, and Anna's fine. "It looks beautiful," he says, because it's the truth. The detail is incredible. "I'm curious about the final levels."

Blake says nothing.

"I'd like to get to them," Miguel adds, injecting an edge of steel into his voice.

"You are very close. Three more."

Miguel inhales sharply, feels the biomech press against his ribs. "What if I said I'd changed my mind, I want help. Nick's noticed the way I'm playing. It's hard not to tell him why. If you make it easier, I won't look so desperate."

"I'd say no," answers Blake, amused. "The offer's not on the table anymore. You don't appear to need my help. When I told you I had a bet of sorts with my partner, I meant it. He has a favorite, as you are mine, and we're both aware of this. He is watching your progress as much as I am, and if it suddenly moves even faster, he will notice. It will be down to the two of you at the end, I am sure of that, but the outcome—" He spreads his long-fingered hands wide. "I'd like to say that I— that is, you—will win, but I cannot say for certain."

Miguel's hands curl into fists. He can clearly see two different futures. Win or lose. Life or death. He's been used to that feeling his whole life, but only in the past few days has the real disease been outside his body, smiling smugly at him. A thing he can hate that isn't himself.

"You bastard," says Miguel. Blake doesn't flinch. "I haven't told anyone. I'm doing what you ask."

"And I am grateful."

Fighting with Blake is like pleading with a thunderstorm. It doesn't care. Miguel backs away, taking notes on Blake's now impassive face, impervious eyes. He could learn a thing or two.

"The virus," he asks quietly. "Will it hurt? Will I know?" With his human heart, it had always warned him: You're doing too much. Slow down. Calm down. Breathe. Check your pulse.

"If it comes to that," says Blake, "it will be painless. Is that the same as not knowing?"

▮LEVEL NINETEEN

Three levels to go. Whether he can do this isn't a question. Whether he can do this fast enough is. He can't explain his impatience to the rest of the team; they all think he already has the thing he wanted.

You are in an old building. It has many rooms. Each room is filled with strange, ancient artifacts.

"It's called a museum, Storyteller," says Leah. Part of him wants to laugh, it's nice to know he isn't the only one who talks back.

They are standing just inside the front doors. It reminds him a little of the library, which isn't that surprising. This is a different collection of human knowledge and endeavor, but a museum is still a library of objects, a concentration of curated memory across all time.

The marble floors gleam as much as the library's wooden ones did, but instead of shelves, glass display cases and cabinets are spread out at intervals across the room. At the far end, an archway leads to another room, beyond that to another.

They spread out to peer inside the displays, though it's a pretty safe bet the overworld didn't dump them in exactly the room they needed to find.

"This is just like a bunch of old spoons and stuff," says Josh, tapping his claw on the glass. "I don't think we need a spoon at the end of all this."

"There's a save point ahead," says Grace. Miguel's come to rely on her sight and how well she uses it. Looking in the right places. It's possible he misjudged her from the start.

"Already?" Leah asks. "We haven't even done anything yet."

"Well, hit it," he tells Grace, who runs ahead to the button, which is displayed on cloth as if it were itself a relic worth treasuring. Nothing happens when she does, but that doesn't mean something won't soon.

Aside from the save point, the next gallery holds ancient chessboards, with tiny pieces of carved ivory and bone, obsidian and slate. Miguel peers through the glass, impressed by their intricacy. People have always played games.

This could be what they're here for, another inside joke. From one of the earliest games to the most advanced one the world has ever seen. Maybe two of them are supposed to play each other.

"Check these carefully," he tells the others. He runs his fingers over the cases, looking for weak points, looking for clues. There are always clues, but there are none he can see here.

Through the next archway into a zoo. Not quite a zoo. His parents had taken him and Nick to the only one in their city once when they were little, but those animals had at least been alive, even if they were caged. These stare at him with glass eyes from behind glass walls, and he shivers. A few feet away Josh sees a snake and crosses the room in a hurry.

So he wasn't lying about that. Interesting.

"This is creepy," says Leah, coming up behind him. He nods. Some of these species have been extinct for a thousand years, or only a hundred, and he remembers the conversation with Nick on the level with the horses. Is this the future they're looking at? Survivors, chimeras full of biomech, will put the most human looking of them into glass cases as both memory and warning.

"Really creepy," he agrees. This is beginning to remind him of the path of fears, this walk from room to room. The knife had been waiting for him at the end of that, so maybe this level's object will be waiting at the end of this. He is suddenly aware of how much time they've spent wandering, looking, inspecting, which they needed to do, any one of the objects they'd passed could have been the thing they're looking for, but time is no longer a luxury he has.

When the time comes, it will be painless. No, asshole, that is not the same as not knowing. He knows now that if he doesn't get to the end of the final level before anyone else, it will be the end of him. It's too late for not knowing.

"Come on," he says, quickening his steps. "We're wasting time."

Through the next room and the next. Ahead, the light is different, both darker and brighter. He breaks into a run, then skids to a stop on a marble floor under a huge dome of colored glass that turns the moonlight to rainbows. Lights placed every few feet around the circular walls illuminate tall stone statues. They're human, sort of, if humans can have horns or the hind ends of goats or talons where their hands should be.

The others are running toward him. Human, if humans can have cameras for eyes or plastic for skin or claws where their hands should be.

In the center of the circle is another glass box, and Miguel knows without looking that it holds what they've come for. Mentally he goes through the contents of the cache for something that will break glass.

"The ax, maybe?" Nick asks.

It hadn't worked to save Anna, but that was a different level. It might this time.

"Cache," he says. "Summon ax." It appears in his hand, the wood solid and reassuring even though his brain knows it is really a collection of pixels, a clever trick. He turns and looks into the display for the first time.

"Uh, Josh?"

"Yeah?"

"You okay with an inanimate silver snake?"

"I'd rather not be the one to claim it."

"You sure? It's kind of your turn."

"I'm sure. Go for it, Captain."

"Okay." Miguel raises the ax. He needs to be careful, not because the snake is an old, beautiful thing, although it is, scales perfectly cast, ruby eyes gazing up, but because he really doesn't want to break it. There was a save point—so that's why there was a save point—and they can come back, but . . .

Time.

He brings the ax down, not hard enough. The glass trembles and doesn't break.

Around the edges of the room, the statues scrape to life.

Oh, great.

He keeps the ax; it's as good a weapon as anything else in the cache. "Get what you can!" he calls to the others as stone legs thunder over the marble. Someone screams. Leah. She is covering her ears, these vibrations more painful to her than to the others.. "Get behind me if you can't fight!" he yells. The statues close in around the five of them. Nick summons a mace, an old-school Chimera weapon Miguel's never found as useful as anything with a trigger.

But guns would be a bad idea in here. There's too much for the bullets to ricochet off, and pulse weapons will be worse than useless against stone.

The ax it is.

He swings at the nearest one, a chimera of its own time, part bird, part something else he doesn't have time to identify. Stone shatters, and he half expects to see blood ooze from the crack spreading up its chest.

Nothing but dust.

Beside him, Josh isn't even using a weapon, just his arm. He throws the statues out of his way, send them flying into the room Miguel just left. Grace doesn't have a weapon either, but she's using one, the best one she has.

"There's a save point in the dome!" she shouts over the noise as Nick lands a particularly successful blow. Miguel looks up for a fraction of a second at the glass fifty, sixty feet above. He's seen things hidden in windows before, but he doesn't know whether he'd have noticed that in a hurry.

And he has no idea how they'd get to it.

A stone punch catches him in the ribs, a blow that would likely have killed him not too long ago. It only winds him, knocking the last ounce of breath from his lungs as he doubles over, gasping.

He's okay.

"Mig?"

"Fine! We need to get that snake! I'm open to ideas!"

He blinks. He's not the only one. Grace, wearing Leah's boots, is climbing up the wall toward the dome. It's slow, he knows how slow, how weird it is to walk like that, but with every step she moves forward, higher.

"Grace!" he shouts. She wobbles, and his slowly returning breath catches in his throat.

"I'm good! Not afraid! Don't distract me, or I'll drop back down and kick your ass."

Okay then. He ducks out of the way of a swinging stone ax that makes his own look like a toy, the ax other axes aspire to be.

Aha.

He glances over his shoulder, past Leah, at the display cabinet. Slowly he starts moving backward, taunting the statue, dancing side to side in front of it.

"Don't hit it until I tell you!" he calls to Grace. He'll take the ass kicking.

"Fine!"

This way, statue. Another few feet. Come on. Come on.

Close enough.

"Get out of the way," he shouts at Leah. She ducks to the side as he feints with the ax.

It works. The statue raises its ax high over its head and brings it crashing down as Miguel dives to the floor. Glass falls around him, slicing his cheek, his arm. He rolls and jumps back to his feet, runs to the shattered cabinet. Brushes the shards away, tiny cuts biting at his fingers.

Where the hell did it go?

A stone arm wraps around his chest in a crushing embrace, drags him backward, away from the broken display. From the corner of his eye he sees Leah trapped the same way, Nick struggling beneath the weight of an impossibly heavy stone foot on his back, holding him to the floor.

"Josh!" he yells. No answer. He looks up. Grace is nearly at the save point, but she can't press it yet. "Josh!"

"Yeah?"

Miguel knows the sound of fear. Josh steps into view, herded by the statues and by a writhing silver snake, undulating across the floor.

Oh, shit.

The snake opens its mouth, bares long, curved fangs. The statues have stopped fighting. Now they're watching.

"Josh," says Miguel, "you have to catch it."

"I can't."

"Yes, you can," says Leah. "Use your claw."

Josh shakes his head. His face is pale, sweat visible from here, a sickly sheen. His chest rises and falls much too quickly.

"Josh, I need that snake," says Miguel.

"C-cache: s-summon g-gun." The weapon appears in Josh's hand.

"No! Josh, you can't kill it," Miguel says. The snake has stopped now, trapping Josh up against the remains of its display. Josh ignores him, aims, fires, but is shaking too badly.

The bullet pings off the marble and spins past Leah's shoulder.

"You're going to kill one of us," she says. "Stop."

Choices. Josh will never catch the snake, Miguel knows it. *This game will teach you who you are.*

Miguel never uses the keypad on his sleeve, he forgets it's there most of the time. He blinks open the private inbox the leaders have been given and types. Everyone else is too busy watching Josh to notice.

[Self: Miguel Anderson] Blake. Help me.

He can almost hear Blake's satisfied laughter.

[Blake] You know what to do. What you have to do.

He needs the snake more than he needs Josh, and maybe it's not venomous. Maybe it'll be okay. "Let it bite you," he says. Wide, horrified eyes meet his. Miguel feels Nick's and Leah's shock. Grace can't hear him. "Let it bite you."

Josh nods, kicks out toward the streak of silver. The snake lunges to sink its terrible fangs into his leg. Too terrified to scream, he slides to the floor. The stone arm releases Miguel, and he drops to the ground, running.

Josh tears the snake from his flesh, and in his hand, it returns to inanimate silver. "Cache," he says with his last breath. High above, Grace is poised, hand over the save point. Miguel closes his eyes, begs forgiveness for what he's about to do. There's no knowing what would happen if he told her now.

What's damaged stays damaged. He can't turn back the

clock. He looks at Leah, Nick, and puts his finger to his lips. They nod. Tears run down Leah's face.

"Okay, Grace!" he calls, loud enough for his voice to carry all the way up to the top of the dome. It echoes off the glass, the marble, the stone of the statues, which have returned to their rightful places.

She presses the button, begins her slow descent. Miguel, Nick, and Leah gather around Josh's body, shielding it as she crawls down. She hops to the floor and turns to them, grinning with pride, a fear defeated.

Another realized. Miguel steps out of the way.

Josh's body lies still on the sprung floor of the gaming room. The room spins, not quiet now, filled with Grace's racking sobs. Is this what they had seen when the boss had pierced his heart? Is this what the others had felt?

There is no reason for Blake to save this one. Miguel watches dully as the doctors come, carry Josh away. He ignores Leah, Nick calling after him, pushes through the doors, and makes his way blindly along corridors to his suite.

This wasn't what he wanted. He didn't like Josh or the way he played, but Miguel didn't want this.

"Fuck you, Blake," Miguel says in the quiet of his room, hoping the Gamerunner can hear him. "Fuck you."

CUTSCENE:
LUCIUS

Lucius frowns at the screen. He didn't *want* the boy to die, and Blake's side claimed him afterward, no question about that, but having his influence out of the way isn't a terrible thing. It isn't the game that causes actual death, he'd seen to that, but the boy's fear and belief had been immensely powerful.

It's not an angelic thought; Lucius has always been surprised by how much of what his side does *isn't* angelic. Good and for the greater good are not the same thing, not at all. When they have to do something unsavory, they can simply hold up their hands and say it's all part of the grand plan. Can't argue with the grand plan, can we? Now do your job, Lucius.

He has always done it well, to the best of his infinite ability.

Blake has been speaking to Miguel Anderson, Lucius knows that. That's fine, Blake can have his little pet. Lucius has one, too. In fact he has several. His side has always played the numbers game. Blake's tends to go in more for laser focus.

That's why Blake is going to lose. Numbers are all that matter now.

"Good morning, Zack."

He says it gently. Blake delights in startling people with his sudden, silent appearances, but Lucius takes no such pleasure. It's not *his* fault he moves so soundlessly, that's just the way he's built.

"Oh, it's you. Morning."

"Did you sleep well? Do you need anything?"

"Yeah. Um. Coffee?"

Zack is too bleary eyed to notice the cup simply appearing in Lucius's hand. The human brain has a magic way of glossing over the actually magical. He's probably assuming it was there the whole time, which makes Lucius generous, not capable of creating coffee from firmament on a whim.

It's pretty vile coffee, to be fair, and Lucius is always fair . . . to a point. There are reasons he and Blake have a proper machine at the office; Lucius doesn't drink this swill except when forced. His superiors apparently can't tell the difference.

Living among humans for thousands of years gives you two things: humor and taste buds.

Oh, and paintball. Lucius had quite liked that before it went out of fashion.

He waits for Zack to sit up and take a few sips. It's the kind thing to do. Lucius before he's had his in the morning is the closest he gets to demonic.

"You are nearly at the final level," he says. "I am merely here to remind you that mistakes will be forgiven if you make good decisions. I will offer what assistance I can, within the rules, of course."

"I'm doing okay so far," says Zack, chest puffed. There is a line between obnoxious swagger and pride in one's work; for the moment Zack remains on the right side of it.

"Yes, you are, and I would be delighted to see you crowned victorious. You have already received some enhancements, well done. Have you decided what you might wish for as your final prize?"

"Not yet. Still thinking." Zack yawns.

"All right. Please don't hesitate to let me know what you decide. I'll leave you to prepare for today's gaming. Your team members are awake and waiting for you."

"Cool."

Lucius can't vanish the coffee cup, Zack is too lucidly observant now. One of the staff will clear it away later. Lucius moves swiftly, silently from Cube Cobalt and summons his hoverboard.

Gentle encouragement. Do good. Be generous to others. Live with honor. His is, if he's honest (and he is always honest), a more challenging job than Blake's. A better one, of course, *of course*, but he gets less sleep.

And he can't rest now. Blake is waiting for him, together they will complete the final touches on the four in the lab at headquarters. Are they beings yet? They cannot move or think for themselves. That will change soon, very soon. Today they get their brains, and after a few more tests, a few more experiments, they will be ready to venture forth on their own.

It will be heaven. It will be hell.

It will be war.

For the greater good.

▌LEVEL TWENTY

The eleventh level passes in a blur, a coin, spotted by the observant Grace, the only souvenir. They quit out for food, sleep. No one is ready to talk about Josh. Miguel feels Nick and Leah watching him, sure they're running through those final moments in their minds.

But they haven't asked. Maybe they just don't want to know, or they want to get out of here as much as he does now.

They step into the gaming room for what is, he hopes, the last time. Miguel can't look at the cabinet that no longer has an owner. He keeps his eyes on his own, carefully wrapping sensor strips around arms and legs and chest. He takes his lenses off last, checking the team feeds one last time.

[Zachary Chan] **Miguel Anderson** Are you ready to lose?

He tosses the lenses in his locker. "Ready?" he asks. He is ready, ready to be finished, ready to see if he can win, ready to see if Blake will keep his word. Blake. Miguel wants to spit just thinking about him. The problem is that Blake keeps his words, they're just never the ones Miguel thinks he's hearing. A diseased heart, a dead teammate.

"Ready," says Leah, stepping across the sprung floor to kiss him. He blinks in surprise. "Let's finish this," she says as Grace turns away, disgusted or angry or both.

"Chimera: overworld," he says. The globe appears, spinning gently. It glows with the light of success, a string of lit markers across its surface.

He touches the final spot with his biomech finger.

They are plunged into absolute darkness.

"Cache," he says. "Summon flashlight."

His hands are empty.

"Did anyone get anything?"

"No."

"No."

Silence. He takes Grace's lack of answer as another no.

"Summon matches?" He tries again. Still nothing.

"All the items we found," says Leah, "we need to use them on this level."

He closes his eyes, nonsensical in the utter black, but it helps him think. Knife, coin, water, oil, sand, book, snake, apple, staff, bell, flame.

"Cache: summon staff, oil, flame," he says.

Only the staff appears. His fingers close reflexively around the wood he can't see.

"I got the oil, and Nick got the flame," says Leah. They summon their objects, the tiny fire lighting their efforts as they coat the staff in oil and set it alight.

Uh-oh. He foresees a problem. His stomach turns over, but he says nothing. He'll see how far they get.

"Good job," says Nick. They are in some kind of tunnel. The light from the torch casts several yards ahead, illuminating damp walls, a stone floor stretching into darkness. There is a wall at their backs. Only one way to go.

"Can you hear anything?" he asks Leah.

"Water, I think. And . . . chewing?"

"Ew, I hate hearing people eat," Grace says before she can stop herself. He glances at her, but she has her lips pressed together as if to keep in any other normal human conversation that might be tempted to escape without permission.

"Can you see anything?" he asks her.

She shakes her head. "Except— These tunnels remind you of anywhere?"

Miguel looks around. The first level. Walking through the tunnels, then being dropped into his path of fears. The demon had surrounded itself with everything its enemies were afraid of. And they were right next to it, right at the beginning.

Clever trick, Gamerunners.

"Okay. Let's go."

The shadows shift, grow, shrink with the movement of the torch as he walks. Their footsteps echo, warning anything lurking ahead of their arrival.

"I see something," says Grace. "A different shadow."

"Thanks," he says. She shrugs.

As one they slow down, peering into the flickering gloom. The flame bounces off wood and glass. Miguel steps up to a table, reaches for the object upon it, and turns it over in both hands. Beautiful and strange, like an 8 made of glass. "Anyone know what this is?"

"I think . . . may I?" Leah takes it from him, turns it over one more time. "It's an hourglass. It used to be a kind of clock, there'd be sand or salt in the top, and it would take a set length of time to fall through to the bottom. But this one's empty."

"We didn't find any sand. Or salt. Salt water, yes, but how would we divide that with what we have?"

Take out what they've used. Knife, apple, water, ashes, bell, book, snake, coin.

"Ashes. Could they be used like sand?" Oh, the Gamerunners' little jokes. The level where'd they'd gotten the ashes had been timed, too. "Leah, that was you."

She summons them, holds the box in her hand, remembering. "You should do it," she says, handing the box to Nick. She holds the hourglass steady on the table as Nick carefully fills it through a small hole in the top. As the last ash lands on the rest, the voice of the Storyteller comes.

You are in a tunnel. You have found an hourglass, which, true to its name, will give you exactly one hour to make your way through. The clocks on your displays have been deactivated. There are no save points, no opportunities to reclaim anything already used. You have one chance.

They may not even have that much, but still he holds his tongue and checks his feed. Zack's team has just entered the level. Eighteen has a head start, but only by a few minutes. He hopes Zack's too stupid to figure out what he needs to do with the torch and the hourglass right away.

Right. Next. They start walking again, Leah carefully carrying their timer. No point in leaving it and not knowing how much time they have left, though it looks like it's already passing too quickly and he has no idea what's waiting for them ahead.

Now *he* hears the sound of chewing. He walks just far enough and stops dead. A scaled, toothy demon, surrounded by a pile of unidentifiable food, raises its eyes to him and grins horribly. It's not that much bigger than he is, but most of that is mouth.

Behind it is a door.

"Feed it?" Leah asks.

Knife, coin, water, book, snake, apple, staff, bell.

Zack has figured out the hourglass. Damn it.

"Cache: summon apple," he says. Nothing happens. Wait. That one was Nick. Nick nods and summons the apple.

"If we can only summon the ones we ourselves claimed," Leah begins, "what are we going to do when—"

She makes connections. "I know," he says. "I'm hoping we'll be allowed to summon them because he can't."

"Hoping?" Grace's voice is choked. "Yeah, okay."

"Got any better ideas?"

She doesn't answer.

Nick tosses the apple at the demon. It plucks it from the air with a creepily tiny hand, stares curiously at it, attempts to take a bite.

And spits it out. Not that then. It rolls across the floor, and Nick picks it up, making a noise of disgust and wiping his hand on his pants. Miguel recites the list again in his head, but it's Leah who tells Grace to get the book. She takes it from Grace and flips furiously through the pages.

"When we were solving the code . . . I saw— Password. Aha." She steps forward, right up to the demon, and says a single word.

The door opens. The book vanishes.

Zack is at the demon. Right behind them, as if they were in the same place. Miguel runs through the doorway, the others following, into a smaller, narrower tunnel. The sound of water is loud and rushing now, a swift underground river. Miguel runs along the tunnel and stops at its bank, looking left and right, up and down. The torch illuminates only a few feet of the black depths in both directions, but there is nothing to see in the pool of light it casts.

He curses under his breath, turns to shine the light on the walls. Hanging from one wall is a broken chain, identical to the chains in the building that housed the horses. He hopes there isn't a horse down here. He's sure he doesn't have another orb with which to slow one down, or Josh to catch it with his enhanced arm.

Knife, coin, water, oil, sand, book, snake, apple, staff, bell, flame. He blinks. Zack's team is still struggling with the demon, trying to kill it with the knife. He wonders where Zack got the dagger; it's unlikely he found it in the same place Miguel found his. He can decode the intricacies later, there isn't time now.

When the time comes, it will be painless.

"It looks like the same metal as the bell," says Grace. "But—"

But Josh got the bell. He tries to summon it. No luck. Nick, Grace, and Leah aren't any more successful.

"Enter cache," says Grace, and disappears so suddenly Miguel stares at the empty space where she stood for several long seconds, seconds he doesn't have, before realizing she's truly gone.

"Is she coming back?" Nick asks.

"I have no idea." Ashes fall into the bottom bulb with a whispering hiss. Miguel swallows. He touches his finger to his wrist. It tells him nothing. He closes his eyes.

And opens them again at the sound of Grace's voice.

"Fuck," she mutters. Miguel doesn't have Leah's hearing, but he knows pain. Grace's hand is covered with blood. In her other, she holds the bell and the snake. Josh's trophies.

"How did you do that?" Leah demands, impressed.

"I didn't think I could summon them, so I actually went into the cache. Josh's locker was damaged, remember? Big hole, right in the glass. Don't look at me," says Grace, jutting her chin at Nick but keeping her eyes on Miguel. "He's the one who shot it. What? I had a better idea after all."

"And what's damaged stays damaged," breathes Nick.

"The hole wasn't big enough, but it damaged the glass. Had to punch through the rest of the way."

"Are you okay?"

"I'm fine." He suspects her definition of *fine* falls somewhere alongside his but doesn't press her on it. Instead he steps back as she reaches up, stretching to the tips of her toes to hang the bell on its chain. He doesn't dare offer to do it for her.

The bell rings, echoing through the tunnels.

And from the darkness a boat slides into view.

There are only four places on the boat, the fifth taken by

a cloaked figure, pushing through the water with a long pole.

He would have chosen Josh to stay behind. Grace looks at him as if she can read his mind and wordlessly passes the coin she'd found to the cloaked figure. A skeletal, metal hand reaches to take it, and the hood nods. Nick jumps into the boat too eagerly, nearly making it tip. Miguel can practically feel the glare from the boatman as Nick helps Grace and Leah step in. Leah reaches for Miguel's hand, but he chooses the seat beside Grace.

"I didn't trust you when we first started playing," he says. He won't mention the desert, Anna. That's gone now. Past. History. "But you've been great. I thought you wanted to sabotage me or something."

"I did," she says impassively. "All I want now is to finish this."

Well. Okay then.

The boat glides down the river. Zack is in his boat, too, though there is no way of knowing whether he is ahead or behind. He's updating frequently enough, much more so than Miguel, who hasn't posted since they entered the level. He doesn't have the time or inclination and doesn't care whether people are rooting for him or praying for his demise. Like Grace, all he wants to do is finish this.

Water, apple, snake, knife. They must be getting close. Something will be waiting for them at the end, and they will need enough time to defeat it, if they haven't used that up already. He peers over Leah's shoulder at the hourglass in her lap. Half full. Okay. He keeps leaning forward, as if that will help the boat go faster.

The boat slows, pulls up to the entrance to another tunnel. The boatman turns, and a shiver runs up Miguel's back. Its hands aren't ordinary biomech; Miguel can see every gleaming knuckle and silver bone as it points. The message is wordless yet loud: get out.

Back to business. He steps out after Grace and jogs down the tunnel, the flame from the torch whipping close enough to singe his eyebrows. An ornate gate brings him to a screeching halt, the others stopping behind him. Through the bars, a large room awaits, lit by sconces on the walls. The knife, maybe? He's picked locks in Chimera before. He passes the torch to Nick and bends down to take a closer look. There is no keyhole. He runs his fingers over the cold steel, and he allows himself one last moment to marvel at the detail the Gamerunners have brought to Chimera. In a quiet gray gaming room, Miguel's body walks, runs, jumps on a sprung floor, a visor covering his face, but here he can even smell the tang of the metal. Whatever pain and horror Chimera has brought, whatever awaits him on the other side of these gates, they have created something remarkable.

And this is the last time Miguel will ever be inside it, win or lose.

"Could they be hydraulic?" Nick asks. Miguel searches for wheels, pipes, channels, Leah and Grace do, too.

"No, but I think you're on to something," says Leah. "Where did we get the water? That ocean level. It's salt water. Salt water is corrosive."

"Cache: summon water."

The bottle appears. He hands it to Leah, she unseals it, and the scent of the ocean fills the space. She'd better be right about this, their only chance.

As soon as the first drop touches the lock, it starts to smoke, hiss, the steel dissolving at their feet. She empties the bottle, staying out of the way of the billowing cloud of steam and rust. Miguel kicks the gate open. The torch vanishes from Nick's hand.

You have opened the dungeon. The boss awaits. Good luck.

One last check. Zack's team is still figuring out how to open the gate.

Snake. Apple. Knife.

The floor shakes, and a *thing* is coming at them: all teeth and claws and scales and spines., fleshy and grinning. They dive in different directions as Miguel shouts for the cache, for the blade found on the tray of surgical equipment. He rolls, searches out Leah. The hourglass is safe, cradled in her arms. What would've happened if it had smashed?

He jumps to his feet. The thing is coming again, right for him. He dodges swiping arms, a thrashing tail. Sweat is already pouring down his face, stinging his eyes. There's no way to get near it. It's twice as tall as he is. Weak points in its feet? He ducks, runs, misjudges. The tail catches him and sends him flying, the knife soaring from his grasp. He hears it, skittering, as he crashes to the floor just outside the gates. He sees the knife balanced on the bank of the river, blade hovering over the water, trembling with every vibration from the boss's pounding steps.

Reaching. Stretching. Praying. His hand closes around the handle. He is panting, shaking. He has no idea how to kill the fucking thing.

"I can't get anywhere near it!" he yells to the others, all busy evading the boss's flailing, angry limbs. "Any ideas?"

"Set the snake on it?" Nick yells back.

"Feed the apple to it?" Grace suggests.

"I don't think it's hungry! Leah, how much time do we have?"

"I can't tell! Minutes!"

Even Zack doesn't matter now. If Miguel is going to die, he's taking this beast down with him. He's stopped too long to think, and pain explodes down his spine. He falls forward, hits the wall, reaches around, and pulls back a hand slick with blood. It only grazed him, but that's enough.

"Grace! Take this and give me the snake!" Leah yells. Miguel can only watch from the floor. She can't throw the hourglass. The boss gets in the way, roaring, and Nick ducks around to wave at its face. Idiot. But the distraction works. Leah and Grace make the switch, though Miguel has no clue what Leah's plan is.

"Nick! Toss me the apple!"

It sails through the air, and she catches it one handed. If he makes it out of this alive, he should tell her how impressive that was.

But it's not as impressive as she's about to be.

Always making connections.

The snake begins to writhe, as alive as it was when it killed Josh. The boss isn't hungry, the serpent is. Its silvery mouth opens, wide enough to swallow the golden fruit whole. Its fangs catch the light and sink into a different kind of flesh.

And it starts to grow. Surprised, Leah drops it to the floor, the silver flashing against the stone. The snake begins to wriggle, undulating as it stretches longer and longer. It's at least a dozen feet by the time it stops, as thick as Miguel's thigh, but it's not done yet. As they watch, it splits into two, then four, then six long, shining ropes. Its head disappears, but it can still move, and the ropes fly through the air and wrap around the boss's arms, legs, tail, and finally around the demon's throat, pulling it to the ground with a crash like an earthquake. Leah covers her ears, the vibrations etched in pain on her face.

"You're bleeding!" Nick says, running to Miguel. Miguel pushes himself up to sitting, standing. "Are you okay?"

Miguel forces a smile. "I'm fine."

More than fine. He grins at the boss. In its restraints, the demon struggles and screams. The silver ropes cut into its flesh, and the faintest hint of light oozes out with dark, viscous blood. Miguel turns the knife over in his palm.

Maybe.

Maybe.

He approaches slowly. He's getting this right or not at all.

A chimera, like him. Like he wants to be. Like everyone. A fusion of machine and flesh. He climbs onto its chest. Raises the blade. Slices. The monster howls a last, echoing howl.

Green light shines up through the wound.

Find a demon. Cut its heart out. Miguel reaches inside and pulls, the tip of his biomech finger reading the edges of the embossed Chimera symbol.

He blinks. Smiles.

"Status update," he says hoarsely. "We win."

LEVEL TWENTY-ONE

Déjà vu. He wakes in a too bright room to the sound of low voices. This time, though, he knows exactly what happened. He remembers winning. He remembers the doctors coming for him, as Blake had promised, and the trip—not to the Cube's medical wing but to one of their hospitals.

He's finished now. It's over.

"We don't understand why it had to be done again," says his mother. His father makes a noise of agreement, support. Funny how even with just their voices, he knows that about them.

He knows the third voice, too. "There was a . . . problem . . . with the original biomech. A malfunction. It saw your son through the competition, but we wished to replace it before it caused any issues. He is fine now."

He'll never tell them the truth.

"Okay. We'll be back when he wakes up." Miguel hears the door close. Footsteps near the bed. He turns to Dr. Spencer.

She's still pretty, and she did his surgery, but those are the only good things he can say about her.

"Am I really okay now?" he asks, staring past her at the wall. Not green. Thank heaven for small mercies. She'd done his first operation, too. If there's something wrong with this one . . .

"Yes," she says finally. Guilt colors her eyes. They both know what he was asking. They both know the accusation he's not hurling across the room, and the fact that she knows it is proof enough.

"I'm sorry," she says, stilted and choked, "that you had to go through this. I was under orders."

"You don't have a mind of your own? You could have chosen."

"And someone else would have done it. This way I was sure you were in good hands. You survived, both times. Hearts are the hardest thing for us to do. They are everything. Only brains could be worse, but we can't do that yet." She sounds like she thinks that's a good thing. He tends to agree.

She touches his leg, a farewell, and disappears. He doubts he'll ever see her again.

He is alone. Very alone. Alone in the way a person can only be when they're not entirely sure where they are, exactly, or where they are in relation to the people who define them. His parents are somewhere in the building still, but he doesn't know where or when they'll be back. Nick, Leah, even Anna:

he has no idea.

His lenses are on the table beside him, folded neatly. He considers sending a message just so he can check the geoloc tag, but then he remembers, again, that he won. His feed is going to be insanity.

What's expected of him now? Interviews where he talks about how glad he was for the opportunity to play? Interacting with all the people who decided to root for his team once it was clear they were going to win?

Nothing, he hopes. He wants to do nothing. Expecting him to keep his mouth shut, not tell the world about Blake, is already asking too much. Oh, he will keep the secret because it's his, too, and he's good at those, but he still fills with rage.

Josh. Racing to the end. Feeling sure, so sure, that he, too, was going to die, and not by his own choice. It's not the same thing at all, though Blake had made it sound like it was, the last time Miguel lay in a bed in a room like this.

The new heart pulses in his chest. Once again, déjà vu all over the place, he pulls aside the gown covering it, watches the function lights beat through his skin.

Can he trust it? Blake? Dr. Spencer?

Does he have a choice?

No.

Say, for a minute, that he believes this one is the one he was supposed to have all along. No virus, no ticking time bomb.

For the first time in his life he isn't sick. It's the second time he's *thought* he wasn't. If this lasts . . .

He can do whatever he wants. If he'd gotten it when he hit Twenty-five, all he would've wanted to do was get back into the game. Be the first to finish the hundredth level. Play the way he had always wanted to play: no weakness, no fear.

Now he doesn't ever want to set foot inside a ChimeraCube again. Even this hospital room is suddenly too much, the walls closing in.

A deep, careful breath. Okay. He doesn't have to.

This game will teach you who you are.

Someone who wants a different life. Maybe the offer of traveling from his parents is still open, a real world to see instead of one housed inside a gray box.

He is alive. That's who he is, all he needs to know.

His new biomech beats in his chest, fruit fallen from a poisoned tree, but he doesn't care. Blake owed him.

[Self: Miguel Anderson] **Leah Khan** Hey.

[Leah Khan] Hey.

[Self: Miguel Anderson] You okay?

[Leah Khan] Sure. We won, can you believe it? Why did you need another heart?

[Self: Miguel Anderson] The first one had a software bug, no big deal. Where are you?

[Leah Khan] Hiding at home. There's an insane number of

reporters outside my place.

[Self: Miguel Anderson] Damn. Did you have your procedure done? Did it work?

[Leah Khan] Yeah, it worked. Can I see you?

[Self: Miguel Anderson] Stay where you are for now. Don't get accosted by the cameras. I'll let you know when I'm getting out.

[Leah Khan] Okay.

In fact he's getting out . . . right now. Over. Done. As Blake so helpfully reminded him, on a day that feels like years ago, everyone here is on his payroll. Miguel doesn't trust anyone in a white coat, the *C* on the lapel.

The trick to getting into or out of anywhere is to pretend like you're supposed to be doing exactly what you're doing. He dresses in the clothes he arrived in, still stained with the sweat of the final level. Gross, but good enough. He walks swiftly out of his room, down the hallway, guessing—wrongly, twice—at the location of the nearest tile. No arrows have appeared to guide him out because he's not supposed to leave.

Stay here. Let Chimera take care of you.

Ha.

But he is alive.

Past the apple tree in the atrium, cameras gather outside.

A few seconds of running, past the reporters and down the street. There has to be a hoverboard station somewhere. He calls up a map, turns left at the corner, sees one a block ahead. They are chasing him, but he's faster, legs toned and skills honed by years of the game. They are players, too, of course, but they aren't him. He stays far enough ahead to pretend he doesn't hear their shouted questions about how it feels, how his upgrade went, what he'll do now, what his next Chimera ambition is.

Everyone runs faster when they're being chased.

A row of silver disks glints in the sun. He pushes past the people in his way, sometimes hitting flesh, sometimes metal. It's been forever since he had to enter his code, but muscle memory takes over. He hops on the board, sending it soaring into the air.

Nothing hurts.

Okay, that's a lie. The new scar does, but he's been *here* enough to know it is the scar, not the biomech inside. The cityscape shrinks beneath him, defined by its landmarks, defined by the gray cubes outlined in shades of neon scattered across it. He half expects one of them to explode, a monster to rise from its wreckage.

He shakes his head into the rushing wind. This is what's real. He may be in midair, but this is a solid, tangible world that the Gamerunners can't manipulate for their own amusement or whatever the point of their game is.

He laughs. By the time his house comes into view, he's convinced himself that Blake got the worse end of their deal.

Sure, Blake won the bet he had or whatever, but Miguel got the thing he always wanted.

At too high a cost, but that can't be changed now.

More reporters are gathered outside his house, a dark smudge on the sidewalk. He skims over their heads, jumps off the board at the front door, and touches his finger to the lock with all the satisfaction of hitting a save point.

A million new followers every day for a week: all the people who like him because he won. He can't even look at his feed anymore, let alone post any updates. He can't think of a single thing he could say that would be interesting or funny to that many people.

A healthy percentage of them are girls, but there's only one he wants to talk to, and she's not answering his messages. He doesn't get it, she'd said she needed to speak to him. Now nothing. Maybe she'd only liked him because he was the only option while they were shut in the Cube.

His parents have finally gone back to work after hanging around for days, a mix of proud, concerned, and trying to act like everything is totally normal. He won't pretend it hasn't been kind of nice, but he's glad to have the house to himself.

He still hasn't been outside since the trip home, which had taken some explaining to his parents, but he's fine, so they're fine. Getting used to being back here is hard enough.

No demons lurk behind the door to the living room, there is nothing to collect, the knives in the kitchen drawer are all ordinary, a matching set.

His dreams have Chimera's detail, the sharpness that makes the rest of the world look fuzzy.

Maybe going outside would be a good idea. He waits for his parents to go to bed and steps out into the night, passing the few lingering, half-asleep reporters who are way too dedicated to their jobs. The neighborhood hasn't changed, and that feels surprising even though it shouldn't. He wasn't gone for that long in the grand scheme of things, but everything is different, and his life stretches ahead of him, as long as anyone's.

Maybe one day the Cube glowing bloodred that he can see several blocks away will hold some appeal again, but for now he's happy that no monsters are lurking in the buildings he walks past, nothing sinister is hiding around the corner.

"You are coming to a crossroads," says a voice in his head. He smiles and crosses the street, not going anywhere in particular, just walking, shrouded by the safe darkness.

He left his lenses at home. He is disconnected, and it feels amazing. He has always liked to walk, and now he can be as fearless as Grace. Beneath his skin, function lights flicker and pulse, just visible at the surface when he takes his shirt off. If he can trust Blake on this one thing, the biomech is safe, will keep him alive as long as the rest of his body holds up in the poisoned atmosphere and broken earth.

He wonders what Blake won from the other Gamerunner. The bet must've been a good one.

Or maybe not. They're rich, crazy geniuses, they have to be. Maybe they'll play with people's lives out of boredom.

He doesn't care either way.

The next day he consents to an interview just to get the reporters to leave. He points at a reporter at random and invites her into the living room, even offering her a cup of his mom's synthmint tea. She shakes her head, makes herself comfortable.

"So, Miguel, are you ready to talk about the competition?" she asks. There's a strange hunger in her camera eyes, but maybe that's normal for these people. It doesn't matter what she looks like, he's the one being watched, the video streamed online. Some of his millions of new followers will be watching, others will scroll through and find it later. Another thing to be added to his Presence. Teenage boy, Chimera champion, hates the lab-grown olives his dad buys in jars, loves his mother's photographs.

He's been quiet for too long. "Uh, I guess so," he answers. "I don't really know what to say."

"Are you surprised that you won?" She leans forward.

He coughs. "Yes, of course. I didn't follow the other teams as much as I probably should have, I was too busy concentrating on my own game, but I know I was up against some good players."

"You were," she says. "It was . . . interesting . . . to watch."

He narrows his eyebrows, doesn't know what to say to that.

"What was the most difficult part?"

There's a right answer and a true answer. They aren't the same thing. "Obviously that sea creature caused me some problems," he replies, "but of course I have to say that losing Josh was the most difficult." But not for the reason everyone watching must think. His death had solved a problem for Miguel in the end, one he didn't know he'd have.

It was the choice, one he made knowing exactly what would happen. Josh made the choice, too, but only because Miguel told him to.

Blake and his obsession over choices.

Blake. He winces, the reporter puts her hand on his knee. He moves away. "Are you all right?" she asks.

"Yes. Just . . . remembering."

"Of course," she says sympathetically. He's tired of this now. She asks him a few more questions: what playing in the new Chimera had been like, how he'd gotten along with the team members he hadn't known before he started, whether he was well taken care of in the Cube while he wasn't playing. He answers, a forced smile on his face, and hopes this will soon be over. Why did he decide to do this again? Oh, yeah, because it might make them leave him alone.

"Well," she says finally, "it seems Chimera's surprises aren't yet fully revealed. We have just received word that the Gamerunners have another announcement for us. Will you be watching?"

They're probably going to tell the rest of the world when they get to play version 2.0. "I'll watch," he says to appease her, and manages to get her out of his house a few minutes later.

He won't watch. He doesn't even sit at his computer and look at anything, let alone his feed.

He's lying on his bed when someone knocks on the door. It's too early for his parents to be home, the sky is still on fire outside, and his mom will be shooting it, his dad doing . . . whatever it is, exactly, that his dad does in the lab all day, trying to make bananas taste like the memory of bananas. And he thought he'd gotten rid of the cameras. When he'd last looked out the window, they were gone.

"Coming," he mutters, opening the door. A smile spreads instantly across his face.

"Hey," he says.

"Hey." Leah looks past him into the house. Yeah, the cameras are gone, but he doesn't want to stand here with the door open either.

"Come in," he says. He leads her to the living room, she takes the same seat the reporter had. Nerves flutter in his stomach; something about her expression makes him feel like that's not a coincidence.

"What's going on?" he asks, wanting to move closer to her but keeping his distance. She's as beautiful as ever, even with the shadows under her eyes. "Did we end when the competition did?"

She doesn't answer. "I saw your interview," she says instead.

"Uh, okay?"

"You said you were sorry about him, but you knew what would happen with Josh and the snake. You knew when you told him to let it bite him that he'd die. I could see it on your face."

His heart sinks. Real or biomech, the sensation is exactly the same. "Yes," he says quietly. "I knew."

"Why? Why not find another way?"

His living room hasn't changed since he was a kid, but he looks around it, taking in every detail while he wonders exactly what Blake will do to him if he tells her. Blake could be sitting in a Chimera building somewhere with his hand on a button. One click.

Painless isn't the same as not knowing.

He opens his mouth. Another knock comes from the front door, and he glances at her, helpless, before going to answer it.

It's Nick. Maybe telling them together will be easier.

"Did you watch the announcement?" Nick asks. There's an

edge to his voice that Miguel doesn't recognize.

"No. I figured it was them talking about when they're unrolling the new game to everyone. Come in, Leah's here."

"It wasn't that," Nick says, following Miguel inside. "It was just one of the Gamerunners," Nick continues, "and what he said was pretty interesting. Hey, Leah."

"Hi."

"Okay, what did he say?" Miguel asks.

"They're saying," says Nick, "that someone cheated."

He shouldn't be able to feel the biomech beat, its pulse speed up, but he does. He touches his finger to his wrist, forgetting that it wouldn't tell him anything even if he was wearing his lenses to see the display. Leah gasps.

"What?" he asks. His voice sounds normal to his ears, which probably means it sounds anything but. He hadn't, he'd told Blake not to help him, but why would they be saying it at all if it was someone else? He won, nobody else would matter.

"The game got so much easier for us," says Nick. "Other than the thing with Josh and the very last one, we raced through the final levels. You said you were just playing the way you always knew you could, now that your heart was fine, but if it was fine, why did you need another one?"

"Because—"

"The thing is, Mig," says Nick, "cheating *is* the way you've always played."

CUTSCENE:
BLAKE

Oh, yes, Miguel, you cheated. He *had* told Blake not to help him, though he'd changed his mind later, and Blake hadn't done *much*. Made a few levels easier, set up the boy to die . . .

Desperate times. The asking had been enough. Intent is everything.

Good boy. Or . . . not. That was the point.

Damn Lucius for going public with his suspicions, but that doesn't matter much, and he understands why. It is time for them to stop being friends. The end is almost here, and reactions to this piece of information will be as telling as those to the competition itself. Plus, of course, sending out that message was the honorable thing to do.

Which is why Blake hadn't done it.

He could of course have simply *forced* the boy to cheat. Human brains are remarkably receptive to having thoughts dropped into them, but he and Lucius made an agreement way back in the early days. Interfering like that was unfair, they'd decided, and though it goes against nearly everything he is, Blake has kept his word in this one small way. It's so much more *fun* to watch people think up ways to hurt or help one another instead of doing it for them. Not to mention that more than once they've come up with things that make Blake wince and think even he wouldn't go *that* far.

"We want them released by the end of the week," says the voice. It's different from the voice of the Storyteller, but that's where the inspiration came from. Disembodied voices, telling you what you want to hear, whether or not it's helpful.

"Yes, Masters," he answers. There isn't one; there are many. The same is true on Lucius's side, which is where humans have mostly gotten it wrong. But there *are* sides, which is where humans have mostly gotten it right.

"Are they ready?"

"Yes, in fact I think you will be quite pl—"

"We will be pleased when we win, Blake. Cooperation has been essential up to this point, but that time is now over. The agreed-upon hour has arrived."

"Yes. Um. How did that happen exactly? Did you all meet over lunch?"

"Blake."

"Sorry."

"Good-bye."

They've never been ones for drawn-out farewells, and neither has Blake. He returns to his office, to a stack of virtual paperwork, paperwork one of those things that are, in his opinion, really just pushing the limits of decency. He's not a monster. Predictably, Lucius has read and signed everything already: the kid who does his homework long before it's due. Blake sighs. It's been a good run, really.

He signs his name to the documents that will lead to the worldwide dissolution of Chimera.

It isn't necessary anymore.

LEVEL TWENTY-TWO

"I didn't," Miguel insists. "But something's going on. Come to my room." His mind races. Something really fucking strange is happening, and he doesn't know what. It's a feeling, a tight ball of dread in his belly.

He's lost all faith that anywhere is secure, private, but his room is the best he's going to get. Leah and Nick sit on his bed, Miguel takes the chair at his desk.

"I didn't use the sim," he tells Nick.

"Wait." Leah holds up a hand. "What sim?"

"I have a simulated version of Chimera. Nick knows I invented it years ago, learned how to code so I could help myself progress through the game faster. Just a sim to try out different situations and strategies. It's probably not the only one in existence." Thinking that makes him feel better. "I was trying to get to Twenty-five as fast as I could. A couple of months before the competition was announced, I realized I wasn't going to get there no matter what I did. The game was getting harder, and I was getting weaker."

Leah winces, then looks mildly impressed.

"Okay," says Nick, "so you didn't use that." His jaw is clenched. Always too concerned with doing the right thing. "You did something."

Miguel inhales. Now or never. "It's more like . . . someone did something to me." It must sound like he's searching for an excuse, a lie they'll believe, a justification they'll accept. Leah raises an eyebrow.

"One of the Gamerunners came to see me in the medical wing after my first transplant."

Leah's other eyebrow joins the first. Nick blinks. "What?"

Back to the beginning.

"At first he just seemed concerned. Nice, almost, though pretty weird. He wanted to know if I was going to keep playing. I said yes. I thought they didn't want to lose a leader, like they were concerned about the publicity or something. I thought that was the end of it."

Nick and Leah are silent, their arms folded over their chests.

"But it wasn't." Miguel continues. "After we hit the desert level . . . Anna . . . I told him I was done. I didn't have to go on, and I didn't want to if it meant I was going to see shit like that.

"Turns out, it wasn't that easy," Miguel says, swallowing.

"The biomech they put in me was infected with a virus. The Gamerunner knew all about me. He knew about that," Miguel says, gesturing to the sim. "He knew—" No, he won't tell Nick, or Leah, about the night on the ledge. "When I told him I was done, he told me what *he'd* done."

Nick shakes his head. "The fuck? Why?"

"There are two Gamerunners, apparently they had some kind of bet, and this one, Blake, wanted to win. Each of them picked a favorite leader. He told me if I won the competition, he'd exchange the sick heart for a healthy one. He made it sound like I owed him some kind of favor, because if it hadn't been for his putting the sick biomech in me, I would've died anyway. It's like you said," he says, looking at Leah, "when you die in your dreams, you die in real life. My body thought I'd died that day on the boat. So he did save my life, he just didn't give me much more time. In exchange, I think he made the game a little easier for us, though I told him not to. To the outside world, I mean, how would they know? It was a different Chimera, they didn't know what was supposed to happen. To the other teams it probably just looked like we were really good. Even to you guys, it just seemed like we were progressing quickly, though Nick noticed."

Nick wants to believe him, his expression a mix of skepticism and hope that Miguel can identify only because they've been friends for so long. He and Leah don't have that kind of history.

"Nobody's ever *seen* the Gamerunners. How do you know it was even one of them and not someone playing some kind of sick joke, trying to make the competition more entertaining?"

"I do think he was trying to make it more entertaining," says Miguel, "but I'm sure he was one of the Gamerunners."

"How?"

"The night before Josh died, he told me it would come down to our team and Zack's at the end. Who else would've known that for sure?"

"That's why you couldn't find another way to get the snake. You didn't have time," Leah says, her voice almost a whisper.

"Yes. Plus I think he wanted me to do that."

"Why?" Nick asks.

"He was really big on making choices. Kept telling me the game would teach me who I was. The Storyteller made a big deal of that in her speech at the beginning, too. I think he wanted to see if I'd choose to sacrifice Josh if I had to."

"How did Josh's dying help us? He was an extra pair of hands, an extra brain."

"Yeah," says Miguel, "but on the final level, there were only four places in the boat."

"So?" Nick asks. "You could've left him behind then."

That's true, but— Miguel thinks. "Grace might would've been pissed if I had. The two of them were close—you saw how upset Grace was—but at least his death looked unavoidable. Like it *wasn't* a choice. Taking him away weakened her. Broke her. It was a shitty thing to do." That doesn't begin to cover it, but he's running out of words. "It meant she didn't have the will to do much other than follow us to the end, though she was helpful because she just wanted to finish the game and then forget about it. And she won't speak to me now." He'd sent her a message, she'd ignored it.

"Okay," says Nick. "Let's say all of this is true. I can see why you'd do anything to save your life; anyone would. It's what you used to do with the sim, I got that. But if one of the Gamerunners *was* helping you, helping us—"

"Why are they going public with the cheating?" Leah finishes. "Yeah. That's the part I don't get."

"Me neither," answers Miguel. "So we're going to find out." He presses a button to project his keyboard onto the expanse of desk, the only thing that's stayed clean since he got home from the Cube. They'll start here. If he can't get in remotely, he'll have to reconsider his options.

But he has a weapon. Two weapons Blake's name and Blake's arrogance. People like that never believe they have a weak point.

"Give me one of those," says Nick. Miguel shoots another keyboard onto the wall behind Nick's head.

"Me, too," says Leah. "I want to know what the hell is

going on. And if enough people think you cheated, they're never going to believe the rest of us weren't involved. If they decide to name a different team as winner, they might reverse my procedure."

He's an asshole. They've been so consumed by this he hasn't asked. "Did it work?"

"I think so. Haven't had a chance to do anything about it, though."

"Help me," he promises, "and I'll help you." It's an unfair trade by any stretch, but it's all he can offer her. She kneels on his bed, facing the wall. The letters and numbers reflect onto her face, making her look like part of the machine.

Breaking into someone else's system isn't easy; he'd have no idea how if it weren't for building that kind of security for himself, his sim. He takes some satisfaction from the payback. If he can't have any privacy, Blake can't either.

His mother knocks on the door, gives Miguel a sly look when he introduces her to Leah. She offers dinner, but none of them are hungry.

The sun is rising when a complex file tree blooms on the monitors, blurring in front of Miguel's dry, exhausted eyes. "Look for communications between Blake and the other one," he says, telling them what to type since their backs are to his screens. He prays that they did exchange messages about revealing the cheat, that they didn't discuss it out loud. He doesn't know if they even spend all their time in the same place. "Wait. Stop. Here's something."

They both turn around, see the message from a guy named Lucius to Blake: "We're not on the same side anymore, if we ever were. I must do the right thing," Leah reads. And a reply: "I know. I was expecting you to."

Not on the same side? What side? Nick and Leah watch as he types rapidly. What's happening to Chimera if they're arguing?

Here. Documents open, their text cramped and confusing. He doesn't speak lawyer.

"They're dissolving the company?" Leah asks, squinting. "Notifying governments?"

"But wasn't the competition supposed to be a beta test for new features? That makes no sense," says Nick. "Why go through that if they don't want to run the game anymore?"

Miguel shakes his head. He has no idea, but he has time now, more than before anyway. So many *whys*. He'd asked Blake why, albeit with a different meaning. And Blake's refusal to give him answers means there *are* answers.

Click, click, click. The tips of his fingers save the biomech one hurt from striking the desk. He doesn't stop. Nick and Leah sit back on his bed and watch. If it wasn't a beta test, it was something else, and that must be in here somewhere.

But he can't find it. He's so close he can feel there's

something *to* find, dancing in his peripheral vision, just out of reach. It's a familiar sensation, one he's felt in Chimera a thousand times.

He throws a game-earned shoe at the wall. Leah jumps.

"Sorry," Miguel says, clutching at his hair. Think. What does he always do in the game when his moves aren't working?

Approach from a different direction. He can't find the answers he needs here, but—click, click—yes, he has one thing. And when you're trapped in a room made of questions, you have to unlock the door from the inside.

"Come on," he tells them.

"Where are we going?"

"Chimera."

"We're going to play? Now?" Nick asks, climbing off the bed. "I don't get it."

Miguel shakes his head. "No. Let's go. And we need to walk, I don't want them tracking us somehow. Don't post any updates either. They might be checking our geolocs."

"What did you find?" Leah demands, her hand on the doorknob.

"Their address."

All this time, and the worldwide headquarters of Chimera had been just a few short miles away. Miguel's not sure what he would've done if he'd had that information earlier. Banged on the door and demanded a new heart?

"They're not going to let us in," Nick says. "The place is gonna have the best security system on earth."

"Maybe," agrees Miguel, "but its owners have spent years teaching us to get in and out of locked places. Ha. They always claimed Chimera would help us in the real world."

"Okay, but it'll be full of people," Nick says.

"They just shut down the company. My guess, it's as empty as it's ever been. If I'm wrong, we'll get out of there."

"This is crazy," says Leah. "What do you think we're going to find out?"

"No idea." Miguel turns to her. "You don't have to come."

Leah grins. "I said it was crazy, not that I didn't want to come."

Nick's laughter bounces off the artificial trees that line the street. "You. I like you. Mig, I like her."

Miguel shoots him a look and takes her hand. "Don't get any ideas."

Nick laughs again, and Leah squeezes Miguel's fingers.

They take the quietest route they can find, not wanting to be recognized, stopped. Once or twice Miguel sees someone across the street staring at them a little too long, but he speeds their pace and turns the next corner. The sun beats down, blinding after weeks in the Cube, where the light had sometimes been harsh but not real enough to burn their retinas.

He's not out of breath, and his chest doesn't hurt, but an even bigger change feels like it's looming. He can't explain it, it's the same instinct that has always helped him in Chimera, knowing when a boss is in the next room or the ground's about to split open. He's played through the levels, assembling what seem like irrelevant puzzle pieces into a coherent finale.

Blake's antics, his manipulations feel like puzzle pieces, and Miguel is sure as fuck going to find out what the picture is.

Miguel stops so suddenly Nick crashes into him. The answers are right there.

Chimera headquarters sit in a maze of identical buildings, nondescript and unremarkable. They're nice, glass fronts gleaming, the bricks well kept, but not nearly as slick as the skyscrapers downtown. They look like the offices of some company that manufactures a small but essential hoverboard component. For that matter, they look like Miguel's father's lab, on the other side of the city, where people in white coats try to make things taste like cinnamon, but if they fail, the world won't fall apart.

"Why here?" Nick asks, his thoughts obviously in line with Miguel's.

"Because they've always wanted to be anonymous," Leah answers. "Or at least show themselves only on their terms."

Through the glass he sees a marble floor, an empty desk that should hold some kind of receptionist, the leaves of potted plants. The front door beckons. It won't be that easy. He remembers his thought in the hospital and amends it: *usually* the trick to getting in or out of somewhere is to pretend you're doing what you're supposed to be doing. There's no way to pretend that here. Other memories are more helpful, like that of their first competition level.

Miguel turns left, leads them through narrow lanes around to the back of the building. He curses under his breath at the mostly flat expanse of wall, no back door. There is, however, an air vent at waist height, and the line between reality and Chimera blurs again. He's done this before.

He curses again, louder this time.

"What?" Leah asks.

"I forgot I can't just summon a screwdriver if I need one."

"Oh. Yeah. Oops."

Nick grips one of the slats on the vent and pulls. It shifts ever so slightly. "Help," he says. Leah and Miguel move to either side of him, and together the three tug on the vent, the screws at each corner grinding against crumbling brick. It wrenches free at one last hard yank, rubble crashing around their toes. Nick throws the metal grate on the ground behind them, and they all stare into the hole.

The vent is exactly like the one Miguel had to crawl through in the game, and he wants to do it exactly as much. There's room for a single body length before it veers off to the right, into the invisible depths of the building.

At least, if he goes first, he'll get out first.

"Stay close," he tells the others, and slowly climbs in, crawling forward on his elbows. The turn is tight, as tight as the walls closing in around him. He takes a deep breath and pulls himself the next few inches, and the next. Pitch darkness comes for what feels like several feet, then the faintest glimmer of light ahead, getting incrementally brighter as he drags his body toward it.

Through the slats of another grate, he sees an empty room. Not just empty of people but completely so: no furniture or computers or even a window. Just walls in Chimera's favorite shade of gray and a single spotlight on the ceiling. This grate is on simple hooks, easy to move aside, and slowly, carefully Miguel climbs out of the tunnel.

"That was easier than I expected," said Leah, following him.

"Don't speak too soon. We still need to find where they keep their tech."

"You think there are cameras or motion sensors or anything?"

Miguel turns to Nick. "Could be, but what are they going to do if they catch us? Have us arrested? I don't think Blake wants me to tell the world he fixed the game."

A shadow passes over Leah's eyes. "They could do

something to that again," she says, pointing at his chest.

He swallows. She's right. Right here, right now, he has to make a choice. He closes his eyes and opens them again.

He'd rather die knowing whatever truth Blake and his partner are hiding than live wondering why Blake cared so much about winning that he was willing to kill to do it. Why they came up with a beta test for a game they never intended to launch.

"Come on," he says, heading for the door.

The corridor feels familiar, like one he's been in a thousand times, as if someone sat in a room in this building and coded a gamescape based on what they saw. That's probably what happened.

"Which way?" Nick asks.

Miguel shrugs. He can't post an update asking for tips on this. "Listen out for people?" he whispers to Leah. She nods.

He heads left, testing door handles along the way. All locked. They might need to come back and break in if they can't find anything else, but for now it seems safe to explore. The light gets brighter as he walks, and suddenly explodes into brilliance as he steps into a large glass atrium, facing the tall windows and front door they saw from the other side. The desk is still empty.

"Hear anything?" he asks Leah. She shakes her head.

"Nothing. You know when a place just feels completely

abandoned?"

He trusts her, but he won't count on her being right just yet. Overhead, four more floors rise, and the edges of a tile mar the marble underfoot.

"Up, I guess," says Miguel, moving to the middle of the tile as Leah and Nick join him. "We'll try them one at a time."

The second floor is only more gray hallways, more locked doors. Maybe Blake and Lucius cleared everything out, sealed it up, and there's nothing to find here. Maybe that's why it was so easy—comparatively—to get inside.

They step back onto the tile. The third floor begins the way the second did, but the corridor is much shorter this time, and an open door at the end reveals a massive room, filled with banks of computers. Bingo.

This is where Chimera lives. What Miguel wouldn't have given to be in this room only a few months ago, crack open the game and discover its secrets so he could progress even faster.

Now he's looking for a different secret. He takes a chair at the nearest desk, wakes the screen in front of him. Nick and Leah hover over his shoulders for the first few minutes, before both finding seats themselves.

There's much less security on the network in here; firewalls hadn't been built to keep out anyone who was already inside the building. Miguel calls up the same files he found in his bedroom, finds the places that kept shutting him out. Now they let him in. His hands move faster than his brain. He goes too far, doesn't realize what he's seen until he's three screens ahead. He flips back. Stares. No. That makes no sense. None.

And then it makes total sense. Bile rises in his throat. He looks for the nearest thing to vomit into, but he's frozen in his chair. Swallow. Burn. He coughs.

"Mig?" Nick jumps up. "Mig? What's wrong?"

Everything. His hand is on his chest. He wants to claw through the muscle and bone and tear out the heart inside. He doesn't believe this stuff. He doesn't know anyone who believes this stuff. All that died out with technology, with science.

Which just made it so much easier for Blake and the other one, Lucius, to hide in plain sight. To take over the world with their fucking game, negotiate with men and women who believe they rule the world and . . . don't.

He coughs again. "Have you ever heard the phrase *Gods play games with the lives of men?*"

CUTSCENE:
LUCIUS

It's almost like being a parent. Lucius steps back, surveying his work with no small measure of pride. And because he's Lucius, he silently gives Blake credit for his contributions.

Neither one of them would have managed it alone. It's sad to think that their partnership is nearly over, but such is the way of the world. Chimera will shut down in a month, enough time for the horsemen to go out into the world and do the jobs he and Blake have so carefully given them.

Their forms, their purposes exist in many mythologies, but never like this.

Technology is a beautiful thing.

"Are we ready?" Blake asks, setting down his coffee cup. "We need to leave. The boy and his friends will arrive soon."

"Remind me again why you want him to come here? And why you think he will?"

"Because we want the truth to come out, but we don't want

to be the ones to say it. History has shown the boy will not be believed, not at first at any rate. People saying the things he will say have been dismissed as madmen since the dawn of time. He'll come because he's curious. I've left him clues. So, are we ready?"

"I think so. Ask them."

Blake does.

"Yes," they say one by one. Their voices are mechanical, false, but the thoughts they speak are their own. Lucius is particularly pleased with the brains. He'd dreaded having to follow each one around, making sure they were acting according to plan. Especially when Blake would have had to do the same, under instructions from *his* superiors, with completely different objectives. What a mess that would have been.

It's still going to be a mess, but the planned one. Both sides are just waiting to clean up.

"Well." Lucius turns to his friend, his enemy, the only one on earth who understands. "It's been a pleasure."

"It's been an absolute chore," Blake retorts, shaking his hand.

"I'm sure I'll see you around, but I'll be busy."

"Me too. Good luck."

"And you."

"Go," says Lucius. He and Blake follow the four horsemen

as they walk out the door of Chimera headquarters and into the world, gleaming creations of the foundations of humanity, war, famine, pestilence, and death, imbued with all the supernatural abilities heaven and hell can provide.

LEVEL TWENTY-THREE

It is so beautifully simple, but even water can make you choke. Kill you. Simple things have power.

Simple choices do. Miguel looks from his screen to all the others, text scrolling across them at a rapid, almost illegible rate. Names. Statistics.

Alignments.

"Look!" he says, pointing. "Every one of those is a person, someone making choices. Good ones. Bad ones." His fists clench.

"That's not possible." Leah's voice quivers.

"They've been data mining our *souls.*"

"No. No-no-no. It's some kind of joke."

But it isn't. "Think about it," Miguel says. "We all basically live either online or in Chimera, which is partly the same thing. Status updates and photo collections. Diaries. Game progress. Grades, statistics, choices. Everything." He points at the computer, the face of what he means. "It's all in there. And when we die, it stays there forever. People have been talking about that for basically forever. You. Me. Immortal in the system. Everything you've ever liked or loved or hated. Everything you've searched for, bought, said. Everything we *are*. What is that, if not a soul?"

"You sound like you believe it."

He doesn't. But he has to. None of this would be here if it wasn't true. And just think of Chimera.

"They've been laughing at us," he says. "They threw gods and demons at us in the game, thinking we'd never figure it out. They designed every level to show us the world they're about to destroy."

"And they've been watching our every move," Leah whispers. "Every decision. Not just ours. Millions of people. Cheer at someone's failure, complain at someone's success . . . Some people were *happy* Josh died."

This game will teach you who you are.

"Now you sound like *you* believe it," Nick says to Leah.

"I don't want to."

Synapses fire, connections made. That's why the balance of the teams had been so important. The spectrum of good to evil. Team leaders the ones in the middle, the hardest to judge, the ones who could go either way had to be tested the most.

Oh, they had tested Miguel.

And he'd failed.

"This— No," says Nick, finally finding his voice. "You were blackmailed into playing like that, into killing Josh. You didn't have a choice, you can't be judged by that. Even if you had a choice, Josh had one, too."

"I did have a choice." A few hours ago he'd been so sure he'd never tell anyone this, but the time for secrets is over. "And Blake knew I'd almost made it once. The night the leaders were announced I left you and Anna in the park and went to—to— I stood on the roof of the tallest building I could get to," he says, hoping that's enough.

It is. Nick's pain is so palpable Miguel has to turn away from it.

"I always had a choice," he whispers, not looking at either of them. "I made the wrong one. For me, for you guys."

"We didn't do anything!" says Leah. "It was your choice. I'm not saying I wouldn't have made the same one, in your shoes, but we didn't know."

Yeah. He doesn't think that matters. He was the leader, there to overrule them, to choose for them even though they had the ability to choose for themselves. They hadn't spoken up, they'd watched him do it.

The truth is too large for this room, though it's held here. It's too large for the enormous world. It surrounds them, a bubble that won't burst no matter how much they poke it with logic and reason.

"We need to tell someone. We need to do something."

Who? What? There is no higher authority than the ones who have been mocking them, that's the point. Leah's shaking fingers fly across the projected keys, and he moves to stop her, thinking she's posting a status update. Too late he realizes what she's actually doing.

She finds her name among billions in a spreadsheet. Tears drip down her face. "I was good," she whispers. *"Was."*

"Leah—"

Years of Chimera have heightened her speed and reflexes. His fingers close around air as she runs, leaping onto the tile at the end of the corridor.

Nick stands, too, leaves, and Miguel is alone.

Stunted trees rise from a dying earth soon to be put out of its misery. There is a wind coming off the water, and Miguel pushes his hair from his eyes for the hundredth time. He barely remembers coming here, it's just where he goes when he needs to be alone or to think.

It's his fault. He made the decision. They followed and are now as guilty.

It's not fair, but life isn't. He's seen that firsthand, even before now.

The sky darkens. The late-summer night is cold, and he

didn't bring a coat. Such tiny considerations are just that—tiny. Unimportant in the grand scheme of things, the grand plan. He missed an entire summer, the last summer, holed up inside a ChimeraCube. He would've even if they hadn't run the competition, but now he feels the loss.

He definitely doesn't feel like a champion.

There's been no more word from the Gamerunners. It might not come at all. After Leah and Nick left, he'd watched his status feed on one screen, the Chimera files on all the others. Human after human, being sorted according to whether they care or not, Miguel's one decision touching millions. Maybe that was all they wanted.

Footsteps. He turns.

"I messaged Anna," she says. "She told me you come here."

Anna would know. It's right that now Leah does, too, for as long as they have left.

"I want to be so angry at you." She sits next to him on the ground. "But that makes it worse somehow. If you hadn't done what you did, we wouldn't know at all. I'd rather know."

Miguel laughs without humor. "I wouldn't."

"Really?"

"I thought I wanted to know. I really did. There was a moment when we were in that first room, the empty one, where I knew we could turn back. I thought I wanted the truth." Painless isn't the same as not knowing, but not knowing is painless. There's nothing he can do about it either way. All his life he's been fighting, and it was pointless, he was never going to live much longer than he has already. Blake knew that. He knew it the whole time, but he gave Miguel hope just to see what he'd do with it. And when that didn't work, he threatened Miguel to see what he'd do with *that*.

Games. A toy. That's what he feels like.

"What did you think their secret was?"

Does it matter now? Miguel shrugs. "I'm not sure. Human experiments? Something to do with the biomech. There've been rumors about a singularity, a collective digital consciousness. Maybe that. I guess I wasn't entirely wrong, but there's nothing we can do either way."

"I think I agree with you," Leah says. "When I ran off, I went to do some reading. Guess what, nobody raving about gods and demons has ever been believed."

"We could show them the proof?"

"Look at the history of the world. Someone will come up with a ridiculous story, which by the way won't be anywhere near as ridiculous as the truth. People are weird. They have their own lives to worry about."

"For now."

"Yeah."

He stands, slowly, legs aching after so many hours on the cold ground. Whether he wants to know or not, he does.

Regret is far behind him. He has to make the right choices now, and the right choice is to let one more person in on the secret. He's told Nick to go to hell so often, laughing the whole time. It's just what people say.

Vision is a fluid, contextual thing. What you see depends on what you know.

He knows too much, and so he sees too much.

Miguel tears off his lenses. This can't be coincidence. Not believing in coincidences is one of the many things Chimera has taught him. Everything found, everything learned is needed, relevant later.

His eyes ache from reading, books on one side, status feed on the other. They'd started to blur, converge.

Miguel reads Leah's message on his monitor. "Did you read the news?"

Yes. A small war in a peaceful country, rapidly becoming a large war in a violent country. Citizens are taking refuge in their local Cubes, where there is food, clean water, shelter. More of the limitless resources to which Blake and Lucius have access, but at least Miguel has an explanation for that now. Life must be so much easier when you don't have to obey the laws of physics.

Also when that life is eternal.

Miguel's stomach turns. He ate that stuff. Maybe it was real food, it had tasted real. It's just that he doesn't know the difference between real and not real for anything anymore.

The world is going to end. That's real.

His hand in front of him. That's real.

Mom knocking on his bedroom door. That's real.

"Dinner," she says.

"Yeah, I'm not really hungry."

"And I don't really care," she retorts, smiling. "We've hardly seen you all summer. Come sit with us, I won't force-feed you."

How can she smile? Oh, yeah. Because he hasn't told them. He turns the arguments for and against over in his mind like he has been for the past week and a half, and pushes his chair away from his desk. His mother puts a plate in front of him at the table, and he stares at it. Is this real food? It was synthesized in a lab, does that make it better or worse than what Blake and Lucius might be serving in the Cubes?

There's no answer to that. Focusing on small questions temporarily saves him from having to look at the bigger ones.

In this case, the biggest one, the question that has consumed humanity since the dawn of time. Preoccupation with it has faded in recent centuries, but that's only made it easier for Blake and Lucius to pull off their plan.

"What do you think happens to us when we die?" Miguel

asks. He wasn't going to ask. He'd opened his mouth to put his fork in it, but the words had other ideas. His parents look up in surprise.

"You're not going to die, sweetheart." The unspoken *anymore* hangs over the table like the lamp illuminating their faces.

"I know." Miguel's unspoken "Yes, I am, we all" are lurks in the darkened corners of the kitchen. "I'm just asking."

"Nothing," says his father firmly. "Your life ends, so does your consciousness. There's nothing after that."

"That's what I think, too," says his mother. "All the more reason to enjoy life while we have it."

"Right."

"Your new girlfriend seems nice." His mother winks slyly. "Is that still a thing? She hasn't been back since that first time. Did we embarrass you too much?"

The feeling of watching himself, all of them, from overhead is sudden, consuming. Small lives, small worries, small pleasures and sins. This is what Blake and Lucius are concerned with, this is what they are collecting. A grain of sand plus a grain of sand plus a grain of sand eventually add up to a beach.

For one of them, it will eventually add up to victory.

"She's fine. It's still a thing."

He hasn't eaten a bite. He watches his parents instead.

They're still young, relatively, and look younger than he can remember their having done so for a long time, their biggest worry erased by a surgeon's laser. He won't put those lines of concern back on their faces, smoothed now but lingering just under the surface.

His father stands abruptly, blinking furiously behind his lenses. "Excuse me," he says, almost to himself, heading for the living room and shutting the door. Miguel and his mother shrug, silent and waiting until his father returns.

Pale, furiously grabbing his coat from the hook by the door. "I have to go," he says, still blinking. "Accident . . . lab . . . something really wrong."

The door slams.

"This worries me," Leah says.

"Oh, really?"

She slaps Nick's shoulder. "No, seriously. Like this is all part of the plan. War starts breaking out, that makes a twisted kind of sense. A computer error causes a meltdown at Mr. Anderson's lab, and others, too. Their systems are linked. That means food shortages, and that makes sense, too. So now people are hiding inside the Cubes, where there's food and doctors and shit, right? Except in all of human history, when have diseases run rampant? When people are living in close quarters. That's the third one. Gather everyone together, it's going to be easier to infect them with some virus or something, isn't it?"

"Won't people leave once they start getting sick? Go home?"

"If they're allowed to," says Leah grimly. "Right now the war is halfway across the world, but it'll come here, and everything else will follow. I know it will."

War. Check.

Famine. Check.

Pestilence. Check.

There's only one more, and it comes with all the others. They should have studied this more in school. The monsters of myth and legend, the demons that hide in fire.

A face dances in the flames. Miguel shifts away from the pit he, Nick, and Leah have built in the park, burning preapproved, environmentally friendly fuels. He almost laughs, but the face winks at him. The others can't or don't see it.

Leah was right. He keeps his mouth shut, afraid of sounding like a lunatic even to those who already know what he knows. They don't know what to do about it, but the knowledge unites them.

Which explains one thing. For days Miguel's been trying to wrap his head around the idea that Blake and Lucius could work together when surely their aim divides them more completely than anything has ever been divided. Now, though, he gets it. How much lonelier would he feel if Nick and Leah weren't here?

He has counted every one of the twenty-two times he's tried to tell his parents, opening his mouth and shoving food into it instead.

They might believe him. They might think that they just got their son back, healthier than ever, only for him to lose his mind.

He's heard of people going crazy after procedures, claiming to have seen something weird while they were unconscious. A few neuro tweaks and their status updates make sense again.

The face in the fire opens its mouth, forms a word Miguel can't decipher. He moves back again.

"Too hot," he explains, letting go of Leah's hand to wipe his clammy one on his leg.

"We really need to decide what we're going to do," she says.

"What *can* we do?"

"I don't know!" She glares at Nick. "Is sitting around here waiting for the world to end really the answer? I've been reading—"

"Of course you have."

"Shut up. I've been reading everything I can get my eyes on." She taps her lenses. "Our souls aren't the only thing living forever online. There are—were—a million and one theories about what happens at the end times. Some pretty weird stuff. Rains of fish and plagues of locusts. The world just disappearing as if it were never here; one minute we'll be sitting in this park and then nothing. A nuclear explosion that wipes out all of humanity."

"There're no fish in the oceans, but they're going to rain from the sky?" Nick raises an eyebrow. "Okay."

"A few days ago you didn't believe in any of this," Miguel says. "Neither did I. I'm not sure we can draw lines around what makes sense anymore. Besides, according to her, there's no such thing as a fish anyway, so maybe it is unlikely."

"I tried to tell Anna this morning." Nick shakes his head. "I couldn't do that to her."

Ignorance is bliss, until it isn't. She's going to find out sooner or later. Blake and Lucius have been sneaky, clever up to now, but they probably can't hide Armageddon. Unless the world-disappearing thing is right. Like just going to sleep and never waking up. You'd never know.

Painless.

"We don't know *when*," says Nick.

Miguel shakes his head.

Leah's face is shadowed; suddenly it clears like clouds after an acid storm. "I'm going to do what I set out to do," she says, standing up. "The game is supposed to teach us who we are, give us the skills and enhancements to do what we need to, right?"

Miguel nods.

"Fine. Then if our souls really exist, if there's really some kind of heaven or hell, I'm going to make sure my sister's is at peace before all this ends. That's the right thing to do, and if I do the right thing, it might not be too late to save myself. We don't know when they're going to stop assessing us, we only know where we are right now. Just accepting it is *not* the right choice." She pushes herself to her feet and bends down to gather her stuff.

Does this really matter now? Does anything matter anymore?

Leah reads the question on his face as easily as if it were research. "Yes, you idiot, it matters. Little things matter. Lives matter. *Stories* matter, human stories, our experiences. They need to be shared, passed down, remembered. The Gamerunners and their bosses might not get that, but I do. If I'm going to do one last thing on earth before we all go to actual, literal hell, it's going to be something that *matters*." She's yelling now, and a security guard in a green uniform exactly the shade of the grass moves slowly toward her. "We're going to try to stop this."

CUTSCENE:
BLAKE

The two men meet on a hill overlooking a city. It doesn't matter which city. They weren't expecting to meet again at all.

Below them a battle rages. Somewhere out there, the horsemen are lurking. Close enough to have an effect, but hiding from view.

"Do you know what this is about?" Lucius asks. He's not talking about the war.

"We have been summoned back," says Blake.

"I *know* that. Do you know why?"

"I do not."

"Would you tell me if you did?" Lucius asks.

"Possibly." Blake carefully keeps his face blank. There is no one on earth or anywhere else better than Lucius at reading his expression, and he doesn't want to show how worried he is.

Although, perhaps, he isn't alone. "We could just . . . not go," says Lucius. A very un-Lucius-like thing to say. "They'll come and find us wherever we are."

A shadow falls across the hilltop. Blake swallows, looking over Lucius's shoulder. "They already have," he says, gazing at the tall black horseman. "What are you doing here?" he asks it.

"Performing one of my assigned tasks," it says, huge metal hand gripping a weapon. "Though you were not the one who gave me these instructions."

Lucius steps forward, edging his shoulder in front of Blake. "Who was?"

"Your superiors. They suspected you might not obey your instructions if you guessed why they were given. You are no longer needed, you see. I have been directed to tell you that you have performed your jobs admirably, but they have come to an end. Now you are simply in the way."

"Wait," says Blake. If he had a heart, it would have stopped by now. Skipped a beat at least. "They still need us. People are hiding in the Cubes here. We're the only ones who know everything about the Cubes and the game inside."

"I think you'll find that is not the case," says the horseman. "And we are intelligent, you created us to be so. Artificially intelligent, ha-ha."

"We invented you." Blake's mouth is dry.

"And I can speak for all of us when I thank you for it. Now, come."

"I don't understand," says Lucius. "If you're going to do

this, why not do it here? Why must we go back?"

"Because your respective superiors have a sense of humor. They wish to see your end in the place where the end began." Around the horseman's feet, a spreading patch of grass is turning brown.

"We can talk about this," says Lucius, his eyes cutting to Blake. "Give us a chance to tell the ones upstairs—and downstairs—that we can still be useful."

"I'm afraid that time has passed. And soon so will you." The weapon raises another inch. It would not kill a human.

Blake swallows.

Is this what it feels like?

He doesn't want to die.

"Follow me," says death. "I will not ask again."

LEVEL TWENTY-FOUR

"I'm going back to Chimera headquarters," says Miguel.

"We're coming with you." Leah stands and brushes off her jeans.

"Guys, no. You can live a little longer, however much longer there is. They don't have to know you're involved at all. And you," Miguel says, looking at Leah, "you have something else to do. You need to find out what happened to your sister."

"We don't actually know what they know," says Leah. "They're . . . gods, or close enough. They probably know everything. They could have been listening to every word we've ever said. We have to assume we have no secrets. You hear that?" she says, louder now. "We're coming for you. And what happened to my sister can wait. I can't save her. We might be able to do something about the rest of us."

Miguel shakes his head. "We got lucky; it was empty last time. That might not happen again, and if it doesn't . . ."

"Then bad luck for us," says Nick. "But there's still no chance in hell you're going alone."

Miguel winces at the word. He never used to. "I don't want it to be empty," he says. "I want to find Blake. I want him to tell me the truth. I want to see it in his damned eyes."

"You really think that's smart?" Nick asks. "What's going to stop him from killing you?"

Nothing. Absolutely nothing. But that's going to happen no matter what. He can *try* to make it happen on his terms.

"That's the fourth," Miguel says, looking from Leah to Nick and back again. "I've been reading. War, famine, pestilence, death. Technically I've already cheated death once. Probably not lucky enough to do it again, so let's make it happen."

"Mig—"

"If this is all really happening," Miguel says to Nick, "I don't want to watch it. Come or not. I'm going."

They take hoverboards this time. Miguel hopes Blake and Lucius are tracking him. In the air it's too windy to talk, which gives him time to think. From what he saw last time, the computers in the building control and gather information only from Chimera and the various online services it's plugged into—there hadn't been any files on Blake's and Lucius's entire . . . pantheon, or whatever. Miguel probably can't do anything to them from there or anywhere.

But he can speak to the world.

He still means what he said to Leah, that given the choice he'd rather not know at all, but that choice doesn't really exist anymore. Everyone's going to find out sooner or later, and the sooner they do, the more they can prepare. Already people across the world are gathering inside Cubes because it's where they think they're safe. They're trusting the very last people they should trust.

He can stop that, or he can try. Guaranteed people are going to think he's crazy. Better to be crazy than complicit.

The building comes into view, its windows faintly aglow with the light cast from monitors busy measuring, filing souls on either side of an arbitrary line. Miguel grits his teeth, commands the board to descend, and lands right at the front door. Screw it. He's not crawling through the vent again.

"Anything?" he asks Leah as the boards rise again, soaring off to return to their station.

She cocks her head. "I don't think so."

The door is unlocked. Miguel would've broken the glass if he'd had to. He knows where he's going now, and Leah and Nick have to run to catch up with him on the tile, seconds before it ascends.

On the third floor he sits at the same desk he had a few days earlier, in the same chair from which he'd watched Leah and Nick run, the truth too much to take. It had frozen Miguel in place; he'd sat here for an hour, watching millions, billions of names scroll past.

He wonders now if this is where Blake or Lucius sat when they made the first competition announcement. Probably not, but there's still a pleasing symmetry to being in this building when he does what he's about to do.

Attention, Chimera gamers of the world.

Miguel takes a breath. The microphone light on the computer blinks in time with ones in his chest.

Okay. It's time.

Leah puts her hand on his shoulder. She offered to do the talking, so did Nick, but Miguel won't let them. Very little of this is his fault, but it is his responsibility.

"Status update," he says.

Attention, Chimera gamers of the world. No, this is not your Gamerunners, but it is your champion. Far more people follow him now because of the competition. A wider audience. He's counting on that. *And I'm here to tell you that everything you think you know about Chimera is wrong.*

Replies start appearing. He ignores them.

You may think Chimera is just a game. You may think it was invented for the benefit of humankind, because we have all benefited from it. In speaking out, I might lose what I've won . . . permanently.

His biomech heart flickers. *Just in posting this message, I'm risking my life. Remember that as you read. You're going to think*

I'm crazy, a lunatic. You're going to think something happened to me during the competition that messed with my mind. That's not totally wrong, but I promise you, this is the truth. Or at least, if it's not, the lie comes directly from the Gamerunners. I found it in their systems.

There have been rumors that someone cheated in the competition. It was me. I admit to it. I could explain why, but it doesn't matter anymore. It wasn't just to win, I'll tell you that much. I did it because I thought I had to.

More replies now, an endless stream of them as his words are shared from his followers to their followers to their followers. He ignores these, too. Leah squeezes his shoulder again. Nick holds his breath, blinking behind his lenses.

I'm doing this because I think I have to, too. Chimera wasn't invented to save us. It was invented to sort us. The men you know as the Gamerunners are rivals playing a game with our lives. Some of us are good. Some of us are evil. The Gamerunners want to know who is who, and every moment we spend online, or in the game, they are gathering that information. They are looking through everything we've ever said, every choice we've ever made, and deciding.

Something bad is coming. It's already started. Read your news feeds and look around you. These wars aren't accidents. The problems with the food supply aren't human mistakes.

Chimera was invented to start Armageddon, and it's coming.

Believe me, or not, but it's coming.

He turns off the microphone. Nick starts to speak, but Miguel shakes his head. He doesn't want to know what people are saying, at least not yet. One weight lifts, replaced by a new one. This should never have been his job; this shouldn't *exist*.

He's done everything he can do. It's up to other people now.

"Okay," he says, standing. "Time to get out of here, I guess."
It's disappointing—that actually isn't a strong enough word—that Blake isn't here, but he might never come back. Miguel can't just sit here waiting for him.

They're halfway back down the corridor when Leah slams her hand into his chest, forcing him to stop. Nick bumps into both of them. "Wait," she says urgently. "I hear something."

"What?" Miguel asks, trying to speak and hold his breath at the same time.

"People," she answers. "And something else. Not sure."

Even he can hear the front door open, the voices that come in with the wind. A light in the atrium blooms to life before them.

"You really don't have to do this," says a voice, amplified by the glass. "We can come to an arrangement."

"You have already given me the only thing I could ever want," says another. "You gave me life. You made me into *this*. There is nothing else."

"Who gave you these orders?" asks yet another voice, and Miguel's shoulders stiffen. That's Blake, he's certain of it.

"I have already told you. I feel now that you are simply trying to buy time, but I'm afraid, gentlemen, that there is none for sale. You have been assets for a long time, but now you are liabilities. Too influenced by the humans around you. Say your good-byes."

Miguel feels Nick try to grab him, but he's too quick. "Wait!" he yells, reaching the end of the hallway, feet skidding to a stop where the tile meets the edge of the floor.

For a moment he thinks he's inside Chimera again. A horse waits outside the building, so out of place as to be laughable if anything, anything could be funny anymore.

He's seen that horse before. There are three others like it, of different colors, out there somewhere. It stomps its foot, blows air through metal nostrils.

Its rider stands in the atrium below, huge, black, robotic, gleaming. A skull formed of metal bones, a kind of weapon he's never seen before in the rider's hand, and he's seen a few. It turns at the distraction, glowing eyes staring up at Miguel, Nick, and Leah now. Behind it, weapons appear in Blake's and Lucius's hands. Well, Miguel's so glad to be of service.

"Mr. Anderson," says Blake, "how nice to see you. Why don't you come down here and join us?"

Miguel had wanted Blake to come here. Now he's

reconsidering. "Uh, I don't think so."

Blake snaps his fingers. "It wasn't a request," he says, as Miguel, Nick, and Leah land on their feet on the atrium floor. "You're outnumbered," Blake tells the horseman. "I don't think they're going to take your side."

"And what makes you think we'll take *yours*?" Leah demands. Her voice doesn't shake, and when death itself is facing you, that's a thing.

"You want answers."

"You can read our minds now?"

"Oh, sweetheart."

Triumph flickers briefly across Blake's face and shatters when the horseman wheels around again. "You think I can't kill all of you?" it asks. "That's what I'm for. My name and my purpose. You built me this way."

"Wait," says Nick. "You built this thing?"

Lucius smiles weakly. "In a manner of speaking, yes, but it is no longer beholden to us."

Miguel watches the Gamerunner, the one he hasn't met before. Dressed in white, which is appropriate, if a little clichéd. He smiles more sincerely, staring into the eyes of the horseman. The appearance of the gun in Miguel's hand is so sudden, unexpected, he almost drops it.

Giving him a weapon isn't very angelic. Nick and Leah have weapons, too.

They want to live.

And they are afraid.

"Let us answer him," says Blake, meeting Miguel's eyes. "He has come this far. He deserves this much."

The horseman nods impatiently.

"You invented Chimera to sort us," says Miguel. This isn't a question, he knows it. He's told the world already. But he wants to see Blake tell the truth for once.

"We did. Our superiors needed more results, and technology makes things faster, you know. Automates the process."

"Your superiors—"

"We don't call them by any of the same names you do, but the base of every story, good and evil, is correct. Those are hard to hide."

"Story," says Leah. "The Storyteller, the story mode of the game. The twelve labors, that's a story. And death, at the end, is a kind of immortality."

Miguel stares at her, impressed. It isn't the first time he's marveled at her ability to make connections.

"Story is important," says Lucius. "Story is what defines people, story and memory. You know that as well as anyone. Besides, some of them are funny."

"You think this is some kind of joke?" Miguel can feel the anger radiating off Nick, silently begs for him to calm down.

If this all goes to, ha, hell, he won't get the rest of the answers he wants.

"When you've been alive as long as we have, you'll look for amusement anywhere. Trust me on that."

Miguel doesn't trust them on anything. Blake can read his mind, shrugs. A "fair point" kind of shrug. The weapon in the horseman's hand twitches.

"So why did you pretend you were helping the planet? Humans? All the biomech, saving us. Why make us think we were going to survive?"

"Because the easiest way to go about our business unsuspected was to make it look that way. And because we had things we needed to test."

"Like the horses."

"Not only them, but we needed to see how they moved, behaved, yes. Animals are more difficult than people, more unpredictable. Our first experiments with them were dismal failures, but we wanted them. They're one of the best parts of the story, any story. Not to mention that they are known, identifiable, effective. When people see them, see what they do, they will know what's happening. Powerless to stop it, of course, but they'll know."

"War, famine, pestilence, death. All the things you need to bring about the end of the world."

"Yes," agrees Blake, "and this is the most important thing:

all things that humanity *does to itself*. What we can do to you is nothing, and I do mean nothing, compared with what you have always done to one another. But it is time for all that to end."

"Any more questions?" asks the dark horseman. "I have a duty to perform, and then I must join my fellows."

So many more. But he knows he's not going to get the chance to ask them all.

Unless . . .

He won't take their side, either of them, but for now he wants them alive, and they have—albeit indirectly—spent years teaching him to defeat monsters. With four people to help him. Years teaching him to defend himself with weapons that just appear in his hands.

Years showing him heaven and hell and the world they have set out to destroy. They're not very creative, but maybe that's a good thing here.

The horseman advances on Blake and Lucius. It's saying something too softly for Miguel to hear, though he's sure Leah can. He can speak with silence, he hopes.

Nod your heads if you can hear me, he thinks. Blake and Lucius do. It looks like fear.

He has an idea.

"Wait," he says, taking one step toward the horseman. "They both built you, right?"

The horseman half turns, irritated. It nods.

"So you'll happily kill us, or them, but there must be some sense of good in you. Something . . . Fairness." Lucius wouldn't have let Blake get away with making the thing entirely evil.

"Death is the fairest thing there is," says the horseman. "It happens to everybody."

"Okay," he says. "Then give us—and them—a chance."

"What are you doing?" Leah whispers.

Playing.

"If we fail, we die. The boss we couldn't beat. That's fair."

"You will not beat me."

"Then you have nothing to lose," says Miguel.

The horseman appears to consider this. Nick and Leah are staring at Miguel wide eyed. They don't know what he knows, haven't lived his life. Every day certain that he was going to die. He's been moments from it. Cheated it once, with Blake's help.

He remembers the ledge. Okay. Twice, with Blake's help.

"Lock the doors," the horseman orders. Blake waves a hand, steel shutters slide down over the windows, bars over the door.

You are in a room. He's spent so much of his life in gray rooms.

"Is that the only way out?"

"Yes," Blake tells the horseman. "We didn't want people getting in. More entrances only mean more weak points."

That's a lie. Miguel glances at Blake.

"Excellent." The horseman turns to Miguel. "I will stay here. You have five minutes to get into position, and then the game is on. This will be fun, I haven't played in too long." It folds its arms across its chest.

"This way," says Lucius. "Come, quickly." He leads the way to the tile; the five of them squeeze on and rise, up over the head of the counting horseman.

"What did it mean, it hasn't played in too long?" Miguel demands. Suspicion burns in his belly.

"You mean *he*," says Lucius. "It was a *he* once."

Blake stops the tile on the third floor. Miguel steps off and turns to them, Nick and Leah beside him. "You didn't completely build that thing from scratch," he says, another nonquestion to which he wants a truthful answer.

"Were you listening to me before?" Blake asks, a tiny smile twitching his lips. "What we could do is nothing compared to what you can do to one another. When we designed Chimera and all the biomech, we realized a secondary benefit. We didn't need to construct the horsemen, we needed to *find* them."

Miguel's mouth opens. Closes. Get your words in order. "I thought nobody had ever finished the game."

"You thought what we wanted you to think. Everybody did."

"So I just challenged the best, most experienced Chimera player—the best, most experienced *chimera*—in the world to a game."

"You did."

"Good job, Captain." Nick jokes weakly.

"You could have warned me," Miguel says. But they couldn't have, not really.

"Your impulsiveness is sometimes in your favor," says Lucius. "It was certainly in ours, as it kept us alive. Thank you for that."

"It won't drag this out," says Blake. "It wants to get this over with and get on with what it's really supposed to be doing. Although part of what it's really supposed to be doing is killing us, but after that, it has a lot to do. It's going to be busy. It will make this quick if it can."

He snaps his fingers. The air changes, the room changes like an overworld. The banks of computers disappearing, replaced by a familiar scene: the open square on which they defeated their first boss in the competition. Skyscrapers of glass and metal surround them, the concrete underfoot sparkles in artificial sunlight. Cars line the streets around the square. Empty crates litter the sidewalk. Reality and Chimera blur. Like the game, he knows his body is in a room, he can see the doorway, the corridor, but the air that fills his lungs is fresh, clean.

"How did you do that?" Nick asks.

"We're *gods*, Mr. Lee."

There's really no reply to that. "Will these things work?" Miguel raises the weapon in his hand.

"They're what we have," says Lucius. "We invented them . . . just in case. They'll fuse out its circuitry, we think."

"Why didn't you shoot it when you had the chance then?"

"It's not that simple."

Because they'd be in trouble with their superiors if they did. Miguel catches Blake's nod from the corner of his eye. Fine. But he won't be in any trouble, at least not any *more* trouble than he's in already.

The end of the world changes your perspective a little.

"Can we touch . . . that horseman thing??" asks Nick.

"Yes."

"I mean, without dying."

"Laying a hand on it won't kill you, but if you get close enough to do that, it's probably too late."

"He's coming," says Leah. He still trusts her hearing.

"Okay. You two"—Miguel points at the Gamerunners —"get behind it."

In that first level, Josh and Grace had been behind it. Distracting enough that Miguel had been able to fire off a shot just in time. It would have gone a lot smoother if Josh hadn't spotted the thing with the arm, but they got out of it in the end.

They'll get out of this one, too.

"Don't get shot," Lucius cautions. "The bullets kill biomech on contact."

His heart. Good to know. But he wasn't planning on getting shot.

"It's almost here," Leah whispers.

The replica is perfect, the same things to hide behind. Miguel crouches behind a car, peering around the bumper through the doorway and down the corridor, waiting for the huge dark monster to come. Cleverly, it didn't take a tile up, it must have used stairs somewhere. The tile would've given him an easy shot at its head.

He sees the glint, light on metal. The horseman strides into the square, footsteps heavy enough to shake the floor. Its—his—eyes cast around, seeking out its—his—five enemies. Leah is a few feet to one side of Miguel, Nick a few feet to the other.

Miguel lifts his gun. Aims.

Movement behind the horseman catches his eye. For a split second he thinks Blake and Lucius are aiming, too, but it isn't only their guns rising, it's them. They wait until the horseman has locked its gaze on Leah.

And they run. Through the door, down the corridor, out of sight.

"Cowards!" Miguel screams. "Come back here!"

The horseman screams, too, its rage echoing off the rendered buildings. He spins rapidly back and forth, wanting all of his prey.

"They're going upstairs!" says Leah. "Chase them or stay here?"

"Here!"

Nick springs to his feet, runs, seizing his chance. He advances on the conflicted horseman, meeting it in the middle of the square. They are only a few feet apart, Nick's back to Miguel and Leah. Miguel wants to scream no!, but his voice dies in his throat. The horseman dodges the first fired bullet, a dark blur. Leah raises her gun, but there is no safe shot. Miguel won't, can't risk Nick.

"Get out of here, Mig," says Nick lowly. "You can't just die now, after everything."

"No."

"You think you have a chance? At all?" The horseman taunts him, recovering its wits, refocusing on the three of them. "I'm not saying this isn't fun, but I have places to be."

"You won't get him."

Miguel stands. Leah's strong fingers wrap around his ankle.

"You seem to be laboring under a mistaken impression," says the horseman, "that I care who I get. Fair is fair. I have no preferences, make no judgments. I have only orders."

"Then what's taking you so long? Come on!" Nick fires again. The bullet smashes a pane of glass. The room is fake, but the rain of shards looks so real.

Damage. Not the right kind.

"Oh, enough," says the horseman. It grins widely, metal teeth in its black skull. A long arm reaches out.

Time slows. Stops.

The horseman strikes.

Miguel jumps up, dives over the hood of the car. The gun slips from Miguel's slick, trembling hand as he lands, slides across the floor, comes to a stop close enough to see every agonizing detail.

Nick's feet rise into the air, tossed as easily as an insult by the dark hand that closes around his throat. His body falls with a sickening crunch.

"Nick!" Miguel screams. He thinks he hears Leah, too, but a roar fills his ears as he drags himself over in time to watch the life disappear from Nick's eyes.

Miguel can't breathe.

Cannot. Breathe. He wraps his arms around Nick, waiting for the blow he's sure is coming. It will probably be painless.

He's heard that before.

But nothing happens. Miguel drags his forehead from Nick's chest, looks up. Leah is standing, frozen in shock, mouth twisted in horror. The horseman is still grinning.

"Kill me," he says. Leah shakes her head. Maybe she's just shaking. "Do it."

But death has taken its price, sated its thirst. "Where are they?" the horseman asks. "I have orders. I must find them. You may live for now, I will have you in the end. You will see me again, Miguel Anderson. Enjoy the show."

In an instant it is gone. Miguel can't move. He grips Nick tighter, feels Leah's arms wrap around him from behind.

For long moments neither of them speaks. Finally Leah does.

"Those fucking cowards," she says. "They escaped on hoverboards from the roof, I heard them. They were lying about the front door's being the only way out."

Miguel nods dully. There was the vent, too. They'd had contingency plans, even for this. He had lied, cheated to save his own life. He shouldn't be surprised that the Gamerunners would do the same. They are not human, but maybe for some things that doesn't matter. Survival above all.

They are alone. The horseman is gone, though he will be back for them. He will be back for everybody in the end. Blake and Lucius have escaped. Nick is gone in the most final sense.

Slowly the square fades around them, the room returning to its normal state. Blake and Lucius could be too far away by now to control it, if that's how it works.

He doesn't really care how it works. His eyes skim over

the banks of computers, their screens forever darkened. There was a time when he would have given every other one of his organs for a glimpse into this room, for the chance to dig into the secrets those computers held about Chimera.

The game that wasn't really a game, or was the truest game of all. Designed to test them, divide them, sort them. To link up with their Presences and label them, thumbs up or down.

He never wants to play again.

Slowly he releases Nick, turns into Leah's embrace. She feels real, the only thing that does, the only thing that isn't a nightmare. Outside the windows, artificial trees wave in a wind that is only the precursor to the storm that is about to come. It is tempting, so tempting, to stay here, on this floor, and watch it all burn.

He has been wrong, and wronged, and wrong again.

This is how the game really begins. Right now.

Acknowledgments

For their help and support on a thousand fronts, I would like to thank the following:

My family, who are understanding even when they don't quite understand.

Britt and her pointy shoes.

Tom Pollock, for the light-hearted chats about humanity, math, and the nature of existence.

Den Patrick, sanity provider and coffee buddy.

James Bennett, and his library of niche research books.

Virginia Duncan, the fairest, smartest, and toughest editor a writer could ever hope to have, and all at Greenwillow Books.

Brooks Sherman and everyone at The Bent Agency.

William Gibson, for a sixteen-year-old girl who discovered *Neuromancer* and was never quite the same.

All of London's genre scene, for the open arms.

And you.

■ ■ ■